Fighting Back

Mercy's Angels Book 2

Kirsty Dallas

D1501699

Kirsty Dallas

ISBN: 1493793861
ISBN-13:9781493793860

FOR MY MUM AND DAD,

WHO TAUGHT ME THAT TRUE STRENGTH IS MORE
THAN JUST A PHYSICAL ATTRIBUTE

CHAPTER 1

Rebecca

Have you ever had one of those moments where you look up, open your eyes and wonder, what the fuck am I doing? Like you've been under some sort of hypnosis and someone finally snapped their fingers and you woke up? I hope I haven't been clucking like a chicken or imitating an orgasm in my hypnotic state. I feel dazed and bewildered. How the hell did I get here, to this moment? It's like one second I was moving forward, albeit slowly, and the next minute—BAM!—I'm on the floor, down for the count. I can't really say it happened suddenly, not if I'm being truthful about this moment of rousing clarity. No, I'm just surprised reality took as long as it did to finally bitch slap me—it's been a long time coming. Perhaps weeks, if not months of wallowing in self-pity has led to this moment of lucidity. This is not me, this is not who I am. I've always been independent, driven and confident. Lately I've been feeling needy, dispirited and apprehensive. Even after my parents died when I was nine, I handled it with as much grace and dignity a nine year old could muster. Of course I grieved, I cried enough tears to end droughts in several countries and then some. Then I picked myself up, dusted myself off, and moved forward. I even picked up my little sister Emily and dusted her off. She moved forward, but in a different way, like full throttle, faster than the speed of light and all that bullshit. Emily didn't just move, she flew, straight out of Claymont as soon as she turned seventeen, not long after Grandma died. I, on the other hand, moved at a slow leisurely pace, enjoying the sights and held firm to the only remaining relic of my family heritage: my grandma's house. I laughed, I thrived and I didn't care what other people thought of me. I lived! Hell yeah, I am Rebecca Fucking Donovan, hear me roar! Well, at least I thought I was. My roar now sounded something more like a timid and pathetic whine.

My eyes had been glued to a grubby stain on the wrinkled white table cloth in front of me for no less than fifteen minutes now. I knew I would have to face him sooner or later, I couldn't exactly sit and stare at the damn table cloth for the entire date. I take a long, deep, calming breath, and return my gaze to the man before me. Luke Hollywell, Claymont's Mr. Dickhead Of The Century, and yes, I, Rebecca Fucking Donovan, hear me roar blah, blah, blah, was on a date with him. My eyes narrowed a little as I looked him over, desperately trying to find a reason as to why I had agreed to this date. He was good looking enough, I guess. His blonde hair was buzz cut short with an angry looking jagged scar breaking his hairline to one side. His eyes were a non-descript hazel color and were perhaps a little too close together. His lips were full, opening and closing as he rambled on about God knows what. I seriously haven't heard a word he has said since the moment we sat down. He has a damn fine body, maybe that's what lured me in. Or maybe it was the whole bad boy thing. Luke was a brawler, a troublemaker, and had seen the inner workings of the Claymont lock-up more than once. And again I ask myself, what the hell am I doing here?

He was looking at me expectantly, and I realized he had asked a question that obviously required an answer.

"I'm sorry, what did you say?" I asked with a sincere smile. If I wouldn't have been checking out his wide shoulders and impressive looking chest, I might not have gotten away with the blunder. Luke just grinned, but it wasn't sexy, it was downright creepy and made my skin prickle with unease.

"Why do you dress like that?" he repeated his question, nodding towards my attire.

I looked down at myself wondering if I had been in too much of a daze tonight that maybe I was wearing my PJs. Nope, I still looked utterly fabulous. I was wearing a fire engine red, vintage style dress with a gathered bust, and peasant style fitted waist. It fell to my knees and hugged my body like a second skin. I had accessorized it with black pumps and a black-faux fur knee length coat. My hair was artfully styled on top of my head in a fifties fashioned do that took longer to arrange than my entire outfit. I sighed. Misunderstood, that was the only way to forgive those who looked at me like I had lost my marbles.

"Not that I'm complaining or anything. Hell, you've got a fuckin' great rack. If ya got the goods, ya might as well display 'em, right?" Luke rambled on, now leering at my breasts.

WHAT...THE...FUCK...AM...I...DOING? I was horny. That was my problem—I needed to get laid! Did I really need to scrape the bottom of Claymont's men barrel to do it though? Hell no! In fact, Ella bought me a surprisingly efficient vibrator for my birthday two months ago. Big Red could get the damn job done without me having to step outside my door. However, Big Red wouldn't cuddle with me after one of those mediocre battery operated orgasms. Big Red wouldn't keep me warm and or kiss me like I was an exquisite treasure. So maybe I wasn't just horny, I missed intimacy. I missed sharing my whole self, not just my body with a man. I wanted intimate touches, hand holding, and hugs. It's been over two years since my last committed relationship and twelve months since I have been intimate with something other than an inanimate object. It's been twelve months since Charlie Cole. I sighed and forced that beautiful train wreck out of my mind. What I really wanted, I suddenly realized, I would not find in Luke Hollywell, that much was for sure.

"Luke, this is a little embarrassing, but I don't really feel well." He cast me a disbelieving look. "I had lunch at that little café down the road from

Bouquets, you know the one, they were charged with that health violation last year. I know, I know," I raised my hands in self-defense," "it's supposed to be the single most unsanitary café in Claymont, but I couldn't resist. All that heavenly deep fried awesomeness was just calling my name." I tried not to scrunch up my nose up at the thought of all that hellish stomach churning deep fried horror. "I mean, I literally couldn't help myself. Now my stomach feels like an eruption is imminent." I rubbed my hand across my stomach and allowed a pained look to cloud my features. "Hell, if I end up with an assquake over my inability to avoid consuming deadly and dangerous food, I will spank my own ass!" Luke's look of disbelief morphed into shell shocked horror and sick intrigue. I almost lost my façade trying to keep a straight face. "Maybe we should do this another night, you know, when I don't feel like I'm ready to explode."

Luke stared at me a moment longer before leaning away from the table. The look of skepticism was back. He flipped his fork nonchalantly for a moment before settling it back down on the grubby looking linen. "Sure, whatever floats ya boat, sweetheart. Want me to drive ya home?" He grinned again and I felt myself wanting to puke.

"My car's outside, I'll be fine." I stood and grabbed my coat from the back of my chair. All the while, Luke's eyes watched my body with unconcealed desire. "Sorry to bail on you like this." Luke nodded and licked his lips as his gaze finally returned to my face. It made my skin crawl. With a forced smile, I turned and walked away from the table.

As I left the warmth of the restaurant, the icy air outside hit my face, shocking my senses to life. A thin layer of deadly black ice lay like a frigid blanket covering the ground, and I was wearing five inch heels. Don't say I didn't like to live dangerously. I finally made my way to my car and slid in, turned on the ignition, cranked the heater up to full-blast, then drove down the quiet and empty streets towards home. I loved Claymont, and I couldn't understand why my sister had been so desperate to flee this town. It had an old world charm, but thanks to the college in town, it was always bustling with life and activity. Emily openly declared her hatred for Claymont from the moment she learned to talk. A week after her sixteenth birthday, not long after Grandma died, she left for the big city lights never to return. Her disappearance almost sent me into a state of catatonic shock. I filed a missing persons report and spent a week living on the razor's edge of fear and anger. When she called to say she was safe, that she was living with a friend of a friend in Vegas, I had mixed feelings. Relief that she was safe, disappointment that she left me alone, guilt that I didn't jump on a plane and drag her adolescent behind home immediately. In the end acceptance won out, Em was born for the bright city lights, and Claymont was too dull for her spirited heart. For the first six months, I heard from her every week.

She was full of hopes and dreams, always happy and excited. Our phone calls made me smile and cry. I was happy for her, but I missed her. Gradually the phone calls became few and far between, until they stopped all together. Em had moved on, and as her sister, I was nothing more than just a distant memory, Claymont nothing more than a place of disappointment and sadness. . So after eight years of little to no contact, I have heard from her five times in the last month and it has me more than a little curious. Oh, I knew what she wanted, but there wasn't a chance in hell she would ever get it and she knew that. Nevertheless, she has been persistent. Emily wanted me to sell Grandma's house. Our house, my house. When Grandma died, it had been left to both of us, even though Emily hadn't been there to stake her claim, nor had she ever attempted to, until now. My lawyer had advised me that I could buy out her share, but he obviously didn't realize the crumbs in my bank account were just that—crumbs. Re-establishing Bouquets with Ella and Annie into the coffee shop/art gallery/floral shop that it was, Mercy's Angels and Bouquets had all but bled my account dry. Money was filtering back in at a trickle, so funds were definitely a little tight right now. I could borrow on the substantial worth of the property, but I was reluctant to get myself into debt when I was finally debt free. Emily was persistent though. My head hurt just thinking of her relentless phone calls. No doubt she was one of the reasons for my recent muddled existence. Crazy sister—check. Too many hours working—check. Not enough money—check. Longest dry spell in history—check. My thoughts returned to my neglected central loving station and I thought back to the last man who had paid it any sort of attention—Charlie Cole. I sighed again at the thought of him and it made me want to slap myself. Get over it, Rebecca, Charlie is a straight up, plain and simple man whore! Yes, he may have rocked my world, and, yes, the thought of him rocking it again turned me into a mushy mess, but I wasn't going to go there again. I had more pride than that and Charlie's lack of enthusiasm to continue rocking my world said everything I needed hear.

As I pulled into the driveway of my pint sized home, I embraced the feeling of contentment this place never failed to give me. My house was sandwiched between mansions, and maybe they weren't mansions according to Beverley Hill's standards, but in Claymont talk, they were impressive. They weren't just big homes, the houses in this neighborhood were ridiculously colossal, like Gone With The Wind mammoth. My miniscule slice of heaven was the bane of my neighbors' existence. Several people on my street have offered to buy me out; offering enough money to make my knees weak. But they didn't understand that this property was more than a number, this was all that remained of my family. My parents rented a few homes when we were children, so we never really found a place we grew attached to. Grandma and Granddad bought this piece of land and built this house before any of the others on the street existed; it was one of the first properties in this suburb. This was the house my dad had grown up in. This was the house where I baked my first cake. It was in this backyard, overlooking the foothills of the Claymont Mountain Ranges, where I learned to ride a bike. Emily and I shared a tiny pocket of a room in the back corner, and although Emily struggled to be content in this home, in this town, we spent many nights just lying there gossiping about school and boys. I would never sell my home. There wasn't a price high enough to convince me it was worth giving up.

Once inside I took a long hot shower and slipped into my favorite flannel PJs. Climbing under the thick feather quilt, I moaned in satisfaction. The incessant blinking of my cell phone at my side alerted me that I had a message. Reaching over, I swiped the screen and smiled when Ella's crazy face stared back at me. Ella could only be described as my partner in crime, my best friend, and my savior of sanity. We've only known each other for a little over a year, yet it seemed as if she was the light that had been missing in my world. Little Ella, who has seen more violence and hate than any one person should ever see. She was a fighter, a tiger! Before Ella, I've never had someone whom I might call a best friend. I had friends or more accurately colleagues and casual acquaintances. I'd never let anyone get too close because in my short twenty-eight years of life I quickly learned that losing people you cared about hurt, a lot. I'd lost my parents, I'd lost my granddad, my grandma, and I inevitably lost my sister. When I began dressing 'differently' than everyone else, it became a whole lot easier to keep people at arm's length. Most people thought I was a little crazy in the head, and who knows, maybe they're right. Screw 'em, I didn't need a world full of fake friends. Somehow Ella had wormed her way into my heart, and call me selfish, but I was keeping her. Ella was as real as they came and she kept me laughing. It was safe to say Annie was my friend now, too. Not only did she fill me with an ever constant supply of caffeine, Annie was also loyal and dependable. She had a quietness about her that radiated past pain, and she was a great listener. You didn't need to tell Annie when you were having a bad day; she just somehow knew and would be the first in line to offer a comforting hug. She also put up with mine and Ella's dirty jokes, potty mouths and childish humor without complaint. Lola was the latest curious addition to our small and humble group of friends. I employed her four months ago to help out at Bouquets since Ella was now an in demand artist. Lola was painfully shy, quiet and forlorn most days, dressing in every drab shade of black one could imagine. But she was a hard worker; she was honest and occasionally she came out with little random pearls of wisdom that would have Ella and me laughing like hyenas. Like the time she told us a balanced diet was a piece of cake in each hand! And her number one golden rule was: Don't squat with spurs on. What the hell? The girl was truly peculiar, but I loved peculiar—I understood peculiar—it beat most other personality traits hands down. So, I had let a few people in and I knew I risked feeling the pain of loss again. Last year, Ella almost died and I had lost my shit for a little while. Someone I had cared about was nearly taken away from me, again. I became increasingly anxious and a little clingy where Ella was concerned. Letting her out of my sight was difficult even though I knew somewhere in the recesses of my mind that her and Jax needed quality time together, to recover. Thankfully, Mercy helped guide me through my fears. She spent a lot of time just hanging out with me talking. She helped me see that living a life where I constantly feared losing everyone and everything wasn't really living at all. I needed to let those fears go. I needed to accept that death was an ugly part of life and embracing those we cared about here and now was what was truly important.

I opened Ella's message and quickly read it.

ELLA: How was ur date with weirdo Hollywell? Jax wants to know if he needs to send out search and rescue?

I laughed. I needed to respond pronto because the thing about Jax and search and rescue, he would totally see through on it. His ex-military buddy, Dillon Montgomery, had recently established an office for his security firm here in Claymont. If Ella had cause to worry, she would be on Jax's case in a heartbeat, and I would have one sexy as hell ex-soldier beating down my door. Hmmmmm. My mind went over the possibilities there. But unfortunately, the man appeared to have eyes for only one woman—Annie. I knew he adored her and her six year old rug rat, Eli. Dillon's dark and mysterious looking cousin, Braiden, had possibilities though. He oozed sexual confidence. His dark scruffy hair framed a face that I wasn't sure belonged on an angel or devil, was masculine yet beautiful. No matter how hot the guy was though, there was something underneath that screamed 'run'. His quiet and intense gaze was intimidating. When he looked at you it was as if he was looking beyond all the clothes, skin and bullshit, almost as if he was trying to see into your soul. So while he had a face and body that caused women drool like mindless fools, there was a darkness about him that kept me from getting too close. Or perhaps I was just too chicken shit to get involved with someone who might have more baggage than my own.

REBECCA: Don't send reinforcements. Home safe. Date was a disaster, I bailed before the meal. Tell Jax I owe him that case of beer!

ELLA: Do u think Jax's ego needs stroking? I'll just tell him you cancelled!! Sorry it didn't work out. I miss you, but not the snow!! XOX

Ella was in Hawaii with the fine hunk of American goodness that was Jaxon Carter. Lucky bitch, but if anyone deserved it, Ella did. She needed this break—her nightmares and panic attacks were justified and she still fought them every day.

REBECCA: I hate u right now, but only a little cause I'm jealous. C u in a week. XOX

Sliding deeper under the covers, I allowed the cocoon of warmth to lull me to sleep.

* * *

I don't know what it was that dragged me from my blissful oblivion. Perhaps a noise, or maybe something as simple as raw human instinct screaming at me that something wasn't right. As my heavy, sleep laden body slowly roused to wakefulness, I noticed a dark figure looming at the end of my bed, slamming my mind quickly into sharp reality. Though my mind was now alert, my body lagged behind, and before I could move, the unfamiliar figure crushed me into the soft mattress. My wrists were quickly pinned to my sides and I was face to face with a nightmare hovering above me, staring at me with blatant rage. I tried to move my arms, but they were pinned down too tight to the bed. All fatigue from my slumbering body was gone, replaced with full blown fear. Instinct kicked in and I began to struggle against the heavy figure. It was definitely a him, I could feel it pressed against my thigh and horror filled my veins. His face was covered with a ski mask, and only his eyes were visible, the white a startling contrast against the black surrounding them. He ripped at my flannel pajama top, the buttons flung off in all directions. Under the muted feeling of disbelief, I realized what was happening and I screamed with a manic fury I never thought I possessed. One of my hands had become free as my attacker wrestled with my clothing and I tried to push him away. A heavy blow to the side of my face killed all sound and movement instantly. One meaty hand gathered my small wrists above my head as he continued to maul my body. A big hard hand grabbed at my breast and squeezed so hard I couldn't contain the whimper of pain that escaped my lips. He was now grappling at the waistband of my pajama bottoms, and the violation and vulnerability of this situation made bile rise in my throat. No, I would not be sick and I would not wig out when my life depended on me being strong right now. I wouldn't go down without a fight and I would make this fucker wish he had never been born with a dick. Raising my knee, I tried to kick him, but I missed—he had me pinned too hard against the bed. Taking a deep breath, as his too eager, too desperate hands tried to reach into my pants, I screamed again. Surely that would wake the dead, the sound was frightening and unrecognizable to even my own ears. The scream was again lost to another sharp slap to my face, followed by another and another. Even though my mind was cloudy and my eyes had darkened for a moment, I instinctively continued to fight, bucking under his heavy weight.

His hand ripped at my panties, his fingers grabbing with frantic violence at my most sacred of places, pushing into me with a relentless force that stung with sharp pain.

"Noooooo!" I screamed as my body bucked and thrashed, fighting for all that it was worth. In an attempt to hold me down, his hand left my wrists. Now partially free, I slammed my fists into his face. Scratching, hitting and tearing at the looming horror before me, tears blurred my vision momentarily. Somehow he tugged my pajama bottoms from my hips, and my panties were torn aside. "Noooooo!" I screamed again, so loud my throat felt instantly raw. He fumbled with his own pants, trying desperately to free himself. In one last ditched effort, I lifted my hands and dug my thumbs into those hate filled eyes. For the first time since I woke to this stranger above me, he let out a noise, an animalistic growl. He levered himself off of me a little, his fist pulled back ready to strike. With the small space between us, I found enough room to raise my knee and I rammed it into his hard dick. He groaned and fell beside me, giving me an opportunity to scramble from the bed, my clothes hanging off my body like shredded rags. Not even stopping to think, I bolted from the room and stumbled over furniture as I ran blindly through my house. With the front door only a few feet before me now, I lunged forward, freedom and safety within my grasp.

"I'm going to fucking kill you," came a roar from behind me. He slammed me against the front door and the air left my lungs in a sharp, painful hiss.

"Rebecca?" The pounding on the other side of the door caught my attention and I slammed my hand against the wood, unable to speak as my lungs begged for air. The stranger at my back became immobile against me. His muffled breath was hot against my cheek and, for some weird reason, I noticed how clean and minty he smelled.

"We'll finish this later, sweetheart!" he whispered, pushing me into the door a little harder before the pressure of his body disappeared.

"Rebecca, it's Don from next door. I've called the police, are you okay?" I took a deep breath and felt my ribs throb in pain. My knees gave way and I sank to the floor. Big ugly sobs broke free from my lips as my mind floated into a haze of disbelief and fear. What the hell had just happened? This had to be a dream, an ugly nightmare, a God awful ugly fucking nightmare. The distant sound of a siren reverberated through my conscious thought. I wrapped my hands around my knees and clutched my body in the fetal position on the floor.

"Just a nightmare, just a nightmare," I whispered to myself, struggling to make sense of what just happened. In that moment, my heart shattered and my soul cried for something I had just lost, for the woman I would be no more.

CHAPTER 2

Charlie

Sitting on the side of the bed, I rubbed a hand through my tangled mess of hair. What the fuck was I doing? I found myself thinking. Getting the fuck out of here before she wakes, came the voice of reason. I rubbed the tight muscles in my neck and reached for my pants, careful not to disturb the naked beauty behind me. After finally finding my sock under the bed, I finished tying the laces on my boots and took one last look at the woman splayed unapologetically bare before me. She was hot—long legs, long strawberry blond hair, a great set of tits, and those lips, hell, just thinking of how great those lips felt wrapped around my cock made me hard. "Down boy," I murmured as I snuck out of the dark room. Yeah, she was hot, but she wasn't her. No matter how many women I found myself inside, they weren't her. An entire fucking year had passed and I still couldn't stop thinking about Rebecca Donovan. That platinum blonde hair, those big beautiful blue eyes, and perfect pink lips. It wasn't just what I saw on the outside that got my blood boiling though; it was the woman on the inside, too. When she laughed, people were drawn to it, and she laughed often. She teased, she joked, and she was always smiling. She was sassy, confident, successful, and didn't give a shit what anyone else thought about her. She was perfect. And she was perfectly unattainable. Oh, I had touched and tasted, just once, and, at the time, I had every intention of touching and tasting again. Rebecca had a heart and body full of warmth and desire. I had found myself thinking that I, Charlie Perpetually-Single Cole could find my way home to that warmth every night, from here to eternity. But forty-eight hours after our one night of fucking heaven, Rebecca didn't want to have anything to do with me. Jax had informed me that Rebecca saw me out with Caitlyn Brown, two days after our night together, and it had tripped her jealousy switch. The fact that she had been jealous made my chest swell with pride, the fact that she refused to take my calls and allow me to explain just pissed me off. Caitlyn had been a business date, nothing more, nothing less. The fact that she was a lesbian didn't seem to help my cause one little bit. So, in true Charlie fashion, I had deleted Rebecca's phone number and forgot all about her. Well, I had every intention of doing that. The fact that her number was still in my phone, and not a day passed by where I didn't think about her was just plain crazy.

Leaving the warmth of—Jane? Jenny? Jill? Gym Girl!—I slipped out her front door and into the freezing night air. It was almost four in the morning and the ground was slick with ice. I was tired as hell and just wanted my own bed and a few hours of blissful sleep. The irritating vibration from my back pocket was easy to ignore; there was no way I was answering a call this time of the night, or morning. By the time I was in my truck and on the road, the damn thing kept ringing and a knot of worry seeped into my bones. Who the hell would be trying this hard to get ahold of me at four in the morning? Reaching for my phone, I glanced at the screen. Mercy Carter, the mother of my best friend Jax, and the owner of the local woman's shelter. Jax was away in Hawaii and Mercy's husband, Dave, was out of town. My stomach suddenly turned with apprehension.

"Mercy, what's wrong?" I demanded as I brought the phone to my ear.

"I'm okay, Charlie, but I need a favor." I could tell there was something up, the tone in her voice was off. She didn't give me time to ask though. "I need you to pick up something from the shop to board up a broken window and drop by Rebecca's."

Rebecca has a broken window? What the fuck? "Mercy, you sure this is something that can't wait till the sun's up?"

"Charlie," the anguish in her voice made my heart suddenly beat hard with panic, "please just come as soon as you can."

"I'm on my way, be there in twenty." I threw the phone on the empty passenger seat beside me and stepped on the gas.

My heart was pounding and my palms were sweaty. Something was wrong, really wrong. A broken window wasn't really something to get all flustered over. Rebecca lived in a nice part of town; in fact, it was one of the wealthiest suburbs in Claymont. Her house was a matchbox amongst the palaces, but it was neat and tidy, and from what I gathered, she got along with all her neighbors well enough. My brain either wouldn't or couldn't process what had Mercy so upset, so I simply moved with purpose, grabbing a few supplies from Jax's business, Carter Constructions. I managed the business, and was currently living in the small studio apartment above the office, so I already had keys to the place. I could have had my own apartment and up until six months ago I did. But it just felt empty and I hated being there. At least at the office, the moment I found myself sitting around feeling sorry for myself like a pussy, I just worked. When I wasn't there, I was at Lee's Gym, pounding the bags and lifting weights. I still trained and sparred with a few of the other fighters, even though I haven't fought in the ring in over five years. After all, kickboxing has been in my heart since I was a kid, ever since I saw Jean-Claude Van Damme in Universal Soldier I was hooked. My competition days were behind me though, I didn't like the way competing made me feel. I would become immersed, completely focused and unreachable when I drifted into that mindset, that place where nothing mattered except winning. My mood would tilt from blissful and carefree to angry and bitter in a heartbeat. When the anger consumed me, what was left wasn't pretty. An irrational storm of rage would pull me under and it scared the shit out of me that I could possibly, unintentionally hurt someone when I was like that. So instead I used the skills I learned in a more positive manner now, teaching self-defense one day a week at Mercy's Shelter. When I started teaching, Ella and Annie were the only women who showed up, and I'm pretty sure they only did so because they felt sorry for me. I adored those two like sisters, especially Ella. She was Jax's girl and, to be honest, if I hadn't already experienced the pleasures of Rebecca Donovan when I met the little fire cracker, Jax would've had one damn jealous best friend on his hands.

The self-defense class quickly grew to eight, and then twelve. Now I had fifteen to twenty students a week, depending on who was in the shelter at the time. It was rewarding to give something back to the community. My talents were limited, unlike Jax who had gained a multitude of valuable skills courtesy of the US Army and could craft exquisite furniture from a blank canvas of lumber. I could keep a business running smooth as a baby's backside and I could fight, but that is where my strengths began and ended. The classes at Mercy's were not only fulfilling, but they was an integral part to the healing process the women embarked on when they stepped over Mercy's threshold. Learning to protect yourself, having that sort of strength and confidence was as empowering as leaving the asshole fucker who had abused them in the first place.

Pulling onto Rebecca's street, my foot instinctively moved off the accelerator as I took in the flashing lights of two patrol cars. My heart began to hammer even harder as I approached them and realized they were parked in front of Rebecca's house. An ambulance was sitting with its doors open in the driveway. Without conscious thought, I pulled to the curb and jumped out of my truck, leaving the keys hanging in the ignition. At this point I didn't really give a fuck.

"Sir?" a clean shaven, barely legal looking police officer called out as I crossed the icy lawn. I ignored him as I took the old porch steps two at a time. Another officer greeted me at the front door, his hand on my chest pushing me away from the doorway. Peering over his shoulder, I noticed the mess in the living room—the coffee table had been knocked over and a vase of flowers was smashed on the hardwood floors.

"Sir, you can't go in there." The officer leveled me with a stare. I guess some people would've been intimidated, but the cocky attitude that underlined the official persona just pissed me off.

"Just try to fucking stop me," I all but growled.

"Charlie?" Mercy's determined voice caught my attention and I looked over the officer's shoulder again. She stood beside Frank, the should-be-retired officer that has been front and center of Claymont's police force for over thirty years now.

"Let him in, Dawkins," Frank commanded. I gifted Officer Cocky with a raised brow and may have given him a slightly cocky grin of my own. As I entered the house and took in the disarray of Rebecca's small living room, my legs became numb, moving on their own accord. Two paramedics stood off to one side, unopened bags and stretcher at their feet. Mercy's shoulders were back, her head high, but her eyes were full of unshed tears. Something bad must have happened, something really bad. God, no, not Rebecca. I gripped the wall as my head spun. Mercy was quickly in front of me, her little hands on my cheeks drawing my gaze down to her.

"She's okay, you can't go freaking out on her though. You need to keep your head and stay calm." Mercy's hard eyes were full of resolve and I gave her a short nod. Mercy has always been direct and straight to the point, and I've always appreciated that about her. It never failed to break through my temper, centering me, focusing me.

"What happened?" I asked through gritted teeth.

Mercy took a long deep breath and glanced over her shoulder at Frank.

"I'll go see if I can convince her to come out," he said, walking down the narrow hall.

"What the fuck? Where is she?" I demanded.

Mercy drew my attention back to her. "Someone broke in, they smashed the window in the laundry room and forced the latch open." Mercy looked at the mess around her.

Someone did a whole lot more than break a window here. I rubbed my chest, trying desperately to ease the pounding of my heart. It hurt and I was beginning to think that I might be having a heart attack. Was that even possible? I was only twenty-eight, and I was fit and healthy. Fuck me, the thought of Rebecca hurt was causing me to have a heart attack.

"Charlie!" Mercy snapped again. "Rebecca was hurt and she doesn't need you freaking out. Take a deep breath and get control of yourself," she said matter-of-factly.

I wanted to throttle her. My eyes slipped closed and my pounding heart began to echo louder in my ears. A familiar stirring in the pit of my stomach made me feel physically ill. Anger. I have struggled with my temper all my life and I've finally learned how to stow it, until now. The thought of someone hurting Rebecca, placing their hands on such pure beauty had the fury inside me churning. I was caught somewhere between abject horror and mind numbing anger. I clenched my fists and the bones cracked with tension.

"Damn it, Charlie Cole!" Mercy's sharp voice forced me back to the here and now. "Control yourself. Rebecca's really shaken up and we're not sure of the full extent of her injuries because she refuses to let the paramedics look her over, and she won't go to the hospital. She took a beating—she has blood on her face and she could have a concussion. Frank called me and I came right away. She was doing fine until Frank began asking her questions, then she panicked. She's been locked in the bathroom for an hour now." She gave me a worried look. "Maybe you could try and talk to her." My eyes instinctively moved to the hallway where Frank was leaning against the door, talking softly. "I know you guys have history, but I also know she adores you, Charlie. She has for a long time, even if she is too stubborn to acknowledge it. Please, just try." Mercy's voice had lowered, and her pleading tone broke through the haze of panic and fury.

I nodded, unable to speak. My legs again moved without thought, drawn to the fragile beauty locked away in the room at the end of the hall. Frank moved aside as I approached, and when I could go no further, I leaned against the door, and rested my forehead on the cool surface. My hands splayed against the wood, wanting desperately to reach the girl on the other side, to comfort her, to protect her.

"Rebecca," my voice was husky with emotion. I don't know if she recognized it, hell I didn't recognize it. I cleared my throat. "Betty Boop, how you doing in there?" I murmured. There was no response, it was silent and it took all my inner strength not to break the damn door down. "Honey, please, just tell me if you're okay or not. I mean, fuck, I know you're not, but do you need help, a doctor maybe?" A faint sniffle broke the silence. Thank fuck for that. "I know you're scared, baby, but there is no one here who wants to hurt you. It's just Frank, me and Mercy. We just want to know if you need medical attention." There was still no response and I took a long deep breath as I began to do the only thing I could think of: I talked. I talked about all sorts of shit. I told her about how Jax had pushed me into the sand-pit in kindergarten when we were toddlers, and to make up for it he had to share his juice box with me. I told her how when I was fourteen my parents had introduced me to the girl they believed I was destined to marry. Poor little Claire ran long and hard from that visit, because apparently, she didn't find breaking wind as funny as I did. I talked so long that I finally ran out of things to say. "Betty Boop, I really need to know if you are alright," I whispered, defeated.

"I don't know." Her husky voice soaked straight through my heart.

"Baby, unlock the door for me, please. Just me, you don't have to see anyone else if you don't want to." I leaned against the door for the longest time before I heard the gentle click of the lock. Breathing a long sigh of relief, I refrained from busting through the door and scooping her up into my arms. Instead, I gently turned the handle and pushed through. Her back was turned, and her shoulders were slumped forward.

"Please close the door," she whispered hoarsely, her throat sounding raw and painful. I quietly shut it behind me, reaching through the shock and fog in my brain for something to say. My mouth opened then shut again—no words would come—there was nothing I could say that would make any of this alright. Instead, I moved towards her slowly and reached out until my hand rested gently on her shoulder. She flinched at my touch, but I didn't pull away, I couldn't. Her shoulders began to shake and she turned slowly to face me. Her hair was a tangled mess, stark red blood from a cut above her eye was a shocking contrast to the platinum white of her soft hair. I pushed it aside and got my first real glimpse of her face. God, she was a mess. A pained groan escaped my lips. Her hands immediately covered herself as she fell back against the wall and sank to the ground. I fell to my knees before her.

"Fuck, I'm sorry, baby." I hated my reaction to seeing her hurt like this, my reaction that forced her to retreat. I needed to hold it together better than this. "Don't hide from me, I need to see that you're okay," I gently whispered, pulling her hands away from her face. Tears fell down her bruised cheeks. One eye was swollen shut, the side of her face an angry shade of purple. The cut above her eye that I had already caught a glimpse of had stopped bleeding, but I could see the trail of blood it made down her face to her chest; there was a nasty cut on her lip that had also stopped bleeding, but it was caked in dried blood. "We need to get you to the hospital," I murmured, afraid to touch her for fear of hurting her. She shook her head.

"Please don't make me," she sobbed.

I leaned my forehead against hers. "Why not, baby?" I said, my throat tight, my own tears threatening to fall.

"I don't like hospitals," she murmured.

I suppressed the urge to smile at the childish defiance in her voice. "I'm not a big fan either, but you really need to be checked out."

She shook her head vehemently. "I can't, Charlie. The first time I went to a hospital my granddad died; the next time was when my mom and dad died; and then ten years later, the last time I visited the hospital, my grandma died. I don't want to go, I'm not ready to die."

Shit! I backed away from her so I could get a better look at her injuries. "You're not going to die, Betty Boop." She shook her head again and began to sob harder. "Okay, okay, I'm not going to force you to go, but that means I'm going to check you over." I gently lifted her head, forcing her gaze back to mine. "If you don't want me to, there are paramedics outside who can do it."

She seemed to take a few deep breaths to compose herself. Her nod was barely noticeable and hesitant. "You," she whispered.

I was moving before the word left her lips. I found wash cloths under the sink and I wet one with lukewarm water. Going back to kneel in front of her, I used my finger to raise her chin and began gently wiping away the blood. The cut above her eye looked deep and would probably need a stitch or two, but the one on her lip would be fine. She more than likely had a concussion and I would have felt a whole lot better if I could get her to go to the hospital.

"Are you hurt anywhere else?" I asked, wiping away the last of the blood from her swollen cheek.

Her hand moved to her ribs. "It hurts here. If I take a deep breath, it's pretty painful."

"Your ribs could be broken. Will you let me take a look?" She looked scared as hell, but my eyes were set on hers with fixed determination. "Or we can go to the hospital?" She shook her head in defeat and carefully lifted her shirt. A slight discoloration suggested definite bruising, she could easily have a fracture. I gently felt around her ribs and pulled away when she winced. "Rebecca, if your ribs are broken, you could end up with a punctured lung or something. You really do need to go to the hospital." A tear escaped her eye and I was quick to brush it away, unable to stand seeing her pain.

"He tried to rape me." Her words hit me like a fucking truck. "He touched me, Charlie, I tried so hard to fight him off, but he touched me anyway."

The wail from her lips was enough to crush the strongest of hearts. I collapsed down beside her, wrapping my arms around her shoulders. She leaned in to me and cried like her soul had been ripped to shreds, and in that moment, I was pretty sure mine had, too.

CHAPTER 3

Rebecca

I sat on the bathroom floor and felt myself break into a million pieces. The horror of what had happened to me bled deep in my soul and I cried so hard, I thought I was going to be sick. Then, much to my embarrassment, I was. I scrambled from the floor to the toilet bowl and threw up what little food I had in me, while Charlie held my hair back. When I was finished he painstakingly wiped my face with a warm washcloth, whispering words that I couldn't hear over my own fucking sobs. He wrapped his arms around me and held me so close and tight it actually hurt, but I didn't care. I felt safe and protected in these strong arms. Whatever history Charlie and I had, whatever lay beyond this moment, I could care less about. All that mattered was his strength alone was keeping the soul eating fears at bay.

"Shhhh, take a deep breath, Betty Boop. Nice long deep breaths, come on, breathe with me."

I found the hypnotic quality of his voice lull me into some resemblance of calm again.

"You're going to go to the hospital," he gently ordered me.

I knew it was an order, even though his voice was tender. I knew he was worried as hell and wasn't going to take no for an answer this time. I was terrified of hospitals, I hated them—the smell, the sounds, the sights. I hadn't stepped foot in a hospital since the night my grandma died, but I knew my injuries really did require professional medical attention. I had to suck it up and stop being such a baby.

"I'll be there with you," Charlie hesitated, "or Mercy, if you would prefer. The doctors are going to check you over, then you can come home and get some rest, okay?"

I shook my head as panic began to flood my body. I couldn't control it; it simply washed over me like a tsunami. "I don't want to be here, I don't want to be in that room," I whispered. The thought of stepping a foot back in my bedroom flooded my body with fear.

"Okay, no problem. You can stay with me, or even Mercy. You know she'd be happy to have you."

Right now the thought of not being with Charlie filled me with a peculiar sense of dread and the thought confused me. I haven't even spoken to Charlie in a year, and now I felt completely reliant on him all of the sudden. I had been sitting on the floor of this fucking bathroom for God knows how long, scared out of my mind and it had been Charlie's whispered voice from the other side of the door that had calmed me. His presence alone settled me, made me believe that everything might be okay.

But there was also a hint of fear at being alone with a man—any man. Even though I knew Charlie wouldn't hurt me, even though I felt safe in his arms, the thought of spending the night alone with him was unsettling.

"You think Mercy wouldn't mind if I stayed with her?" I whispered. I felt so weak and pathetic, and if I didn't hurt so much, I would kick my own ass. But no matter how much I wanted to feel strong, I couldn't, I was terrified.

"You know she wouldn't mind," Charlie said easily.

"Dave is away, she's all alone in her house," I whispered, realizing that too made me a little uncomfortable.

"If it makes you feel better, I'll crash there too. You, me, and Mercy, we'll have one big happy sleepover. For me it will be like old times, except Jax won't be there breaking wind every five minutes." I tried to smile but my lip stung like a bitch. "Here's what we're going to do. Mercy's going to sit with you while I get some materials from my truck and leave it with Frank to secure the broken window. Then you can pack a bag and we'll go to the hospital, all three of us together." I nodded, grateful that he was doing the thinking for me. I didn't want to think, I didn't want to feel for that matter. Then the thought of packing a bag sent a jolt of panic through my veins once more.

"I can't," I whimpered.

"Can't what, baby? he asked, still sitting beside me, his arms around me, holding me, protecting me.

"I can't go in my room, I can't pack my bag." I started crying again and it pissed me off. I haven't cried since my grandma died over nine years ago.

Charlie pulled away to look me straight in the eye. He cupped my cheeks gently. "Not a problem, Betty Boop. I'll pack your bag while Mercy sits with you, okay?" I nodded. "Anyway, I'm dying to see what else you've got in that top drawer with those pretty red lacey things you wore the last time I was here."

A small smile tugged at the corner of my mouth and my stinging lip made me wince. A tear slipped free again, a reminder of how quickly my life had descended from peaceful to chaotic.

"I'm sorry, honey, it really isn't the time for jokes. I'm a prick."

I pulled him closer and held onto him for dear life until I finally found some control again. "Just don't open the drawer beside my bed, please." Somewhere in the panic and fear, embarrassment over Charlie finding Big Red seemed about as bad as it could get.

"I'm intrigued, but I promise I won't go near it," he whispered.

I could hear the smile in his voice, and as much as I wanted to give him a playful punch and make him pinky promise, my heart just wasn't light enough.

"Thank you," I simply whispered. My throat was so sore from screaming that I would have given anything for some warm tea with a dash of honey right now. Tea? Since when did Rebecca Donovan drink fucking tea? Coffee, yes. Wine, hell yeah. Vodka, most definitely. But tea? Never!

"No need to thank me, we are friends after all." Friends. Yes, that's what we were. The word actually hurt as I let the idea roll around in my mind. I had always wanted more with Charlie, even when I denied it like a cold hearted bitch to anyone who would listen. I couldn't lie to myself though. I couldn't refute that my heart adored this man and wanted more. Over the past year I thought perhaps 'friends' was even a stretch, so I should be grateful we are at least that.

"Come on, sweetheart."

I shivered at the term of endearment. Suddenly I was back against the front door, that monster's body pressed against mine, his hands ripping at my clothing.

"Rebecca?" Charlie said sternly.

My gaze returned to his; he looked worried, confused. "Please don't call me that," I whispered, tears falling in a steady cadence.

"Rebecca?" he asked, his brow furrowed with worry.

I shook my head. "Sweetheart," I managed to say without throwing up, "he called me that," I explained.

Charlie's nostrils flared with what I assumed was anger before he gave me a sharp nod and scooped me up from the floor. My ribs ached in protest, but I would deal with it just so I could stay nestled in the warm safety of Charlie's arms. He walked me out into the living room where Mercy immediately began to fuss over me. The paramedics swooped in and wrapped a brace around my neck and began shining things in my one good eye, asking me questions, inspecting my ribs. Frank stood close by and I could see he was eager to ask me his own questions. I couldn't handle all this attention on me; it was just too much. The tears began to fall again and Mercy gripped my hand tightly. My eyes searched for Charlie and panic threatened to consume me when I didn't see him. Then he appeared, tall and strong, my bag thrown over his shoulder. His green eyes found mine and never left them, not even as Frank stood and talked to him. That alone gave me the strength I needed to focus and get through this.

As I was wheeled into the hospital, I kept my eyes closed. Charlie still had hold of one hand, Mercy the other, but I didn't dare open my eyes. I didn't want to see where I was. The sounds and smells were enough to make my breathing labored, opening my eyes would destroy me. Finally, the gurney became still and I heard the sound of curtain hooks sliding over metal.

"You can open your eyes, Rebecca, the curtains are closed and the doctor is here to check you out," Mercy whispered from beside me.

Trusting her word, I opened my eyes. The curtains had been pulled closed. I saw that the room was small and bright with standard medical equipment spread strategically around the room. A kindly looking female doctor smiled down at me and I clutched Charlie's hand tighter when she began to check my injuries. I felt so lost, so broken, so not me. Rebecca Fucking Donovan didn't cry, she didn't beg and she sure as hell didn't find herself completely dependent on a man. Rebecca Donovan was a free spirited, liberated, self-reliant woman. Don't get me wrong, I wasn't some sort of snooty feminist. I liked a man to open doors for me, I wanted my chair pulled out for me, I wanted romance, to be wined and dined. I knew that wasn't necessarily real though, so, I opened my own doors and pulled out my own chair. I took home my own bouquets of flowers and cooked my own dinner. Right now I didn't feel like that girl anymore though. I felt frail, I felt weak and I hated it.

After x-rays, a couple of stitches, and more poking and prodding than I could handle, I was finally given the all clear to leave. The sun was up, the bright cloudless day shone through the window, filling the small room I had stayed in. Charlie handed me some clean clothes and Mercy helped me get changed in the bathroom. He had packed me freakin' sweats to wear! The man clearly didn't know me at all. Nevertheless, I didn't have the energy to argue, and really, the bruised, bloody mess that stared back at me from the mirror was tragic. Pretty clothes were not going to lessen the bruises or make the nightmares of the previous night go away. When Mercy pulled me back into the hospital room, Frank was standing by Charlie, and his sorrowful expression turned my way. I knew he had questions, and the least I could do was attempt to answer them. That's what a self-reliant, strong woman would do, right? I gave his silent questioning gaze a brisk nod and sat down on the side of the bed. Mercy thankfully stayed close and continued to hold my hand.

"How bout we start at the beginning. Tell me what you were up to last night before you went to bed," Frank suggested.

I almost snorted a laugh. God, he was going to love this, all three of them would. "I had a date," I murmured huskily. It would have been kinda hot, like Demi Moore hot, if the circumstances of how it came to be this way had been different. I had literally screamed my voice away. Charlie raised a brow but said nothing.

"With who?" asked Frank.

I would give anything not to answer this, embarrassment was about to come my middle name. Wow, did I really care? I had just been assaulted in my own home, in my own bed. I had been hit, touched, and a man had attempted to rape me. Did I really care how pathetic my extra-curricular activities had become? "Luke Hollywell."

Frank and Mercy did well to contain their surprise. Charlie not so much.

He groaned loudly and shook his head. "Luke Fucking Hollywell?" he growled.

"Charlie!" snapped Mercy. Both of us pinned him with a death glare. I guess if my face didn't look like it had been through a round with Mike Tyson, mine might have been as intimidating as Mercy's.

"How did the date go?" Frank ignored Charlie. If he could I could.

I turned my attention back to Frank. "About how you would imagine. The guy is a walking, talking, self-absorbed ass." It was Frank's turn to raise a brow, but before he could say anything, I added, "I left before we even ordered, I told him I felt sick."

"How did Luke take that?" he asked.

I shrugged. I really didn't think he cared one way or the other. "There was a certain amount of disbelief, but I'm sure he wasn't too fazed."

"He didn't get angry, make any threats?" Frank was fishing.

I knew Luke hadn't done this. He might have been a loser who was renowned for causing trouble at clubs and bars, but hurting women was not Luke's style. He liked women, he had a certain reputation as a man who loved to pleasure women; he didn't need to take it by force.

"No, Frank, he wasn't angry, he didn't even break a sweat." Frank scribbled furiously in a little notebook held in the palm of his hand. He peered over the glasses that were perched low on his nose.

"Did Luke leave with you?"

"No, I left him sitting there. He probably ordered dinner and ate before he left."

"What time was this?" Frank glanced up from his notebook.

"I bailed at around eight. I was home and in bed before nine."

Frank nodded. "The 911 call came through at two-fifteen this morning," he continued. I just sat and stared, feeling suddenly disconnected from the conversation, from this room. This is where things went to shit, this was where my heart began to pound and my mouth became dry. Reaching for the glass of water, I raised it to my lips and winced when the glass brushed the cut there. "Tell me what happened. Did you hear the window break?" I shook my head. It was a known fact amongst my small circle of friends that when Rebecca's head hit the pillow, nothing could wake her. I was a deep, heavy sleeper.

"I'm not sure what woke me, maybe it was a noise, but I'm not sure. When I opened my eyes, he was just there," I choked out the words, and Mercy gripped my hand a bit tighter. Charlie moved to my side, his strong hand rested on my back, helping me regain some of the strength I was fumbling for. I took a deep breath and continued, "He was just standing at the end of the bed, and as soon as I realized he was there, he pretty much threw himself on me and held down my hands." I took a deep breath, hoping words wouldn't fail me now.

"Did you get a good look at him, see any scars, tattoos?" urged Frank.

I shook my head as a tear slipped free. "He had something over his face, I could only see the whites of his eyes. He looked angry." Charlie settled down beside me, the warmth of his body at one side and Mercy's at the other filled me with comfort. "He ripped my top and touched me," I cried, pulling my hand from Charlie's and rubbing my chest, careful of the bruises that he left.

"What about an accent?" I shook my head. "Did he seem nervous or angry?" I thought carefully, and although he barely spoke, he definitely radiated clear anger and confidence.

"He seemed to know what he was doing and he didn't seem worried about getting caught. He was confident." I remembered those narrowed eyes of fury peering down on me. "And angry."

Frank stood patiently, not pressing me continue, but I knew he wanted me to. "He tried to pull my pants down." Fuck, I was breaking again, the wound still so fresh on my soul was tearing open once more. "He touched me there, too," I sobbed. "He was trying to rape me so I stuck my fingers in his eyes and kneed the fucker in the balls." Charlie kissed my temple.

"Good girl," he whispered.

"I got out of the bedroom and made it to the front door. He slammed me into it so hard, I think that's when my ribs got bruised." No fractures, thank God. To be honest, the bruising was painful enough, I didn't think I could cope with broken. "Don from next door was yelling from the other side of the door and I guess it freaked him out."

"It was Don Brugner who called 911. Your attacker left through the back door. There was a garbage can against the fence that he most likely used to stand on." I nodded woodenly. Reliving the experience, on top of recently having lived it, had drained me. I had nothing left.

"Okay, honey, one more thing and then I'll get out of your hair. Have you had any weird phone calls? Perhaps noticed someone who seemed a bit out of place hanging around the street, maybe even hanging around Bouquets?" My sister's phone calls could easily be considered weird, but completely unrelated to this. I shook my head a little despondent. I really didn't feel like I was giving Frank much to go on.

"Frank, Rebecca needs to get some sleep. Maybe you could call us if you need anything else," Mercy suggested. Thankful for bringing things to an end, I gave her hand a gentle squeeze.

Frank flicked his notebook closed. "Okay, if you can think of anything else, you call me right away." Frank gave me a stern look. I felt about twelve again, standing before the principal, awaiting punishment for turning on the fire alarm at school. I nodded obediently.

"What about Luke?" Charlie said through gritted teeth.

"We'll check him out, see if he has an alibi. Right now we don't really have anything but a bad date. That's not much of a motive and it's certainly nothing to base a case on."

"He said we'd finish it later," I whispered, my mind skipping back to those final moments. Frank, Mercy and Charlie's heads all swung my way. "He said, 'we'll finish this later, sweetheart' before he left the house."

Frank and Charlie looked at each other, while Mercy rubbed a soothing hand over my back.

"Perhaps it would be best if you stayed with someone until we wrap this up. It was probably just an idle threat. It's not common for a random criminal to come back for a second attempt, but it's better to be safe than sorry," Frank confessed.

"What if it wasn't a random attack?" asked Charlie, his eyes blazing with anger. As far as I was concerned it had to be; there wasn't a single person I knew that had it in them to do this—not even Luke Hollywell.

"We'll figure it out, Charlie, sexual assault investigations take a little time though. The case rarely solves itself then falls into our lap all gift wrapped and nicely presented. Just call me if you think of anything else." Frank gave me another of his pointed looks over his silver rimmed glasses.

"And you'll call if you find anything?" Charlie countered. Frank nodded and left the room. Charlie rubbed the back of his neck; he looked tired and worried. I knew just how he felt, probably more so. "I'm going to go sort out the paper work, I'll be right back, okay?" I nodded. It was all I could manage. Talking was too hard, my throat was too sore. I had nothing left inside me to offer so non-committal head movements would have to do.

"Rebecca, I'm going to have to call Lola and Annie. You need someone to take care of the store for a few days. What do you want me to tell them?" Mercy asked. Shit, I hadn't even thought about Bouquets, which was in fact now called Mercy's Angels and Bouquets, but Ella and I still referred to it as Bouquets. Old habits die hard.

"Ummm...maybe just tell them that I'm sick?" I shrugged.

"Perhaps I can tell Annie what happened. She would understand and you've known her for quite some time now. You aren't going to be able to explain the bruises easily; she'll find out soon enough. We'll just tell Lola you're sick and she can take care of Bouquets for a few days, okay?" It all made sense and I knew Lola and Annie would take care of the store for me. I also knew Annie would understand what I had been through. She had faced her own demon, in the form of her ex-husband, who physically and mentally abused her. She had fled to Mercy's Shelter eighteen months ago. Annie had trusted me with her past, with her nightmares, the least I could do was be honest with her about my own.

"That sounds fine. Lola needs to get the order for Mr. Benoir out by this afternoon. Tell her the order is in the book."

"How about you get a ride back to my place with Charlie and I'll stop by the store and talk to the girls. Charlie can help get you set up in the spare room at my place; he has a key." I nodded. Whatever...I no longer really cared what happened or how it happened. I was so tired I thought I might fall asleep standing.

Charlie sorted out the discharge instructions, he collected the prescriptions for pain medication and, much to my horror, sleeping pills. Seriously, sleeping pills? I slept like the dead as it was. If I had any trouble, my good ol' friend Hangar One Vodka would help me pass out—it was just as effective. Charlie and Mercy walked, one on each side of me, as a nurse pushed me along in a completely unnecessary wheel chair, navigating the hospital corridors with ease. I closed my eyes and ignored the sights and sounds that frightened me so much. Once Charlie helped me climb up into the ridiculously high cabin of his Ford truck, my head leaned against the cool glass of the window and my mind drifted. I couldn't believe how different I felt compared to yesterday, when my dramas included a nagging sister, bills, and my need to get laid. Now part of me was dying to hear my sister's voice, the bills could take a flying leap, and the thought of getting laid made me ill. Oh God, the last person I had sex with was sitting right beside me, and it seemed as though he would be the last person who ever touched me in that way. A tear rolled down my cheek. The thought of anyone touching me intimately made me shiver. He had touched me, he had taken away my choice and turned something that was supposed to be beautiful and exciting into something ugly and scary.

"Rebecca?" Charlie's voice broke me from my sorrow.

The car had stopped moving and I hadn't even noticed. I turned to face him, not bothering to wipe my tears. It hurt too much anyway. My face was aching, throbbing in fact. It made me think about Ella and the abuse she endured at the hands of her stepfather. My heart broke a little more for her.

"Baby," Charlie whispered, cupping my cheek, "you're going to be okay. You're going to get through this and that beautiful face of yours will have a smile on it again, if it's the last thing I do."

My nod was involuntary, because the reality was, I didn't believe him. I couldn't imagine ever smiling again. But Charlie's conviction required a response and I found myself not wanting to let him down.

"I'm going to run in and get your prescriptions filled, it should only take a minute or two. Will you be okay by yourself?"

I looked around. We were in a busy parking lot, surrounded by shoppers, people going about their everyday, mundane lives with a blissful ease I now envied. Would I be alright? His words echoed through my mind.

"I'll be fine, Charlie, just hurry up, please. I'm really tired." My head found its way back to the cool glass and I heard Charlie sigh and slip out of the truck.

The windows were dark, thank God. Otherwise, my horrid face would probably scare the shit out of the people walking by. I couldn't recall the moment I began to fade away, the moment my eyes became heavy and on a burdensome flutter, closed. Sleep pulled me away from my pain, away from my sorrow and blissfully far away from my fears.

CHAPTER 4

Charlie

I was only in the drug store for twenty-five minutes. I stood sweating and shuffling from one foot to the other nervously, feeling a little like a teenager about to get busted for buying condoms. I didn't want to leave Rebecca alone for long though, not after the night she had endured. I should have given the damn prescriptions to Mercy, but I had been so eager to get her away from the hospital, I had forgotten. When I made it back to the truck, I found her fast asleep. She looked so small and fragile with her head rested against the window. I managed to shove my jacket between her and the glass without waking her up, then navigated the busy morning streets to Mercy's house on the outskirts of town. It was on the same road that led to Jax's place, but not quite as far away from civilization. Mercy's house was a big, two story colonial with a wide sweeping front porch. I loved it here and I visited often. I even lived here for a couple of years after Jax left for the army. He didn't want to leave Mercy all alone and I needed to escape my parents before I did something truly damaging and irreversible. The preaching and fanatic religion that I grew up with fuelled hate and anger forced me to distance myself from my family. I haven't seen my parents in three years, and at the risk of sounding like a hypocrite, halle-a-fucking-lujah for that. The degree to which they demonstrated their so called faith was excessive to say the least. They had strict rules: no music, other than church hymns, no brand named clothing, because apparently the devil owned Prada, no alcohol, no fast food, no books other than the bible, no computers or electronic devices, outside of the microwave, fridge and dishwasher, hell, we never even owned a TV. It was all a little too cult-like and antiquated for a kid born at the end of the twentieth century. Mercy's was the kind of home I dreamed of growing up in. She was the perfect mom who baked on Sundays, laughed often and filled her home with music and noise. She let me ride a motorcycle, she didn't bitch when I got my first tattoo, and she never cursed my existence as being attributed to Satan himself. I hadn't been by in almost a month and just pulling into the driveway helped relax me. It was like coming home, to a real home, with a real family.

I somehow managed to open the passenger door without Rebecca falling out. She didn't stir as I lifted her carefully from the car and carried her up the steps. I've never carried a woman like this before, and I found her slight weight in my arms strangely comforting. It felt good to be taking care of someone like this, or perhaps it was simply the fact that I was taking care of Rebecca like this. I wanted to keep her buried against my chest for eternity, where no one could ever hurt her again. After an awkward shuffle and a few frustrating minutes, I managed to get the key in the lock. As I kicked the door shut behind us, a possessive need descended over me—the need to keep Rebecca here with me, the need to keep her safe. Rebecca was a free spirit though, not a girl to be locked away from the world. Once she healed, I had no doubt she would make her way home the first chance she could. The only reason she had turned to me for comfort was because she had been through a traumatic experience, and she felt safe with me. I wasn't stupid enough to think that Rebecca Donovan wanted anything more than to simply feel safe right now. If safe is what she wanted, then safe was what I would give her. I adored this girl; I've adored her for a long time now, but I let her get away. Seeing her beaten and bloodied face in her bathroom had broken my heart in two. Her tears had undone me, her fear, her need, it was all so unlike Rebecca. But she had every right to those feelings and I would be whatever she needed me to be. If she needed to feel safe, then she would feel fucking safe. If she needed someone to take care of her, I would fucking take care of her. When it came time to let her go, I wasn't sure how I would do it, but I would.

I laid her down on the bed in the spare room on the ground floor. Mercy and Dave's bedroom was upstairs, as well as the study and a large bathroom. The downstairs bedroom was smaller, but no less comfortable, and there was a bathroom was right across the hall, next to the living room. I'd be close to her on the big couch in the living room. I grabbed a blanket from the closet and spread it carefully over her tiny body, tucking it carefully under her chin. Her hair was still matted with dried blood. She needed a shower, but I couldn't bring myself to wake her. She was exhausted, both emotionally and physically. She could shower when she woke. I stood and stared at her for the longest time. I didn't want to leave her alone, but I needed to make a call to Lee's to let them know I wouldn't be available to spar with Brent tonight. I needed a shower, I needed to go home and grab some clothes, and then I needed to sleep for about twelve hours straight. I would have to wait until Mercy got home before I left though, there wasn't a chance in hell I was leaving Rebecca alone. I had a pair of jeans and a shirt in the closet that I left here last time I visited, so I grabbed them and made my way to the bathroom. I had some of Rebecca's blood on my shirt, but that wasn't what bothered me. It was the scent of Gym Girl that was lingering on my skin. The fact that I had gone straight from her bed to Rebecca made me feel ill. I wanted to wash every woman I had ever touched, except Rebecca, from my body, from my mind. I wanted to be clean for Rebecca, I wanted to be untainted. I wanted to turn back the clock and be buried deep in Rebecca's willing body, in her bed, in her home. I wanted to take her out to dinner, wine and dine her, spoil her. I wanted to take away her pain and give her back the beautiful, worry-free life she'd been living.

"Fuck," I groaned as my dick began to harden at my thoughts. I turned the hot water off and almost yelled like a pussy under the painful ice cold water. It turned my libido and wanting off as quickly as thoughts of Rebecca had turned it on. I dried and pulled on the clean jeans and shirt. I checked on Rebecca one last time before I took to the couch. I was sleeping like the dead before my head hit the pillow.

* * *

A blood curdling scream had me rolling off the couch and hitting the floor in a painful heap. I had been in a deep, dreamless sleep and was now wide awake. I scrambled from the floor and, for a split second, had forgotten where I was, but seeing Mercy rush down the stairs, her face full of angst as she moved with determination, reminded me quickly. I got to Rebecca's doorway at the same time Mercy did and we both stopped for a second to see Rebecca thrashing around in the bed, trapped in a violent nightmare. Mercy ran to her side and tried to hold her down and wake her, but Rebecca was fighting hard. I slipped into the room and helped Mercy gently hold her arms down.

"Rebecca, your safe, wake up," Mercy whispered gently. She was still fighting and screaming and it was breaking my heart.

"Betty Boop, open your eyes!" I demanded with a little more force. Thankfully her pretty blue eyes flew open. For a heartbeat I expected her to come at me with a feisty little right hook, instead she surprised me by launching herself right past Mercy and into my arms. Her entire body shivered and I held her close, trying to infuse some warmth into her. I peered at Mercy over Rebecca's shaking shoulders. Mercy knew what Rebecca was going through; Mercy's ex-husband had spent years beating the ever loving shit out of her. That was before my time, but I've witnessed the nightmares that still plagued her.

Mercy reached out and placed a sturdy hand over mine that was holding Rebecca's head against my chest. "I'll go make some coffee," she whispered. It was still dark out, but I could see the faint distant glow from the rising sun through the window signaling the rapid approach of another day. We had slept right through the day and most of the night. To be honest, Rebecca had done better than I thought she would. She had to have slept no less than fourteen hours straight. When I felt her body begin to relax, I pulled back a little to check her over. One eye was still swollen shut and the other was red from crying. She tried to pull away and I knew she was embarrassed about the way she looked. I didn't want her to feel that way around me so I gently leaned in and I pressed my lips to her forehead.

"They're just bruises, Betty Boop, the swelling will go down in a day or two. You are just as beautiful as ever, there is no need to hide." She didn't respond for the longest time and I thought maybe she drifted back to sleep until she eventually pulled away from my arms. My fingers twitched with the need to fold her into my chest again.

"I've never been inside Mercy's house," Rebecca murmured, her voice still husky and strained.

"It's warm and cozy. You'll like it here, hell, I love it here." She looked around the dimly lit room. "How are you feeling?" I chanced asking her the one question I was pretty sure I knew the answer to.

"Sore." She shrugged, raising her hand lightly to cup her bruised cheek.

"How about I run you a bath? It might help for you to soak a while." Her nod was despondent and it pained me to see her this way. Mercy brought in a hot cup of coffee which I left beside the tub as it filled. Rebecca quietly closed the door to the bathroom, separating me from her. Not being able to be with her, to tend to her, pissed me off. I don't know why I felt such entitlement where Rebecca was concerned; it's not like we were together or anything. I went to the kitchen and sat at the table.

"I fucking hate this," I murmured, watching the gentle fall of snow in the backyard. The heaviest falls of winter had passed, but a soft coat of snow and ice still greeted us most mornings. In another month, it would be gone. Mercy had already started cooking a feast: bacon, sausage, eggs, biscuits and gravy, and hash browns. It was overkill but the thing about Mercy was she liked to coddle and she liked to cook. I watched her flip the bacon in the pan, my mouth watering and stomach growling. It would be almost as good as Benny's all day breakfast at The Pit Stop, almost.

"She is going to have nightmares for a while, and she will most likely suffer from panic attacks. She might even have PTSD. She'll also cry a lot more tears. It will be good for her to talk to Dave when he gets home." If anyone knew about the stresses of living a life of pain, it was Dave. Although he hadn't lived through anything as such himself, he was a psychiatrist who worked at Mercy's Shelter. He spent every day talking to the women who crossed their threshold. He didn't work in a fancy office with his degrees plastered on the wall, instead he worked in the shelter, making beds, cleaning bathrooms, fixing shit and being the ear many of the women needed, and more often than not, the voice of reason. Even Jax and I have spent time sitting with Dave, getting our heads on straight and dealing with our own shit. Rebecca could definitely benefit from talking to him.

Breakfast was cooked, sitting, and waiting, but Rebecca was still in the bathroom. I began to worry and stared at the closed door. Feeling like a complete and utter perv, I left Mercy loading our plates up with too much food while I pressed my ear to the bathroom door. The gentle sobbing from the other side literally hurt my chest. Unable to stop myself, I knocked.

"Betty Boop, I'm coming in." I gave her a moment to protest. When she didn't, I opened the door. She was sitting in the tub, her knees drawn to her chest, her face resting on them, her blonde hair still matted with dried blood. I sank down beside the tub and brushed her hair back.

"I'm sorry," she quietly sobbed.

"There is nothing you need to be apologizing for, baby."

She shook her head stubbornly. "I haven't cried this much in a long time. I feel like a helpless, weepy female," she confessed with a sniffle.

I smiled as I got up and grabbed some shampoo from the shower, then went back to kneel down beside her. "In case you haven't noticed, you are, in fact, female and the events of the last twenty-four hours warrant weeping. Helpless?" I paused. "Not a fucking chance, Betty Boop. You fought that fucker off. Things could have been a whole lot worse, but you fought back. You're a fighter, it's who you are. So, no, you're not helpless." I encouraged her to tip her head backwards and gently wet her hair before squeezing in some shampoo and lathering it in. I've never washed a girl's hair before. Was it weird that it was kinda turning me on?

"I don't suppose that shampoo is for color treated hair, or that it has vanilla bean extracts in it?"

I couldn't help the laugh that escaped my lips. "I wouldn't have a clue. Considering I'm the only one who has used this bathroom in the last year, I would say not."

She sighed. "That's okay, but I'll need to get my own shampoo from home. My hair will turn into a bird's nest if I don't use it."

It has been a long time since I lived with a woman and that had been Mercy. I hadn't taken much notice of what a woman required to survive on a day-to-day basis, other than food and water, so it was safe to say women's grooming was a little foreign to me. As a man who liked women, I certainly appreciated such things though. If Rebecca needed special shampoo, I would damn well provide it for her. After rinsing the soap from Rebecca's hair, I grabbed a clean towel from under the sink.

"You need me to stay?" I asked, not sure if I should go. Her answer was to simply stand, water running rivulets down her beautiful body. I might have become instantly hard if the bruises against her pale skin didn't draw my attention.

"It's nothing you haven't seen before," she admitted without emotion.

As soon as she stepped from the tub, I wrapped the towel around her and grabbed another for her hair. Once she was rubbed dry and glowing a pretty shade of pink, I left her to dress while I joined Mercy in the kitchen.

When Rebecca finally meandered out of the bathroom, she looked nervous. I raised my brow wondering what the hell had her so uncomfortable all of a sudden. She glanced down at her clothes.

"You only grabbed pajamas and sweats," she murmured.

I nodded because, yeah, I realized that. What did she want? Those sexy as hell dresses and a pair of heels? "I was thinking of comfort, not fashion."

Rebecca shook her head with frustration. "I know and I'm just being stupid." A tear slid free, just one, lonely fucking tear. "I mean, you're right, I feel like a Mack truck hit me and I'm upset that I don't have my normal clothes. I don't know why, I can't explain it." She sank into the chair beside me.

"Rebecca, it's normal to feel this way, you're out of sorts, out of your comfort zone. Your clothes make you feel comfortable so it's perfectly natural that you'd want them," Mercy said quietly from beside us. She leaned over and pressed a gentle kiss to Rebecca's forehead. Fuck, I hadn't even thought about that. As far as I was concerned all she needed were loose fitting, baggy, comfy clothes.

"I'll stop by your place today and grab your shampoo and some more clothes," I offered. Rebecca looked up at me with a shy smile playing on her lips. Just seeing that smile, as small as it may have been, made me feel ten fucking feet tall. I helped create that smile, I brought her that moment and I'd be damned sure it became my number one priority to create more of them. "I know you're probably not hungry, but try and eat something, then you can take one of those wicked little pills and zonk out for another twelve or so hours." I gave her a wink.

"I don't want any pills," she growled defiantly. There was the Rebecca Donovan I remembered.

"It's not permanent, Rebecca, it's just for a little while. It's normal to have trouble sleeping after you've been through a traumatic experience," Mercy reasoned.

Rebecca's eyes were filled with stubborn determination. "I just slept an entire day and then some, I'm pretty sure I'll be fine."

"Make you a deal. We'll try no pills first, but if you have trouble sleeping then you have to take them, without me or Mercy having to hold you down."

Rebecca grimaced and eventually relented, "Fine, but I won't need them."

The look on Mercy's face suggested otherwise. We already witnessed one nightmare and it wasn't pretty. As Mercy had already explained, Rebecca would probably be plagued with plenty of nightmares, flashbacks, and a bucket loads of tears. There was a time when such things would have sent me running for the hills, but not anymore, not with Rebecca. I'd endure anything for this girl, I'd take her pain, her nightmares, and her fears in a heartbeat. If only it were that easy.

CHAPTER 5

Rebecca

The thing about Charlie...he was always right, and damn it, it pissed me off. I have no idea why something so small was making me so angry. Over the course of the next few days, my life had become a Charlie Cole I-told-you-so merry go round. Mind you, he never actually said I-told-you-so, but I knew when he was thinking it. Even if he was nothing but patient, understanding and charming. Thank God Mercy has been there to smooth over my tantrums. We tried it my way—without the sleeping pills—and it didn't work. I was plagued with nightmares which led me to do everything humanly possible to try not to fall asleep. The getting to sleep part wasn't the problem, it was once I was there. Almost immediately I would transport to a dark familiar room, my bedroom—a room that had once been a sanctuary of comfort and peace—and then he would appear, hovering over me with those cold eyes. I would be pinned down, unable to move, his hands roaming freely over my body. I would wake up screaming and sweaty. On one occasion, I vomited everything that was in my stomach all over Mercy's floor. Humiliation filled my heart and soul. On top of losing my mind, I felt as if I had also lost my dignity. Charlie had brought me more clothes, my usual clothes, and I tried to wear them, but I felt silly sitting around in pretty dresses and pencil skirts, so sweats became my begrudging fashion choice. The swelling in my face had started to go down, and though my face no longer looked like a swollen elephant, it had gained some curious coloring. I still looked like a Mack truck had done a number on me. My ribs still ached, and I had frequent headaches that throbbed. I was going stir crazy sitting around Mercy's all day and night. All of this free time had me thinking too much, I needed to keep busy. Part of me wanted to be at home, that was the old part of me, pre-assault Rebecca. Post-assault Rebecca was terrified of returning to the scene of my assault. What if I could never return? I'd have to sell the house and the thought made me feel even worse. To lose the cottage would mean losing a part of me, and in the last few days, I had already lost too much of me to risk losing anymore. Staying at Mercy's has been comfortable and Charlie has been here every night. I would get anxious and restless when he went off to work during the day, but as soon as he got back for the evening, I would immediately relax. I was such an idiot, after all, hadn't I chalked Charlie Cole up as my one big mistake. It was one night that tilted my world off its axis—he did things to my body that still made me blush an entire year later—but a mistake nonetheless. Consequently, I had joined the vast collection of notches on Charlie Cole's bed post. Finding comfort in his presence seemed like such a mistake, but at the same time it felt curiously right.

34

After we got settled at Mercy's the day after the attack, Charlie wanted to call Ella and Jax immediately, but Mercy and I persuaded him not to. They were having the vacation of a life time in Hawaii, and there was absolutely no way was I getting in the middle of that. Ella would freak out, like ballistic freak out and insist on coming home early. No way was I okay with that. So instead, Charlie called Dillon Montgomery and his cousin, Braiden Montgomery, who have recently set up a second office for their security company here in Claymont. Dillon and Braiden were like ninjas of the security world. While Braiden was apparently sprucing up my non-existent home security system, Dillon was looking into the police reports to see if he could work his own case behind the scenes. I don't even know if that is legal, but to be honest, I don't care. The more people out looking for the fucker who turned me into a damn skittish meerkat, the better. I had become so nervous and anxious. I was paranoid, too—I had the feeling as if someone were watching me—it felt like there was a constant prickling at the back of my neck. I hated that feeling. I hated the dark now—waking to a room shadowed in darkness made me feel physically ill—I had to sleep with the constant glow of a lamp to guide my nervous thoughts to calm resolve in the middle of the night. I have never been scared of the dark, not even as a child. But this was my life now: fear and trepidation.

Luke Hollywell had a good alibi. After I left him at the restaurant, he proceeded to order a steak, well done, a side of fries and a salad. He then left for a club where he was filmed on CCTV footage getting into a brawl somewhere around two that morning. My attack was said to have happened between one and two. Luke couldn't have made it to my house in that time. Anyway, Luke had an endless supply of women coming and going. One failed date didn't seem like it would have rattled him at all. To think someone like Luke Hollywell didn't see me as a challenge or suitable conquest, sat uncomfortably in my stomach. I really shouldn't have cared, after all it had been me who had rejected him. But I couldn't stop the nagging feeling of self-doubt that insisted on being noticed, desired. Charlie hadn't wanted me, and apparently not even the dregs of Claymont wanted me either. What was wrong with me? I've never lacked confidence, until now. Now I was second guessing myself, doubting my choices, and doubting my self-worth. I sat on the back porch, watching the stars twinkle in the clear sky. I felt like drifting up there to join them, where nothing could touch me or hurt me; where my worries would cease to exist. Being surrounded by a void of nothingness seemed so appealing right now.

"Jill, I'm sorry," came a hushed voice from the doorway beside me. Charlie slipped out and stood on the porch with his cell phone pressed to his ear. He didn't seem to know I was there. "Sorry, Jenny," he seemed to wince, "I had shit to deal with Saturday and I had to bail early." My stomach dropped. "Yeah, I had a great time, too, and I'm sorry I had to sneak out." He was quiet for a moment. He had shit to deal with Saturday? Was I was his shit? "Look," he scratched his head in what appeared to be aggravation, "Jenny, I did have a great time, hell, I had a fucking fantastic time, but that's all it was, just one night of fun. I think it would be best if we just left it at that." Another long pause and I felt ill. I wondered if I could sneak away without him noticing me. I carefully stood up. "I'm not sure when I'll be back at the gym but I'm sure I'll see you around." I took a few steps towards the door, his back was to me now. I thought I had it in the bag, until I stubbed my toe on Mercy's damn doorstop.

"Shit," I hissed.

Charlie swung around and spotted me, the regret in his eyes tangible. I didn't want that: his regret, his pity. I scowled at him then turned to limp back into the house, all attempts at stealth gone.

"Jenny, I have to go. I'll see you around." He hung up and followed me into the house. Mercy was at the shelter tonight so it was just the two of us. Dave would be home tomorrow. "Betty Boop, are you okay?" he called out from behind me. As I made a bee-line for my temporary bedroom, I remember the first time he had ever called me that, how I had swooned under the endearment that he coined just for me. When he used it a few weeks later at the Claymont Christmas tree lighting, I wanted to knock the bastard out for it. Kind of like I wanted to right now.

"Fine, I just stubbed my toe. I'm sure I'll survive," I grumbled.

"I wasn't talking about your toe," he murmured from across the room.

I pulled off the blanket that had been draped over my shoulders and threw it over the back of the sofa as I passed by.

"I have no idea what you are referring to. I'm fine," I said through gritted teeth.

Charlie shook his head in frustration. "I'm sorry," he whispered.

I stopped fleeing and turned to face him. Pissed off, tired, emotional with a dash of PMS to boot, I was not in the mood. "What for? You didn't kick my toe."

"Not for your damn toe, for that phone call. I didn't realize you were out there, I didn't really want you to hear that."

His frank admission made my blood boil. What? Did he assume that I thought he was some sort of saint? That he didn't hook up with every vagina in Claymont? Or perhaps he didn't want me to hear that he referred to me as his 'shit he had to deal with'. I clenched my fists wanting to pound them into his sheepish face.

"Who and what you do in your spare time is none of my business, Charlie. You don't have to sneak outside to make phone calls for fear you might upset little ol' me. I could care less." That was a big fat lie. I cared a lot more than I was entitled to. My words seemed to piss Charlie off.

"She was just a friend," he said, irritation clouding his too handsome features.

"Charlie, it doesn't matter. I told you I don't care," I snapped. "I'm only sorry that my drama interrupted your evening." Charlie's eyes burned with fury and his anger made my heart pound with fear. He looked livid and that's all it took to push me into an anxiety attack. Ordinarily I would be getting ready to sucker punch the asshole, but now, timid scaredy-cat Rebecca Donavan was sweating over nothing.

"You were not the 'shit I had to deal with', it was just an excuse I gave Jill because I couldn't very well say, 'I snuck out because I was desperate to get away from you'."

Well, that sounded a little better, but I was still pissed off and uncomfortable with the anger in his eyes. I couldn't stop the reflexive step away from him. "Her name was Jenny, and, like I said, whatever, it's none of my business."

His eyes flared with fury and I took another hesitant step away from him. Before this could turn into an ugly screaming match that would only result in me balling my eyes out like a two year old, I turned and quickly locked myself away in the spare bedroom. I could hear Charlie muttering and cursing, but at least he made no attempt to come into my room. I sank down on the bed and lifted my knees up under my chin, hugging them close to me. I hated this, I hated everything about this life I was suddenly living. As lovely as Mercy's home was, it wasn't my home. I hated the tears that seemed never ending, I hated the nightmares, I hated the pills I was taking, and I hated the fear. But most of all, I hated the trepidation I had just felt towards Charlie. I knew he would never hurt me, but I was officially no longer in control of my emotions. And now I was fucking crying, again. I cried so hard and long it made me feel sick and my eyes were stinging with the force of my tears. I didn't even stop crying, I just drifted off to sleep with my cheeks still damp.

When I woke the next morning, Charlie had already left for work and Mercy had just gotten home from the nightshift at the shelter. She looked exhausted, which made me change my mind about what I had planned to ask her. I woke up this morning with my mind made up, staunch determination flooding my foggy brain—I needed to go home. I didn't want to go home, but I needed to. I needed to face my fears and be on my home turf again. I needed a ride though, but Mercy looked so tired I wasn't about to ask her to turn around and drive me back to the other side of town. As soon as she retreated to her bedroom for some shut-eye, I grabbed a pen and wrote her a quick note so she wouldn't worry. I packed my few things and called a cab. It arrived twenty minutes later and I climbed in, giving the driver the address to my house. The whole way there I nervously bit at my sore lip. My injuries were healing quickly, most of the swelling was gone, and the bruising had morphed from bad, to worse, to not so bad. My ribs were still sore and would likely take another couple of weeks to repair. It was my head that needed to be worked on now. I needed to cleanse the asshole who had attacked me from my thoughts. I needed to fight the nightmares away, but I had no idea how. Facing my first demon, my home, was my first priority. I didn't want my home to be a demon, I didn't want to be afraid of my one safe place.

As we pulled onto my street, my heart started beating like an irregular drum, and my palms were sweating. I moved on autopilot as I paid the driver and climbed out of the cab. Now standing in the front yard of my little cottage, the double story monstrosities that surrounded it made it look even smaller. It looked just the same as always: light, cozy and homey. I stood there for the longest time, telling myself I was simply admiring the familiar structure, when in fact I was just delaying the inevitable. I picked up my bag and nervously strolled toward the steps that led up to the small porch and the quaint wooden door. Right now would be a great time for a neighborhood emergency that required immediate evacuation of the area. Maybe I should go check out Bouquets first? Problem was my car keys were sitting in a bowl on the kitchen counter. Don't be ridiculous, I am Rebecca Fucking Donovan, I am not scared of my own home. With my shoulders back, I walked up the steps and approached the front door. I knew there was a keypad on the other side now that required a PIN access code to disarm my new, state-of-the-art security system that Braiden installed. The PIN was written on the inside of my wrist, and all I had to do was open the door and punch it in. It occurred to me that I had no idea how much this new security system had cost me; so far I hadn't paid a cent.

I dropped my bag and stood staring at the front door, rubbing the new key for the new lock in my fingers. My hand raised to the door and I hesitated when I saw it was shaking. "Shit," I whispered, pulling my hand back. I tried again and found myself unable to even touch the door. "Fuck it," I sobbed, and the tears began once more. I leaned against the door, and closed my eyes—big mistake. I was flooded with images from the last time I was here, on the other side of that door, fighting for my life. His hands on me, in me. I cried hard and slipped down to my knees, my breathing became erratic and out of control. What the hell was wrong with me?

"Rebecca?" a familiar voice penetrated the haze and watery tears that obstructed my vision. I leaned even harder against the door trying to force myself to calm down. "Take a deep breath, breathe with me, long deep breaths, in and out." I found myself obeying the gentle voice at my side, and when I finally settled down enough to glance in that direction, the damn tears started all over again.

"Ella?" I sobbed when I saw Ella in front of me. Her own tears slipped free as she wrapped her arms around me.

"You should have called me, you idiot!" she cried. I laughed and sobbed at the same time. I turned when another warm hand squeezed my shoulder. Jax knelt at my other side, his gentle grey eyes full of concern. Fuck he was huge—the man was a damn giant!

"I'm gonna go in there and grab whatever you need then Ella is going to drive you to our place in your car, that way you won't be stuck out there without transportation, in case you wanna go somewhere."

I nodded and cried some more. Most of that sounded like a pretty damn good plan, except for one part. "If you think for one second I'm allowing Ella to drive me anywhere, you're crazy."

A beautiful smile broke Jax's concerned features. Ella has only had her driver's license for a few months. She was a contender for the worst driver in history: she drives way too fast and her roaming eyes have trouble staying on the road, front and center.

"Don't be a bitch, I'm a good driver," Ella demanded from beside me.

I glanced back in her direction. "You're driving scares the shit out of me. I didn't survive an attack from some deranged asshole only to die in a blazing inferno from Ella-lead-foot." Ella knew I was joking—mostly. "I'll drive, but I would be really grateful if you would go in with Jax and get some more of my stuff. I'm sure he doesn't need to see the hot gear I wear under my fabulous clothes." Jaxon Carter thumbing through my underwear was an uncomfortable thought.

Ella gave me a wicked grin. "Good idea since the most adventurous my underwear gets are boyshorts and sports bras."

"I can handle underwear, just don't make me carry out any weird plants that look like genitalia and we're good to go." Jax chuckled beside us.

Damn, I had missed these two.

CHAPTER 6

Charlie

I pummeled the bag like it was an enemy of old that required immediate decimation. There was too much anger in me, and I needed to get it out. It has been a long time since I've felt like this, years in fact. For a time, anger had been my way of dealing with shit until I learned to control it. I never hesitated to start a fight and even joined in on those that weren't mine. My attitude sucked, my temper stewed constantly. I hid my battle behind the happy-go-lucky Charlie most people knew. I could joke, fuck around, and tease with the best of them. While on the outside I was carefree, on the inside I felt much darker. My temper could easily flare and it took years of tedious and barely reigned control to keep myself in check. I learned to walk away, to remove myself from situations that could easily become heated battles. At Dave's suggestion I began keeping a journal where I could pour all that negativity into the pages and be somewhat free of the burden of those thoughts. Breathing techniques and meditating helped calm any building tension and beating the shit out of a bag was a great release. Once upon a time I fought, and fought hard; however, now I worked out—lifted weights, sparred and ran. It all seemed to help release the pent up energy that fueled my body, which would make me irate and fidgety for no good reason. My temper was a scary thing when unleashed; it put lives in danger and was one of the reasons I didn't fight inside the ring anymore. Occasionally my inner turmoil would rage and I would battle my way free from it with a brutal training regime. Right now the war inside of me was intense. I was filled with too much anger. I wanted to maim; I wanted to draw blood; I wanted to kill. And it scared the fuck out of me. Every fiber of my being screamed at me to hunt down Luke Hollywell and beat him to within an inch of his life. Frank had assured me Luke had a good alibi, but I wasn't so easily convinced. Someone needed to be held accountable for Rebecca's pain. She was so jumpy and fragile now, so unlike the Rebecca we all knew and loved. Loved? I shook my head in frustration. I didn't have a clue what love was, or what it felt like. My attraction to Rebecca seemed like nothing more than raw male possessiveness and desire.

The heavy pounding and slaps on the leather bag before me were almost soothing. As soon as I finished here, I would hit the treadmill for a few miles then grab a shower. I was desperate to get back to Mercy's house and check on Rebecca. I really fucked up last night, in typical Charlie fashion. I had a niche for fucking things up, especially where women were concerned. I have no idea how the hell Gym Girl got my number. I sure as hell didn't give it to her. I can only assume someone here at the gym did. The last thing I had wanted was for Rebecca to hear the conversation, but instead she heard every damn word of it. Then my general irritation over Gym Girl's phone call had morphed into all out anger over Rebecca's nonchalance. I knew I had made her uncomfortable. I had sworn to bring her smiles, but instead I scared her. Fuck it! I hit the bag a little harder and followed it up with a sweeping round house kick. I bounced around on the balls of my feet and attacked the innocent black bag of sand. Rebecca didn't deserve me losing my temper. I just got so angry because I wanted her to care who I spent the night with. I wanted her to care about me. Damn it! I wasn't some hormonal teenager anymore; I didn't give a shit if a girl liked me or not. Mercy's words rang in my head though, confusing me further: Rebecca adores you. Apparently Rebecca could care less about me, and now, if anything, she was scared of me. Front kick, right hook, side kick, deep breath. Left uppercut, hook kick, punch, punch, roundhouse kick. I kept up a rigorous pace until my body was burning, and sweat was dripping down my face, chest, arms and legs. At this rate I wouldn't be able to run, I would be too worn-out. Settling the swinging bag, I pulled off my gloves and threw them down on the bench along with my towel. I set the treadmill at a moderate pace and began to jog, which I would finish with a sprint. Slipping the buds from my headphones in my ears, I pushed the volume up high and allowed Eminem's Lose Yourself to numb my thoughts. I had been blissfully unaware of my surroundings for no less than fifteen minutes when a tap on my arm caught my attention. I barely contained my eye roll as I pulled the buds from my ears. Fuck, I wasn't in the mood for this shit. I told her how it was from the beginning: one night, let's have some fun then we go our separate ways. I've learned from Jax's mistakes to be up front and blatantly rude to get what I wanted from a woman. No commitments, no cuddling. I wasn't a complete asshole, I always made sure the women had a good time. But I never offered more than I was able to give. With Gym Girl, I had been completely upfront as usual. Yet now I get the feeling she hadn't really heard me. She leaned over the front of the treadmill, her spectacular tits displayed in a tiny pink sports bra, tight black lycra pants wrapped around her long legs. Yeah, she looked good, but not good enough for me to go for seconds, and nowhere near as spectacular as Rebecca.

"Hey," I panted, keeping my eyes front and center.

"You haven't been around much lately, I thought I might have scared you off," she said with a sly grin. I shook my head. It would take more than a one night stand with some girl to scare me away from my happy place. I've been coming to Lee's Gym since I was a teenager; since Mercy slapped me upside the head and made me see the dangerous road I was on. She found this gym and enrolled me straight away. Lee was actually General Lee, a sixty year old ex-marine. His father had owned the gym and when he

41

passed away, General Lee automatically took it over. He ran a tight ship, and kept all fights in the ring, and most importantly, he cared about the fighters who came into his gym. He was a good guy, in fact the best, and a studious combination of the General, the gym and Mercy had set my life on a new path. So it would take a hell of a lot more than a one night stand to scare me away from here.

"Do you think you could spot me on weights when you're done here?" she asked.

Not a chance in hell, I thought.

"Sorry, I have to get out of here as soon as I finish up. Corey is around here somewhere, I'm sure he can help." She looked a little pouty. I hated pouty. Rebecca never got pouty. She got pissy and fiery, not pouty.

"How about we meet up later for a drink, my treat?" she suggested, undeterred by my casual attempt to palm her off onto someone else.

"Sorry, no can do. As I said, I have to get out of here as soon as I'm done. I'm busy tonight."

"Tomorrow night then," she said. I tried not to cringe. She was relentless, I'd give her that.

"Ji...Jenny," I quickly corrected myself, maybe I was a complete asshole. I slowed my jog to a walk then eventually stopped.

"I know, you said one night and I'm cool with that. I just thought we could still keep it casual and make one night two, maybe even three or four. I had fun, I know you had fun, too." Her eyes sparkled.

Yeah, I had fun, but as soon as the fun was over, I was right back to where I was before the fun began—miserable and empty. The only person who seemed capable of filling that gap didn't want me, but that didn't mean I was going to fall into old habits again. I needed to quit this shit and if I thought I might stand even half a chance at winning Rebecca over, I wouldn't so much as look at another female again.

"Jenny, you're a really beautiful woman and you deserve so much more than I can give you. I'm sorry if I led you to believe that there would be anything more than one good night, but that's all I've got to give. There's Corey if you need a spotter." I nodded in Corey's direction, and when she turned to see for herself, I quickly escaped.

Under the hot spray of the shower, I tried to relax. I took long deep breaths and tried to picture myself somewhere else. Specifically at my cabin up in the mountain range that was on the outskirts of Claymont. It was perfect, tucked away in quiet seclusion, surrounded with towering firs, and in the winter, a heavy layer of snow would blanket everything. It was a peaceful oasis that I retreated to when things began to get out of hand. The cabin helped me relax. My anger and frustration would bleed away to complete and utter peace. I would live up there if it wasn't a three hour drive to civilization. I blew out a deep breath; I needed to get my shit together. I needed to rid myself of the anger that was still simmering below the surface. Not only had Rebecca seen enough anger of late, but I had a self-defense class at Mercy's Shelter tomorrow night and those women did not need an angry alpha male leading the class. Those women had fled dominant men who had already hurt and maimed them, both physically and emotionally. I was supposed to be a beacon of safety, not a fucking reminder of the terror they had escaped.

I dried and dressed quickly, slipping out the back door of the gym to escape another run in with Gym Girl. The twenty minute drive to Mercy's helped me settle down even further, and by the time I pulled my truck out front, I felt as close to calm as I could possibly get. I used the key Mercy had given me many years ago to enter and strolled into the place like I owned it. It was probably a bit arrogant and rude, but hell, it felt like I've lived here my whole life. Mercy was as good as my mother and this house was as good as my family home. All was quiet, apart from the low murmuring of Mercy and Dave's voices coming from the kitchen. I didn't see Rebecca and the doorway to her room was wide open. As I strolled into the warm bright kitchen, I stopped and took in the awkward scene before me. Dave had his arms wrapped around Mercy, his lips firmly planted on hers, his hands sliding down her back to cup her ass. Yeah, this was not the kind of thing I wanted to walk in on, and why I probably should've knocked before entering. I was glad Mercy found Dave, or perhaps it was Dave who found Mercy. After the shitty hand Mercy had been dealt with Jax's father, Dave was an angel in comparison and he clearly adored Mercy. However, I did not need to witness those sessions of adoration. They kind of made my stomach roll. I turned my head to look away and cleared my throat loudly. Their eyes swung around to take me in as I stood awkwardly, watching them from the corner of my eye, just to make sure they were decent before I looked at them straight on.

"I need to take that key from you," Mercy scolded as she let her arms fall from Dave's neck.

"You have such great timing," Dave said dryly.

I gave them my best grin as I waltzed in and grabbed a Coke from the fridge. "I guess I didn't expect the kitchen to be make-out central with Rebecca here and all." I took a long drink then froze when I took in the look Mercy gave Dave. "What?" I demanded.

Dave put his hands up defensively and backed away. "Don't look at me, I just got home. I'm going to take my suitcase upstairs." He snuck out of the kitchen and I looked to Mercy for answers.

"She's not here," she said in that rational voice of hers that drove me nuts.

"What do you mean she's not here?" I asked, my voice pitching like some sort of whiny girl.

"I meant exactly what I said, Charlie. She was here when I got home this morning from the shelter, but she left sometime after I went upstairs to get some sleep. She left a note." Mercy handed me a sheet of paper with Rebecca's elegant handwriting on it.

Mercy, sorry to run out while you are sleeping, but I think if you were awake you would have tried to stop me. I need to go home, I don't want to be afraid of my own house. It's the only thing I have left of my family, and I can't lose it. I've already called Braiden and have the security code and my new key. Tell Charlie thanks for everything. I'm sorry I've been such a burden to you both over the past week. Love, Bec X

I glared at Mercy. "Burden?" I said a little too loudly.

Mercy shook her head and took the piece of paper from me. "Settle down, Charlie, don't go getting your panties in a twist."

Considering the seriousness of the situation I couldn't help the bark of laughter that escaped my lips. Mercy didn't swear and she most definitely did not say panties. "I don't wear panties, I don't even wear damn underwear." I chuckled.

Mercy's brow furrowed. "T.M.I., Charlie!" She took the can of Coke from me and emptied it into a glass, handing it back with a frustrated look on her pint-sized face. Why she has this obsession with people having to drink Coke from a glass rather than the can was beyond me. She has always insisted and I have never bothered to ask. As long as I got to drink my damn Coke, I could care less. "You know Rebecca, she is independent, and she hasn't had to rely on anyone in a long time. Being here, being looked after goes against who Rebecca is. She is trying to get back what she lost a week ago, and I don't mean her home. She wants her confidence back, her strength."

"It's too soon, Mercy. If she thinks she can just waltz back through that doorway like nothing ever happened, then she's crazier than I thought!" I felt a little bad as I said the words, but I was too pissed to stop myself. "She shouldn't have left, she should have enough damn sense to know that it takes time to heal from something like this."

"Rebecca is stronger than you think, Charlie," Mercy defended her.

"I don't care how strong she is, it's too soon. Can you seriously stand there and tell me she's fine right now?"

Mercy shook her head and pierced me with that stare of hers that makes my lips seal shut. Not even my own mother could silence me with a look, but Mercy had it down pat. "First of all, Charlie Cole, calm down. I won't have you throwing a temper tantrum in my house." I went to speak and her look silenced me again. "Secondly, I know very well Rebecca isn't all right at the moment—she is far from it—but I am also aware she can't be forced to do something she doesn't want to do. If she doesn't feel comfortable here, then we shouldn't force her to stay."

Thoughts of my cabin started flashing through my head once more, but this time for a different reason. My anger and control wasn't so frayed that I needed it, but I was wondering if Rebecca might appreciate it. The only other person to set foot in my secluded paradise was Jax and half a dozen builders from Carter Constructions. As soon as the roof was on and the front door on its hinges, I've been the only one who has crossed the threshold. Taking Rebecca somewhere as personal as my cabin felt right. Not many people knew the extent of my struggle with anger. In fact, Mercy, Jax and Dave are the only ones that have been privy to the real Charlie. Taking Rebecca up into the mountains and showing her that part of me would mean letting someone else in, and I wanted to let Rebecca in. At that moment, Dave strolled back into the kitchen and wrapped his arms around Mercy, drawing her back into his chest.

"I have to go by and check on her," I murmured, my thoughts caught between wanting to whisk Rebecca away to safety and wanting to see that fiery spark back in her eye, that fiercely independent and stubborn spirit that was so true to her.

"She's not there." Mercy sighed interrupting my thoughts. Before I had a chance to become enraged, Mercy answered, "She's with Jax and Ella. They got home this morning. When Jax called from the airport, I had just found Rebecca's letter. I told him what had happened while they were gone, and he took Ella straight to Rebecca's house. He called me a little while ago. Rebecca is at their place now." The pained look on her face physically hurt me. Dave held her a little closer, obviously sensing she was upset. "She broke down on the doorstep. Apparently she couldn't even open the front door."

Picturing Rebecca in front of her house, broken, afraid and alone pissed me off. She shouldn't have gone alone, she knows that she has friends that are willing to help her through this.

"Fuck," I growled. I didn't know how to fix this, I didn't know how to help Rebecca and it was killing me.

"Just be there for her, Charlie. She needs to talk to someone about this, and until then, all we can do is be there for her. She needs your strength right now, not your anger and frustration over a situation that is out of your control." Mercy knew me well. "She wants to go to work so Ella is going to take her in tomorrow. At least there, she will be surrounded by familiar people, and it will make her feel safe. Working again will also help her regain some sense of that lost freedom." Dave gave Mercy a kiss on the top of her head, then his gaze returned to mine.

"Maybe we can convince her to join your self-defense class at the shelter?" he suggested. I gave him a short stiff nod. "Rebecca is a strong woman—she's a fighter—she was able to fight off her attacker, but she could benefit from learning more about defending herself." I knew Dave was trying to help me find an outlet for my feeling of futility, and strangely enough, it helped. I nodded again with a little more determination. Helping Rebecca learn to defend herself was something I could do.

"Thank you," I whispered, running a hand over my tired face. Mercy broke free from Dave's embrace and moved towards me, wrapping her arms around my waist. I held her tightly. She was so little, almost as small as Ella. They were like little dolls.

"No thank you necessary. You staying? I'm cooking lasagna." I thought about it for a moment. A home cooked meal was appealing but one look at Dave's don't-you-dare stare made me chuckle. He had only been away for a little over a week, but obviously they had lost time to make up for.

"No, I hit it pretty hard at the gym. I'm just going to go home and crash." I backed away from Mercy and grinned. "You could always pack away some left overs for me though, I could pick them up from the shelter tomorrow." She beamed at me, the kind of smile that a mother reserved for her children, and it warmed my heart in seconds.

"I was going to make extra for Jax and Ella. God forbid they try and cook something on their own. They'd burn their house down. You can half it with them." I rubbed my stomach that was already growling in anticipation.

"Well, don't forget Jax and Ella have Mary packing them away meals, too. I've got no one."

I gave Mercy a quick kiss on the forehead. Dave shook his head, a secret grin playing at the corners of his mouth. I nodded my thanks once again and left. I only hoped whatever Dave had planned for Mercy took place somewhere other than the kitchen. If they contaminated the kitchen like that, I would never eat anything from it again. Who was I kidding? Mercy's lasagna was legendary, they could screw around on top of it and I would most likely still eat it.

CHAPTER 7

Rebecca

I could hear Ella grumbling at Jax in the kitchen. I smiled, remembering just how nasty that little tiger's tongue could get in the mornings—she was not a morning person. I rolled to my side and watched the sun slice through the blinds, allowing sharp beams of light into the otherwise dark room. For the last few nights my sleep had been plagued with nightmares. It was always the same dream: I wake up foggy from a deep sleep only to find my body pinned down. Angry eyes stare down at me before hands began ripping at my clothing and violating my body. But for the last couple of nights, the dream has progressed and rather than simply waking the moment I become trapped as my attacker defiles me with his hands, I dream about his body entering mine forcefully. The feeling of complete and utter helplessness fills me and I wake up kicking and screaming like a wild banshee. I was so embarrassed last night when poor Ella stood by my side looking down at me with understanding in those dark brown eyes of hers. Jax stood by warily, while Ella held me as I unleashed another violent torrent of tears. Hours later, I still feel the lingering fear and horror from my nightmare. My eyes felt swollen and puffy from crying. I needed to escape this fear. I felt trapped in a place where my heart constantly thumped with trepidation. Where I felt the overwhelming need to look over my shoulder every five minutes. This type of fear made me feel tethered to others, as if I could no longer survive on my own. My independence was gone, replaced with a deep-seated need for others. Chasing closely on the heels of that fear was anger. Anger I could deal with though, fear was something I was completely unaccustomed to. Slipping from the bed, I made my way into the bathroom and glanced in the mirror, taking in my aging bruises. They were still distinct enough that makeup would not hide them, but not so ugly that it looked as though my face had gone a round with Mike Tyson. My ribs still ached, but at least it no longer hurt to breathe.

After a scalding hot shower, I stared at my clothes. Ella, beautiful, thoughtful Ella had packed all of my favorite dresses and skirts, my gorgeous pumps, all of my makeup and hair accessories. She thought of everything. My clothes have always been like armor for me. When I wore them, I felt invincible—I was strong, defiant, and independent. They no longer felt comfortable though. Maybe they made me stand out and were why I had been attacked. Hell, they certainly had not protected me. Dressing like a fifties pin-up girl seemed ridiculous now, and I began to see what everyone else saw when they looked at me: a fraud. I still had some of the clothes Charlie had packed, and amongst the sweats and boring shirts, I found a pair of jeans, and pulled them on. I marveled at how they looked; it had been over five years since I last wore them. I found a black, form fitting, modest button down top and slipped into the pair of ballet flats that I've been wearing for the last week. I pulled my hair into a high ponytail and applied a minimal amount of makeup—just enough to help cover the worst of the beating I endured, on the outside anyway. A few deep breaths later, my shoulders back, head held high, I left the bedroom.

"Screw you, asshat," I heard Ella grumble as I reached the entry to the kitchen.

Jax laughed out loud. "Angel, you know if you talk to me like that I'm just gonna throw you over my shoulder, march you straight back upstairs where I will make you scream again."

As I walked in, I caught the heated stare Ella was giving Jax, and the wanton desire on the big man's face as he gazed back at her. Jax was wearing nothing but a pair of track pants, sitting dangerously low on his hips, and it took every ounce of self-preservation not to follow the hard, perfect washboard abs down to the magic V that led into the waistband of his pants. The man was scorching hot perfection, but he didn't make my heart race like Charlie. He didn't make my mind turn to slush and my knees go cliché weak at the mere sight of him.

I cleared my throat. "Do you two need me to clear the room?" I offered.

Ella grinned. "No, because he's not getting any, even if he begged me for it." She continued to stare daggers at Jax, who just laughed.

I snorted. "Yeah right, because you are so good at keeping your hands off of him." Jax handed me a mug of coffee and I sighed. Caffeine, the elixir of the gods. I pulled out a chair and sat by Ella, who was staring holes through me now.

"What?" I asked, the mug pausing its ascent to my lips.

"What are you wearing?" she asked.

I glanced down at my clothes. "I can't exactly go to work in sweats," I said, avoiding the real question.

Ella suddenly looked worried, her little smile turned into a concerned frown. "Did I grab the wrong stuff?"

I automatically reached out and took her hand. "No, you grabbed my entire wardrobe of personal favorites, and I'm very grateful. I just didn't feel like wearing those clothes today."

There was a long awkward pause as Jax and Ella stared at me, as if they were trying to read between the lines, which I had no doubt they were both doing easily.

"Where's my friend Rebecca and what the fuck did you do to her?" Ella broke the silence.

I couldn't stop my small grin. "Screw you," I muttered.

"She looks fine, Angel, leave her alone."

Ella's eyes cut through the air to land on her giant piece of man candy. "Of course she looks fine, she looks great! I just meant she looks different."

Jax placed a gentle kiss to the top of Ella's head and I'll be damned if the girl didn't turn into a pile of goo right before me. "We know what you meant. I'm going to grab a quick shower then we'll head into town." Ella watched Jax move to the doorway of the kitchen.

"You're welcome to come help me!" Jax called out.

Ella shook her head. "Not until I get my kitten!"

"Not happening, Angel. I'm allergic to cats."

"Bullshit," Ella muttered, watching Jax climb the stairs to their loft.

"You want a cat?" I asked. Ella didn't seem like a cat person to me. She looked more like a dog person, an angry looking Rottweiler person to be precise.

"Yes, I want a cat, and Jax won't let me have one."

I chuckled. I couldn't imagine Jax not giving Ella something she wanted. That man would give her the moon if he could. I paused and found my heart sinking a little at the overwhelming love this home contained. Jax and Ella's love for each other was the kind of love that poets wrote sonnets about and musicians sang about—unbreakable devotion—and I wanted it. Someone who adored me exactly as I was, someone who didn't question my motives for dressing a particular way, someone who I could feel safe with. Sickly tangled with that desire was the fear of finding that someone, only to lose him, just like I lost my family. But, glancing around Jax and Ella's home, a large piece of me thought that taking the risk might just be worth it. My thoughts lingered to Charlie, the only man whom ever ensnared my heart and made me think of forever. I haven't seen Charlie since the night of Jenny's phone call back at Mercy's. I know he calls every night to check on me though and it makes my heart both flutter with excitement and sink with the gravity of the situation. I was avoiding him because in Charlie, I would only find heartache. I couldn't deal with a broken heart right now, there is far too much of me that needs fixing as it is.

"Are you okay?" Ella's nervous voice pulled me from my thoughts. She looked worried again. Ella's life has been full of so much worry that I refused to burden her with my problems.

"Of course I am. I'm a little tired, but once this caffeine enters my blood stream I will pep right up. I've actually considered inserting an IV line to shoot caffeine straight in my veins. I wonder if that's possible." I wondered out loud. Ella didn't react at my attempt to make her smile. Usually at this point she would say something smart like, "how about I grind you some beans and you can try snorting them."

"You know, it's okay to not be okay. You are entitled to feel a little self-pity and a healthy dose of fear. It's alright to be afraid, I should know." Ever the wise Ella, at all of twenty-three years of age.

I sighed. "I am afraid, Ella. So scared I'm amazed I haven't locked myself away in a self-imposed padded cell where no one can touch me ever again. I understand what I am feeling is warranted, I just don't understand how to fix it. I'm just a little banged up right now, but not completely broken."

She nodded solemnly. "You should talk to Dave. He helped both me and Jax." She took a sip from her own coffee. "And Charlie too, for that matter," she added as an afterthought.

"What did Charlie need Dave's help with?" I asked, suddenly curious. Charlie was a goof, a happy, crazy, whorish goof. I couldn't imagine him needing a psychiatrist for anything.

Ella took her time in answering, obviously not wanting to betray Charlie's confidence in saying too much. "Charlie might come across as easy going and carefree, but, like all of us, he has had his own shit to deal with. From what I've learned, his family is bonkers, like obsessive, clearly crazy, manic, borderline-cult-devout fucked up." I almost snorted my coffee across the table at Ella's eloquent description of Charlie's family. I've heard that they were a bit weird, but Ella put a whole new perspective on them. "Did he ever tell you why he quit fighting?"

My eyebrows raise in surprise. "I assumed he still fought. He spends most of his spare time at Lee's Gym, doesn't he?" I shrugged.

Ella shook her head. "He still trains, works out and spars with the other fighters, but he doesn't fight in the ring anymore."

I waited for her to explain why, but it appeared that she wasn't going to. I bristled at the fact that Ella seemed to know Charlie better than me. It's not like I was supposed to know everything about him. One night spent rolling around under the sheets with him certainly didn't give me any insight into the real heart of the man.

"Mercy said Charlie has been a big help to you, that he came the night you were attacked and he was the only who you would talk to." Ella's statement was almost a question.

No matter how hard I tried to deny my attraction to Charlie, Ella knew the truth of the matter. My thoughts flittered back to that night and I almost winced under the onslaught of the images that flashed through my mind. I pushed the ugly memories away, locked them down tight in the back of my mind and managed a nonchalant shrug.

"Mercy probably doesn't realize her call dragged Charlie from between the legs of his latest conquest." It was Ella's turn to wince, she didn't hide her reaction though. She pulled her long dark hair away from her face and tied it into a messy bun on the top of her head. She was wearing that beautiful long hair back more often now, showing off the stunning, petite features of her pale smooth face. Her eyes, accented with her Asian ancestry, looked at me with seriousness. The scar that sat dangerously close to her right eye was faint though noticeable but it certainly didn't detract from her beauty. My hand unconsciously touched the small scar I now had on one pale eyebrow.

"Like I said, Charlie has issues," Ella worried her bottom lip between her teeth before she continued, "and it's no secret that Jax had his own issues that had him seeking out every woman in this town." For a split second her eyes flared with irritation, but then it was gone. "But Jax loves me and once I allowed him in, his heart became mine and vice versa. Charlie cares about you, Rebecca, a hell of a lot. He's told me so. But if you don't let him in, you'll never truly realize just how much he feels for you. I know that you think you are Miss Independent Ice Queen of the Decade, but I know you aren't. I know you want what any single girl with a heart wants: someone to care about you, to fuss over you, and you want to give that love back just as much. Those other women Charlie was with were just a distraction. I'm not saying they were a good distraction or that it was healthy, but it wasn't love. In fact, it was a hell of a long way from even happiness for him." Jax stomped down the stairs and Ella stood up, taking our coffee mugs to the sink where she promptly rinsed them out.

"Ready?" asked Jax as he entered the kitchen and planted a teasing kiss to the nape of Ella's neck. The exact same spot on my neck tingled, the thought of Charlie kissing me that way filled my body with warmth.

Ella's words roamed around in my mind, making me feel more confused than ever. How could someone, someone who apparently cared so much about another person, so callously use other women? Could I risk letting Charlie in? Could I risk losing him, or losing a chance at love? My head was in such a cloud of fear and uncertainty right now that I wasn't sure I could open myself to such a chance.

CHAPTER 8

Charlie

Jax was keeping a close eye on Rebecca, and I knew I could trust him to keep her safe. Even so, I haven't seen her in over two weeks and it was beginning to drive me insane. I was out of my mind with worry, and I was irritable and pissed off for no good reason. I've lost count of how many times I've turned my truck in the direction of Bouquets, only to chicken out at the last minute. I didn't want to push Rebecca, I wanted to give her space. But at the same time, I wanted to gather her in my arms and steal her away where no one else could touch her. How fucked up was that? There were still no leads on Rebecca's attacker and his parting threat was still lingering in the air, so no one was comfortable leaving the women to their own devices; therefore, Jax had become a hovering pain in their asses. Dylan and Braiden Montgomery have been swamped since opening their second office in Claymont, but between the two of them they were still looking into Rebecca's attack. According to witness statements, no one heard or saw anything out of the ordinary. In the police report they found, there had been no fingerprints left at the scene. All we had to go on was Rebecca's crazy date with Luke Hollywell, who had a solid alibi. A combination of frustration—about a case that was seemingly going nowhere and not seeing Rebecca in what felt like forever—was playing havoc with my blazing, inner fury. Giving oxygen to those flames of anger was the son-of-a-bitch Hollywell, who had the nerve to walk through the doors of Lee's Gym this afternoon. Apparently he had been kicked out of his own gym and was looking for a new training ground. In a moment of uncontrollable rage, I pinned him against the wall, prepared to pound my fist into his face. The General and Corey had to pull me off of him. Instead of tossing the insignificant piece of shit out on the street, the General saw it as an opportunity to teach us both a lesson. We had a problem with each other and it needed to be dealt with. The General only dealt with these kinds of problems one way: inside the ring. He wanted us to fight, get it out of our system, and move on. There was a possibility that this fucker had attacked Rebecca, had attempted to rape her. If it's proved that he's Rebecca's attacker, there would be no moving on. If I was put in a ring with him, there's a damn good chance I'd kill him. The General didn't tolerate fighting on the street, so his answer was to keep it in the ring. In a moment of red hot fury, I accepted the challenge. I was going to fight Luke Hollywell in two weeks. I didn't see it ending well.

I climbed from my truck and pulled my ratty old gym bag from the back seat. It was a little after five, and my class at Mercy's didn't start for another twenty minutes. Inside the shelter, the sweet scent of muffins filled my nose. I peeked my head around the kitchen doorway to find Mary humming along to the song I was positive sounded a little like Snoop Dogg's Drop It Like It's Hot. Mary always seemed to be full of shocking surprises, and recently she revealed her new love for rap and urban R&B. Dressed in a floral dress, flats and a fancy apron full of ruffles, she was a complete contradiction. Her eyes sparkled with mischief when she spied me watching her from the doorway.

"Charlie Cole, I'm sure your momma would have taught you that it's bad manners to sneak up on people."

From anyone else, I would have prickled at the comment about my mom—who was on a plane to crazy town with a one-way ticket, and most of the people in Claymont knew it—but coming from Mary, I knew it was just playful banter. I smiled.

"You know me and manners never really took." I dropped my bag in the doorway and began snooping around the kitchen, looking for the freshly baked treats I could smell. Mary watched me as I checked the still warm oven. Nope, not there.

"Looking for something, Mr. Cole?" Mary chuckled.

I stood up and scanned the kitchen counters. This had become a game for Mary and me. She baked and I ate. But lately, she made me work for it. I checked the large pantry, the kitchen cabinets, and lastly, the fridge—hoping to God she didn't really put my warm treats in there. I found plenty of food, just not what I was after. When I turned to face her, I saw that she was barely holding it together.

"Where are my muffins, Mary? You don't want this to get ugly." I grinned.

She burst out laughing. "Five minutes, Charlie, just five minutes earlier and you'd have your muffins."

My playful grin disappeared. "Who took my muffins?" I demanded.

She laughed harder. "Ella left just before you came through the back door. Actually, she ran; I think she knew you would be looking for them."

That cheeky little brat, I thought to myself. I was definitely kidnapping her precious penis cacti next time I dropped by Jax's. I'd been threatening to unman her cactus for a long time. Now that she had messed with my muffins, that cactus was done for! The girl was going down! Mary's loud laughter finally settled and she reached behind her back to produce one lone muffin.

"I saved this for you." She grinned at me. I moved forward quickly and wrapped my arms around Mary's soft, large body, then quickly drew away, taking the still warm muffin with me. She shook her head. "I think you all love my muffins more than you love me."

"Not a chance," I said through a mouthful of muffin. "Without you there would be no muffins." I grabbed my bag off the floor and made my way out into the wide open living area of what was Mercy's Shelter for Abused Women. There were a few regular faces, and I was both glad and irritated to see a couple of new ones. It impressed the hell out of me that these women found the strength to leave the monsters that dared hurt them, but it pissed me off that such evil existed in the first place.

Mercy came in through the front door, and when she saw me, her hands flew up, palms out. "No, I had nothing to do with the abduction of your muffins. That was all on Ella and Jax."

"Jax was in on it?" I shouted.

"I believe he was driving the getaway vehicle." Mercy laughed.

They were both going down! At that moment the front door swung open and Ella strolled in, followed by Annie and then Rebecca. The air left my lungs on a long drawn out breath. She seemed to be held in a gripping conversation with Annie, while I carefully looked her over. Her hair was pulled back in a high ponytail, giving me an unobstructed view of her face. She looked beautiful. Her bruising was all but gone. There were dark shadows under her eyes, which worried me, but other than that she still looked like the damn ethereal beauty she always had been to me. Ella stood to one side, watching me as I watched Rebecca. Busted. She raised a brow and gave me a sly grin.

"Ms. Munroe, you look mighty proud of yourself," I noted.

"Mr. Cole, I do believe you and your muffins were outsmarted."

I snorted. "Not likely, all you did was show up five minutes earlier than me. That's not outsmarting, honey, that's pure luck. And don't worry, my plan for revenge is gonna leave your head spinning." Ella laughed just as Rebecca and Annie turned towards us from their conversation.

Rebecca's eyes locked on mine, and the look in her eyes made my heart pound hard and heavy in my chest. It looked like she was happy to see me, fucking ecstatic even. Ella and Annie went to help Mercy push some furniture out of the way as Rebecca strolled nervously up to me, her hands tucked away in the pockets of her pullover. I hated that she felt nervous. I smiled in an attempt to ease her apprehension.

"Betty Boop," I whispered, "how are you feeling?" She looked up at me, her eyes held a wealth of pain behind them. She smiled, but I could see the turmoil that was going through her mind and body. She looked away, unable to hold my concerned gaze, and shrugged. I waited patiently until those pretty blue eyes settled back on mine.

"Probably no better than I look."

"You look beautiful." Not even God himself could have stopped my hand from rising to her cheek, the back of my fingers gently caressed the soft skin. She blushed and it caused her face to glow a gentle shade of pink; it was adorable. It took a great deal of effort not to get a raging hard-on right there, surrounded by the women of the shelter. Damn, I was a sick fuck.

"I don't feel like it, Charlie. I feel..." She seemed frustrated. "I feel..." Her eyes dropped to the floor between us. "I feel scared. I feel like someone else is living in my God damned skin right now."

My hand cupped her neck gently and I used my finger to raise her chin so her eyes were back on mine. I wanted her to see the truth in my words; the complete honesty I was about to entrust in her. "I get that, Betty Boop, I get what it's like not to be in control of your emotions. It's like your outside of yourself looking in and you know what the problem is, you can see it but you just can't find a way to fix it. You will get that control back though, I promise you if it's the last thing I do, I'll help you get that control back." Her eyes seemed to search mine for the truth behind my words. Finally, a small smile fell easily upon her beautiful full lips. A cough from behind us got my attention. I glanced over my shoulder to see Ella's smug grin as she stood in line with several other women, all watching with rapt interest at the exchange between me and Rebecca.

"So eager to get started, short stuff." I chuckled. Ella's smile turned into a hard glare. I loved ruffling her feathers; it was definitely one of my favorite past times.

As the one hour class progressed, I could see Rebecca's unease growing. I had teamed her with Ella and kept all their maneuvers clean and simple. I knew it was possible that a certain hold or position could trigger a memory, fuck, I have seen it happen with plenty of women in the shelter since I began teaching my classes here. Thankfully Mercy noted Rebecca's discomfort, and made an excuse to draw her away from the group. Finally the class drew to an end and I guided the girls through a quick cool down and slipped away to find Rebecca. She was sitting in Mercy's office, her legs drawn up in front of her. She looked so young and fragile sitting there all alone. I didn't want to startle her so I knocked on the wall beside the doorway gently. Her worried frown turned to look my way. Her eyes glazed over with tears and before I could say a word they spilled over her lashes and down her soft cheeks. I knelt on the floor in front of her and allowed my arms to find their way around her small frame. She shook as she cried, her hands clutching me close.

"What's wrong with me?" she finally whispered between sobs. The pain and confusion in her voice broke my heart.

"There is nothing wrong with you, Betty Boop. You're scared and you're hurting." She gripped me tighter, trying to hold me as close as possible.

"I don't want to feel this way," she whispered.

"You won't forever. I'll help you," I breathed. "Let me help you," I quietly pleaded. Her subtle nod helped me feel some resemblance to calm. She was handing me a small amount of control, a chance to help fix this, to help repair the damage one person managed to inflict on her bright soul.

"I need to go home," she confessed.

"You will soon enough." It would take time but I had no doubt she would overcome the fear that lingered following her attack.

"No, Charlie. I have plants to water, food that's spoiled and needs to be thrown out, and I need to check my mail."

"I can go do all that for you." She leaned away from me, a spark of determination firing behind her eyes.

"I don't want anyone to do it for me, I want to do it, Charlie, it's my home." She took a deep breath. "It's my family home, it's all I have left of them. I can't lose it."

I leaned my forehead against hers, not wanting any space between us. "How about I take you? We can do it together." Her eyes seemed to flutter shut with relief. "This weekend," I added.

She nodded. "I'm working Saturday morning but I'm free all afternoon."

"Saturday afternoon it is then," I agreed. Her entire body relaxed.

"Shit, I've got to go in to Lee's Saturday afternoon. It should only take an hour, two tops." She lifted her head and being this close to her, I wanted to lean forward and kiss those beautiful lips.

"Maybe I can come?" she suggested.

Now I was tense. Normally I wouldn't have a problem taking Rebecca with me to Lee's, but now I was worried the aggression within the gym might trigger unwelcome memories for her.

She could see the obvious reluctance on my face. "I'm sorry, that was really forward of me." She tried to smile through her tear stained face. "Forget it, my head is in another place right now, things have started coming out of my mouth as if there is no filter."

I couldn't stop my laughter. "I'm fairly confident that pretty mouth of yours has never had a filter, Betty Boop." She smiled and it was genuine. Some of the tension that had seized my body lately seemed to melt away at the sight. "I want to take you, believe me I do. I'll be sparring, it won't exactly be real fighting but it has a tendency to sometimes get a little real, a little brutal. I don't want you to see that."

Rebecca's back straightened, her hands slipping from my shoulders. "You think I'll get scared," she said with a little defiance that reminded me of old Rebecca.

I ran a hand down my face in an attempt to hide my smile. I groaned. "No, maybe," I fought for the right thing to say. Rebecca sighed and seemed to come down from the fit I thought she was about to throw.

"Let me try," she pleaded. "If it starts getting to be too much, I'll just go wait in your truck or something."

She really wanted to come, I could see that in her eyes. I wasn't sure if it had something to do with defeating her fears or something else entirely. I raised my hands in defeat, I couldn't deny her anything, especially when her eyes were begging me like that. "Fuck it, you can come with. If it gets to be too much, you can hang out back with Liz." She gave me a 'who's Liz' look. "The General's wife, Liz, she's always there on the weekends, otherwise she'd never get to see her husband."

There was a very good chance this would come back to bite me on the ass. But another part of me, the caveman part of me, was pleased to be taking Rebecca to my happy place, to be able to show her off and stamp my mark of ownership on her. I was such an ass.

CHAPTER 9

Rebecca

I don't know why it felt imperative to go with Charlie to his gym. As soon as I got the feeling that he didn't want me there, that he didn't think I could handle it—that was it—competitive, stubborn, independent Rebecca reared her head and demanded attention. I was sitting on the old wooden bench in the back of Bouquets, my hands busy with the yellow rose and orange tulip floral arrangement in front of me. My mind wasn't really on the job at hand though. Thankfully, after eight years in the business, I didn't need to focus too hard on what I was doing; my hands instinctively knew what to do. I couldn't seem to get Charlie Cole out of my mind. The protective way he looked at me made my central loving station spasm with appreciation; however, my mind raced over all the 'what ifs'. What if he woke up one day and wanted to sneak out on me? Did he have some sort of sick hero complex which compels him to say and do the things he has for me? Maybe his feelings were misplaced by a simple need to help a friend. Being protective of a friend is a long way from proclaiming undying love. Did I even want that? Of course I did, what woman didn't want something as epic as true love? And as much as I tried to stop wanting Charlie like that, I couldn't. Ella has assured me that Charlie wanted me; that his feelings for me eclipsed friendship, but I was having trouble believing that. Charlie just didn't love and maybe that was for the better, because I wasn't sure if I could either. My eyes began to fill with tears at the thought of never having what Jax and Ella have. My lip curled in frustration. I was sick to death of crying. Everything would make me cry: songs, sounds, smells. And I was scared of everything, especially the dark. I still felt the eerie sensation of someone watching me and had considered speaking to Jax about it, but in the end, I knew it was probably nothing more than unsettled nerves that were consuming all rational thought. The sorrowful looks people cast my way were driving me crazy. Only my inner circle of friends knew exactly what had happened to me, but I'm sure the rumors were in spreading like wildfire; Claymont wasn't that big of a town. Fingers snapped before my eyes, bringing my thoughts back to my present surroundings.

"Thought I lost you there for a moment," murmured Lola. She was dressed in her typical black pants and black top, her black hair held back by a black scarf. Her green eyes were watching me as she took the bouquet from my hands and finished wrapping the stems with twine. Lola noticed me looking over her ensemble and she shrugged. "The world can be quite amazing when you're a little strange."

My eyes flicked back to hers and now she was looking over my clothes. I was wearing a pair of jeans, a plain, long sleeve t-shirt, and a pair of Converse. When Ella took me shopping last week, I picked up a couple pair of jeans and more than a few ordinary, long sleeved shirts. But Ella insisted on the Converses because, and I quote, "they're complete and utter coolness, and just plain badass." My hair was pulled into a messy bun, and I was wearing very little makeup. I looked normal. I didn't feel entirely comfortable with the way I looked, but for some reason I couldn't bring myself to wear anything from my iconic fifties style wardrobe either.

"Do you have a book of quotes at home beside your bed?" I asked.

She ambled away to put the bouquet in bucket of water by the front counter. "I just like to read," she said before answering the phone.

I glanced across the wide walkway that separated my floral shop from Annie's coffee shop. It seemed a little slow over there today. Annie's new girl, Beth, was manning the counter, while Annie smiled shyly from across one of the tables at one incredibly sexy Dillon Montgomery. He was grinning wickedly at her and she blushed, which made me all sorts of curious. The two of them have been dancing around each other in the longest, most drawn out courtship known to mankind. They've known each other for a year now, and still haven't been on a single date. Dillon spent a hell of a lot of time in the coffee shop though and he looked after Annie's son, Eli, often. But they couldn't seem to take the next step. If he looked at me the way he looks at Annie, I can tell you the man would have been flat on his back in a heartbeat. With that thought, darkness seeped its way into my mind and images from that night began to consume me. I breathed away the panic with long controlled breaths, just like Ella showed me. Without causing a scene, I found my calm place again and jumped up from the bench. I glanced out the front window and caught sight of a flashy looking black sedan parked at the curb. It wasn't the car that made my heart skip a beat though; it was the tiny girl, with pixie short black hair that caught my attention. I took a hesitant step toward the front of the store. The girl looked frightened as a beefy looking bald guy grabbed her roughly by the arm. As the girl glanced back over her shoulder, I caught a glimpse of her eyes and gasped.

"Em?" I whispered, observing the familiar looking girl. My younger sister has eyes just like mine, only paler. They were completely unique and unmistakable. The last time I saw Emily, her hair had been long and a dark shade of blonde, her figure beautiful with soft curves. This girl was thin, her skin pale in a sickly way, and dark rings hung under her haunted, striking eyes. I watched, muted and still as she was pushed into the back seat of the sedan. As the car pulled away from the curb, I started to doubt myself. My sister wasn't in Claymont and that girl didn't really look like Emily. My sister was safe, far away from the ugliness in my world right now, living it up, living her dreams. I shook it off and glanced around the store. I needed something to do, I needed to keep busy. I tied off the garbage bag and lifted it easily from the bin.

"I'm just going to dump this out back," I called to Lola, who was still on the phone. She gave me a quick nod to let me know she heard me, and I made my way to the back of the shop, to the heavy door that separated the warm cozy interior of Mercy's Angels to the stinky alleyway that sat beyond. I latched the door back so it wouldn't slam closed and lock me out, then stepped into the alley. My eyes scrutinized everything. There were several large dumpsters that belonged to the other shops along the strip of road we occupied. Some were overflowing, scattering trash across the black, icy asphalt. It smelled dank and spoiled. The shadows made my heart hammer with unease, but I'd be damned if I was going to turn into a chicken shit damsel in distress. Heaving the bag of garbage off the ground, I moved out into the alley, towards our appointed dumpster. I pushed the lid open, and with a small amount of effort, I managed to haul the large bag up and over the side of the dirty steel monstrosity. I nudged the lid shut and it slammed closed. At the same time, another loud bang echoed from somewhere behind me. Glancing over my shoulder, I noticed the back door to the shop had closed. I became rigidly still, my brain coming to the conclusion that if I didn't move, I would become invisible to any possible threat. I stood like that for the longest time, my heart beating so fast and furious I could feel my pulse in my hands and feet, my ears deafened by the loud thundering beat. From the corner of my eye, I thought I noticed movement in the shadows—finally my rigid, paralyzed mobility disappeared—and I ran for the door. I had no idea if there was someone behind me, but every sense I possessed screamed at me to move. When I reached the door, I pounded on it so hard it made my hands throb in pain and I screamed so loud my throat hurt. I heard heavy footsteps behind me, and a low chuckle that made my stomach curl as I continued to pound on that door like my life depended on it. When the door finally opened, I fell through it with such force I would have landed on my face if Dillon wouldn't have been there to catch me. I was quickly moved aside into Annie's waiting arms as Dillon moved swiftly into the alley. I couldn't stop the slightly hysterical sobs that forced their way out of my mouth. As I sank to knees that would no longer hold me, Annie followed me down, rubbing what I guess was supposed to be comforting circles on my back.

"Rebecca," I knew Dillon was now behind me, but I was so embarrassed at my hysterical breakdown that I refused to turn and look at him.

"What the fuck?"

My entire being sighed at the sound of his voice and my sobs stopped. Just like that, his voice forced the panic away, and I felt safe. Charlie's big strong hands pulled me from Annie and I didn't fight him. I allowed myself to sink into his chest, my ear pressed hard against him as I listened to his beating heart, the sound soothing me to my core.

"What the hell happened, Betty Boop?" His voice was a command, and unlike Dillon's, I could not ignore it.

"I...I was putting the t...t...trash out," I tried, hating the sudden stutter I developed. I took a deep breath and tried again, "I was putting the t...trash out, the door shut. S...someone was out there." I glanced around Charlie's arm so I could see the empty alley beyond the open door.

"Did you see who was there?" asked Dillon in what I recognized as his all-business voice.

I shook my head, my eyes watching the alley warily. It looked empty and quiet. Had there been someone there? Maybe my mind was playing tricks on me. With a finger under my chin, Charlie moved my confused gaze back to him.

"What did you see?" he asked.

My brow furrowed as I tried to recall exactly what had happened. "I tossed the trash in the dumpster, and when I closed the lid, I heard a loud bang from behind me. When I turned around, the door was closed. Then I thought I saw something in the shadows, not really a person, just movement." Damn it! I clenched my fists, my anger bubbling under my skin. How the hell did I become this wallowing miserable mess of pathetic female? "I'm going insane aren't I?" I laughed humorlessly.

"Did you latch the door?" Lola asked from behind us.

I didn't even realized she was there until that moment. Great, now my only employee was going to think her employer was completely bonkers.

I hesitated before answering, because as sure as I was that I had in fact latched the door back, a small insecure part of me was beginning to think I was losing my shit. "Yeah, I latched the door back. I was nervous going out there, so I latched it back to the wall and stood at the door just looking at the stupid damn shadows for five minutes before I could bring myself to walk outside." I watched a silent exchange between Charlie and Dillon which pissed me off. I didn't want to be the fragile fucking weak woman who everyone tip-toed around. I'd be damned if they were going to start keeping things from me in a bid to protect poor Rebecca Donovan.

"What?" I growled at Charlie when his gaze returned to me.

"If you latched the door it means someone had to unlatch it, which means you aren't going insane." I could see the desperation in his eyes. He would prefer that I was insane, hell, suddenly I preferred the idea of insane. The only other option was someone was screwing with me, and not in a good way. Dillon called in Braiden to do a thorough search behind the shop, hoping that whoever had been snooping around left behind a clue as to who they were. They also put in a quick call to Frank to let the police know what had happened. Then I spent the next twenty minutes arguing with Charlie about accompanying him to the gym for his sparring session.

"I refuse to be the spineless, crazy maiden who can't deal with her shit."

Charlie raised a brow in my direction. "Maiden? Seriously? What era were you born in, woman?" I glared at him. "You are not spineless, you are not crazy, and you are definitely no maiden. Strong willed, stubbornly determined, intelligent, and one hundred percent sexy as hell woman is a more accurate description. And you have all that without needing to hang out with a bunch of testosterone filled boys in a sweaty ol' gym."

I drilled my nails in a determined beat against the door of Charlie's truck, my gaze in Charlie's direction unwavering. He was not leaving me behind.

"Fine," he threw his hands up in the air before settling them once again on the steering wheel, "like I said, stubborn as a damn mule," he muttered. I somehow managed to hold in the satisfied grin that begged to be let out, and watched the outside world pass by in a blur as we made our way to Lee's Gym.

I climbed down from Charlie's truck—I almost needed a ladder to get in and out of it. I would have clearly thought Charlie was over compensating for something if I didn't know better. Charlie stood by the front door to the gym, a cheeky grin on his face which made me wonder if I had toilet paper trailing from the back of my jeans or something. It wouldn't be the first time the Humiliate Rebecca demon came out to play, making my cool and stylish persona look like a farce—poppy seeds stuck in my teeth, red wine spilled in my lap, broken heel on my pumps, sitting in gum—you name it and I've more than likely faced the awkward humiliation of it.

"What?" I asked nervously, looking down at my clothes and running my tongue over my teeth.

"You know, you look like a damn teenager dressed like that?"

I looked down again at my simple outfit and quirked an eyebrow. "Ella picked it out." I shrugged.

"Ahhhh...that explains it."

"You don't like it?" I couldn't help but blurt out. If he said no, I would most likely burst into tears. It would be completely un-Rebecca like and I would be embarrassed as hell, but my emotions were clearly out of control right now.

"I think you look beautiful in anything you wear," his smile turned devious, "or don't wear." I blushed, just like a fucking teenager! "Come on." He pulled open the door and guided me inside, the warmth of his hand at the small of my back made me feel safe and cherished. His previous words about me being beautiful made me feel hot and possibly the tiniest bit horny—something I never expected to feel again after my brutal attack.

I have never stepped foot in a gym, so my expectations were probably carved from hearsay and movies. Don't get me wrong, I've dabbled in exercise. I ran, well, jogged slowly. Some may call it a brisk walk, but I preferred the term leisurely jog. I attended yoga in the park during summer; it was…interesting. I even attempted a pole dancing class once, which was a catastrophe. Lee's Gym wasn't anything like I expected. I expected to walk into a state-of-the-art gym, full of fancy machines, walls lined with mirrors, and pretentious men and women too obsessed with staring at their reflections to notice the world around them. Instead, Lee's Gym was very understated. There was a small part of the gym sectioned off for weights, the equipment was obviously quite old, yet it was clean and tidy. A few treadmills and exercise bikes lined one wall and on the opposite side of the gym were punching bags and mats. All of the exercise equipment surrounded what was obviously the iconic representation of an authentic gym—the boxing ring. It smelled a little funky, not in a gross way, but used—sweaty with an underlying scent of bleach. There were a few guys pounding on the bags and a few others were lifting weights. The ring was empty. As I followed Charlie, a silver haired man that stood almost as tall as the giant Jaxon Carter, strode towards us scowling. He had to be pushing sixty, but he had the physique of a man that took care of himself. He looked every bit like Beast from Beauty and the Beast that my grandma read to me as a little girl. His irate glare made me instantly nervous.

"Cole," the towering giant growled.

Charlie glanced back over his shoulder and sent me a cheeky grin accompanied with a wink. "You've got that look, General," Charlie said, a hint of humor in his voice.

The gruff looking Beast scowled even further, if that were at all possible. "And what look would that be?"

"The look you get when your wife makes you sleep on the couch because you've been an ass." Charlie chuckled. I stood nervously at Charlie's back. I wasn't sure if this was playful banter or something that was going to end in a brawl.

Beast's scowl broke and a surprisingly gentle smile replaced it. He peered over Charlie's shoulder, his eyes softening as they settled on me. Beast was really nothing more than a slightly rough looking kitten.

"Two nights of couch time and counting. Apparently when your wife asks if she's gained weight, answering honestly is not recommended. Mind you, I did tell her I thought her curves were sexy!" Beast gave me another curious glance. "What is a beautiful young lady like this doing with an arrogant ass like you, Cole?"

Charlie laughed and it made me feel at ease, and a little more comfortable. "General, this is Rebecca Donovan, Rebecca, General Lee, owner of this smelly excuse for a respectable establishment."

The General clipped Charlie on the back of the head as he stretched out his large meaty hand that consumed my tiny one. "The flower lady! My wife talks about your shop all the time." The General beamed.

"Perhaps she's giving you a subtle hint," I replied. "Women like flowers. They might even help get you off the couch." The General laughed and the sound was loud and welcoming. I felt safe surrounded by these two men, protected even. I found myself feeling lighter and more relaxed than I've been in weeks.

"Oh, there is nothing subtle about my wife, darlin'. A wise man once told me that the moment you gave in to a woman's demands, she'd have you by the short and curlies."

Regardless of how barbaric and ridiculous the notion was, I couldn't help but smile. "Then you obviously haven't heard the saying, 'a happy wife is a happy life.'" Damn, I was beginning to sound like Lola. The General's loud burst of laughter made me jump, and Charlie discreetly took my hand and gave it a gentle squeeze.

"You got me there," he said, running a hand through his buzz cut, silver hair. "Cole, Brent is gearing up, go get yourself ready." Charlie dropped my hand and gave me a reassuring smile as he backed away to, what I assumed, was the locker room. "Come on, Rebecca. I'm soon to be your number one customer. Come hang out with me while our boy gets changed and tell me what will make my wife the happiest woman in Claymont." The General was in the process of explaining how his wife, Liz, was due in shortly and would love to meet me, when Charlie reappeared from the locker room.

The General's voice became lost in a fog of lust and desire. Charlie was wearing knee length gym shorts with some sort of padding over his shins. His chest was deliciously bare and smooth, tattoos adorned his perfectly sculpted biceps and his hands were wrapped in tape. I have seen Charlie in all his naked glory before, but the way he looked right now—partially naked, raw and ready to fight—had me all hot and bothered, in a good way. Charlie gave me a knowing grin as he strode with confidence towards the ring in the center of the gym, my eyes following him the entire way. His muscles seemed to flex and move with fluid grace, his back coiled with strength as he pulled himself up through the ropes. As Charlie continued to move around the ring, stretching and bouncing on his feet, a gentle clearing of someone's throat at my side caught my attention. The General was watching me with a mischievous gleam in his eyes.

"Sorry, I missed that," I choked out.

He laughed and shook his head standing. "Not important, little lady. Come on, let's get up close so I can keep an eye on my boys." I followed the General to the side of the ring and Charlie leaned over talk to me.

"You okay?" he asked, genuinely concerned.

"I'm fine, Charlie, stop worrying." I scowled, noticing the General's curious sideways glance.

At that moment, a tall man, dressed almost identical to Charlie, strolled into the gym from the locker room. I assumed this was Brent. He was as tall as Charlie and just as well built. A warm grin—on a face far too handsome for a fighter—graced his features. He was gorgeous--his eyes were a rich chocolate brown that sparkled with the promise of fun and adventure; his dark brown hair was pulled back into a messy bun, which should have looked feminine and ridiculous, but with this man's confidence and sex appeal, he totally pulled it off; his skin was bronze, as if the sun god himself had kissed him with a permanent glowing tan; his body was taut and strong, and not a single tattoo or imperfection marred his lean athletic muscle. I followed the corded trail of abs that disappeared where his distinctive magic V kicked off. My mouth was begging to drop open in a display of shock. Claymont had apparently become heavenly-man central. With Charlie, Jax, Dillon, Braiden, and now this fine specimen before me, I only needed seven more divinely crafted men and we could put together one hell of a calendar for next year! Brent winked my way, or maybe it was meant for the General, either way I was absolutely taking it with a gracious smile.

"Brent," Charlie growled, "keep your fucking winks to yourself."

Brent laughed and began to bounce around the ring just as Charlie had done earlier. "Think you can keep your concentration with your pretty girl watching?" Brent quipped.

"Think you can keep your eyes off my pretty girl before I introduce your cocky face to the floor?" Charlie quickly replied. His girl? My heart fluttered along with my girly parts.

"Both of you stop fucking around and get your heads in the right place," grumbled the General from beside me.

Suddenly, I felt my presence may be too much of a distraction. Maybe I shouldn't have come. "I'm glad you're here, the boys need a challenge," the General added. I was grateful he set my uncertain thoughts aside.

Charlie and Brent turned towards each other and tapped their gloves. There was no hesitation as they began to dance around each other, throwing light punches that barely connected. My eyes followed the gentle boxing match, completely mesmerized by the beauty of it. The two men had perfect bodies that moved effortlessly around the ring. Obvious strength and surprising flexibility were combined for a fight that was varied with punches and kicks. Charlie moved effortlessly around Brent's punches, and swept his foot high for a kick that narrowly missed Brent's head.

"Watch yourself, Cole," Brent hissed.

Charlie grinned. "What's the matter, princess, I scare you?"

As the sparring went on, Brent's assault became a little more determined, but before I could allow worry and anxiety to enter my thoughts, someone murmured from over my shoulder.

"We need to talk."

Four simple words from a familiar voice. And I knew we had an Oh-Shit moment on our hands. I turned around and came face to face with Luke Hollywell. He didn't look angry, concerned if anything, but Charlie Cole was seriously going to flip the fuck out. His eyes didn't scare me like the eyes of my attacker did, they were different. Too pale and not at all crazy enough.

"You son of a bitch!" came the roar from behind me. And here was our oh-shit moment starting now.

"Do you have a death wish, son?" asked the General from beside me.

In an impressive display of agility, Charlie jumped clear over the ropes of the boxing ring and landed gracefully on the floor. His eyes were full of fury, which absolutely freaked me out, but not in the same way those angry eyes did the night I was attacked. In a moment of complete insanity, I stepped into the path between Charlie and Luke, hoping to God that I didn't end up squashed in a brutal male collision. Charlie's eyes looked confused and he became as still as a statue, watching me with his fists clenched at his sides. Behind him, Brent had jumped from the ring and seemed ready to hold Charlie back, as the General took a step closer to Luke, ready to do whatever necessary to prevent bloodshed in his gym.

"Charlie, it wasn't him," I quickly began to explain.

"How the fuck do you know that? His face was covered!" Charlie demanded.

"His eyes, Ella is always carrying on about eyes. And since I've been friends with her, I've taken more notice of them. Luke's eyes aren't dark enough, they're like a pale, baby poo brown, not dark brown."

Charlie shook his head. "It was dark, you can't be sure."

"He was pretty up close and personal in my face, Charlie, I'm one hundred per cent sure about this," I said a little angrily.

Charlie seemed to be battling an internal war. His body was ready to fight, but his mind was conflicted. I took a deep breath followed by a few hesitant steps towards him, and when I was close enough to touch him, I reached out a hand and gently swept away a stray lock of hair that had tumbled across his eyes. "You believe me don't you?" His eyes stayed on mine for the longest time before he cast a quick look over my shoulder in Luke's direction. He gave me a stiff nod. "Please don't be angry," I breathed. At that, Charlie's entire body seemed to melt, his eyes softened and he took my hand that lingered on his arm, and pressed it against his chest right over his heart. His other hand reached for the back of my neck and pulled me in close. He was dripping with sweat, but I didn't care as I wrapped my arms around him.

"I'm sorry, Betty Boop," he murmured in my ear. "I didn't mean to scare you."

I instantly relaxed and even managed to chuckle. "That part where you jumped down from the ring and that bad ass scary look? It was kinda hot." The rumble of laughter from Charlie's chest seemed to thaw the mood in the gym.

"I need a new fucking job," grumbled the General.

CHAPTER 10

Charlie

I still couldn't believe Luke had waltzed into the gym and had the balls to walk right up to Rebecca. When I saw him standing before her, blood red rage clouded my eyes and I was ready to kill. The only thing that brought my temper to a grinding halt was seeing said little blonde hair, blue eyed girl looking at me with fear in her eyes. Not fear of Luke, but fear of me. A few whispered words from her beautiful lips and I calmed instantly. The only other person who came close to handling my temper so effortlessly was Mercy. Under Rebecca's hand that rested on my chest, my heart went from a gallop to a leisurely canter. I relished the feel of her soft feminine body in my arms and in that moment I was filled with an emotion I could reliably say I had never felt before: Pride? Admiration? Love? Hell, call it what you will, but in that moment Rebecca Donovan was once again mine, and I was not letting her go this time. Feeling her warm body against mine helped keep me focused; it helped keep the fury at bay. I glanced over her shoulder, my eyes settling on Luke Hollywell. The arrogant prick didn't back down, he was standing tall, eyes staring me down. I wasn't convinced that it hadn't been Luke who had hurt Rebecca, but I wasn't going to beat him to a bloody pulp in front of Rebecca, or in the General's space for that matter.

"What the fuck do you want," I growled at him.

"I want to speak to Rebecca." His eyes moved over the small crowd that had moved in closer to watch. "Without an audience preferably."

Before I could say a word, the General moved to my side. "You want to talk to him, darlin'?" he asked Rebecca.

She turned to face Luke, but didn't move away from me. I was grateful, her presence between me and Luke was the only thing keeping me sane right now. Rebecca nodded. "You can use my office." I went to protest but the General was quick to shut me down. "But Charlie and I go with you." He pointed at Luke to make sure he got the message. The fucker nodded.

We followed the General to his small, cluttered office at the back of the gym. The door was shut behind us and we stood around rather awkwardly. My body was still tense, I felt twitchy, but somehow I kept my ire reined in.

"What do you want, Luke?" Rebecca sighed.

"I didn't attack you that night. I don't need to force myself on women. If I want to fuck, I have no problem finding someone willing to fuck me." He gave Rebecca a smug smile.

My fists clenched and thoughts of slamming one of them in his face began to cloud my mind again. The General leaned back against his desk, watching Luke thoughtfully. Rebecca, thankfully, was still standing in front of me, keeping my hands from finding the conceited prick's neck.

"I told Frank I didn't think you were involved, but obviously he had to check you out, Luke. You were the last person who saw me before the attack."

Luke shook his head with frustration. "I have an alibi and I'm still being followed. Every time I turn around there is a fucking cop in my face," he spat.

Rebecca shrugged. "I have no control over the police, Luke. You have a problem with them, take it up with them yourself."

Luke took a step forward and immediately the General was on his feet as I stepped around Rebecca, placing her slightly behind me. Luke stopped and finally showed the good sense to look a little nervous. He moved to the doorway and pulled it open with a little too much force.

"I didn't hurt you," he snarled at Rebecca. "You're not even my type. Though I gotta say, the new clothes are an improvement."

"Son of a—" I lunged for the asshole, but was met by a wall of resistance in the form of the General. "Let me fucking go!" I demanded.

"You'll get your chance in two weeks, Cole. In the ring." After what seemed an eternity, I settled down enough that the General cautiously let me go.

"What do you mean, 'in the ring'?" came Rebecca's wavering voice from behind us.

Shit, I had lost my freakin' temper again. I ran a hand down my tired face and leaned against the now closed door in frustration.

"It's what my boys do when they have a problem with someone. Rather than let them battle it out on the streets, they resolve it in the ring, with officials to watch over it and a ref. It's safer that way," the General explained.

"You're going to fight him in the ring?" I turned to face Rebecca. I was surprised to see the anger in her eyes. I nodded. "What kind of barbaric caveman mentality is that?" Her voice grew louder as she glared at both the General and me. "We are not in grade school anymore, we are all adults here. Has anyone ever thought about sitting down and talking out their problems instead of fighting them out?"

Being the asshole that I am, I couldn't stop the laughter that spilled from my lips. The idea of me and Luke sitting in the same room was beyond hilarious. The General did a much better job at keeping his face unreadable.

"You're laughing at me?" Rebecca demanded, her pretty cheeks tinged with red.

She was pissed off and it reminded me so much of the old Rebecca that I smiled again. Dumbass move, Cole!

"Rebecca," the General said gruffly, "this is a place for fighters who are not typically known for articulating their problems. They use their fists as an outlet, it's their way to get their aggression out. Talking does not always work for the people who train here. I've had a lot of experience in handling men like this, both in the military and in this gym. Trust me on this, dealing with it in the ring is safer."

Rebecca opened her mouth to say something, but nothing came out. She looked like a fish out of water, her lips moving but no sound coming out. At her exasperated failure of speech, she threw her arms up and stormed right past me, out of the General's office and into the gym. I followed her, concerned that Luke might still be lingering somewhere out there. Rebecca had her cell phone in her hand, scrolling through her contacts as I approached.

"Who are you calling?" I asked.

"I'm calling Ella to see if she can come pick me up, which says how desperate I am to get away from you right now because she drives like a freakin' mad woman."

Instinctively I grabbed the phone right out of her hand. She was not escaping me again.

"What the hell, Charlie?" she screamed.

I winced and I was pretty sure some of the guys around me did, too. "We are going back to your place, just like we planned. You are not chickening out on me now."

The fury in her eyes was palpable. "I was not chickening out. Ella can take me!"

"You are not running away from me, Betty Boop." She seemed to take a few long deep breaths before calming herself. It was a nice turn around to see someone else losing their shit for a change.

"I'm not running away, we are having a time out!" She reached for her phone again, and some childish part of me saw fit to stuff it down the front of my shorts, right into the uncomfortable briefs I only wore when training. Rebecca shook her head, her face horrified. "Oh, that's just plain nasty! You're all sweaty and gross." She rubbed her eyes and finally sighed in defeat. "Fine, whatever. But I need to get out of here now, Charlie. All this macho man-sweat and aggression is giving me a headache. I need a drink," she grumbled.

"Fine, give me ten and we'll be on our way."

Back in the warm cabin of my truck, I pulled Rebecca's cell phone from the pocket of my hoodie. Rebecca just glared at me.

"I wiped it off." I chuckled.

"You owe me a new phone." When she refused to take it from me I threw it onto the dash and backed the truck out of Lee's parking lot.

"Come on, Betty Boop, after everything we did a year ago, you have a problem with your cell phone touching my junk?" I grinned at the blush that flooded her cheeks.

"That was different," she murmured.

"How so? I was pretty damn sweaty that night and you couldn't keep your hands off me as I recall."

She laughed and the sound was like a break in the storm, it was peaceful and calm for just a moment. "You were unable to keep your hands off me that night. You had my damn panties off before we even got out of your truck!"

The surge of lust that filled my body at the memory went straight to my dick and I shifted uncomfortably.

"Having trouble there, Charlie Cole?" she quipped in a cute sing-song voice.

I gave her a smug grin. "This stroll down memory lane is waking someone up," I murmured.

Rebecca's smile fell a little, and her eyes became distant. "I'm sure there are plenty of women prepared to take care of that for you."

She looked away from me, but not before I saw the sadness in her eyes. In that moment, I wanted to explain to her that I didn't want anyone else, only her. I didn't want to screw up this opportunity though so I kept my mouth shut and went over the words I needed to say. It was only a ten minute drive to her house, but it was the longest ten minutes of my life. The drive was quiet and strained. As soon as I pulled the truck into her driveway and put it into park, I reached across and grabbed her chin, forcing her eyes to mine.

"Baby," I whispered. Her sadness and fragility was back now, old Rebecca, strong Rebecca had fizzled in the space of fifteen minutes. "I don't want any other woman taking care of me," I quietly confessed. "I didn't want anyone other than you back then, I haven't wanted anyone other than you since then, and I sure as hell don't want anyone other than you now."

Rebecca's brow furrowed with confusion. "You have had plenty of someone else's since me."

I cringed at her far too accurate observation. I shook my head and stared out the windshield of my truck. If I told her the truth, if I told her how I fucked to take away the aggression, the restlessness, the loneliness, what the hell would she think of me then? I didn't want to lie to her though, and there was really no other explanation I could give.

71

"You're going to think I'm a complete asshole." I glanced her way and she was watching me expectantly. I shrugged. "Dave calls my escapades a search for the affection and love I lost as a child in the arms of anyone willing to accept me. Apparently it is destructive behavior, and to be honest, I've only recently come to the realization that he's right." Rebecca didn't say anything and I shifted nervously in my seat, my hands gripping the steering wheel so tightly I thought it might snap. "It also helps me blow off steam."

"Okay, so why does there have to be lots of different women, rather than just one?"

I looked her straight in the eye. "I found one. There was a misunderstanding and the stubborn girl refused to take my calls. As it turns out, I'm apparently just as stubborn because instead of banging down her door and demanding she listen to me, I refused to chase her." Rebecca's eyes glistened with unshed tears. "That was one of the biggest mistakes of my life," I told her without looking away. "I won't make it again." A tear slipped down her cheek and I opened my door and quickly made my way around to her side of the truck. I unbuckled her seatbelt and pulled her around to face me, wiping the tears from her cheeks. "If you run, Rebecca, I will follow you. If you refuse to take my calls, I will end up on your doorstep and I will demand you hear me out. I won't make the mistake of letting you go again."

Tears fell down her face but she smiled and somehow managed to laugh. "Your timing sucks, Charlie," she whispered. "All you'll be taking on right now is one basket-case of a woman who wakes up screaming every night, who's scared of the dark and jumps at every little sound. And she's not even sure if she can handle being touched intimately anymore."

I cupped her cheek and rested my forehead against hers. "Betty Boop, just being beside you, near you, just like this is enough for me. I'd be happy for the rest of my life if this was the closest we got. But, baby, you are going to have so much more. That fear is not always going to be there. I promised you I would help you defeat it, and I won't let you down." Her small nod was good enough for me. "You want to do this today? We can come back tomorrow if you want." She pulled away and looked over her shoulder toward the house.

"No, let's just get it over and done with. Anyway, my vodka and wine is in there and I really, really need a drink." She wiped away her tears and I helped her down from the truck.

CHAPTER 11

Rebecca

Who would have thought that the doorway into my own home could make me so nervous? Common sense told me I was safe. Charlie unlocked the door and was keying the security code into the keypad on the wall to our left. I knew I was safe, I knew there would be no figure cloaked in darkness ready to grab me. I was scared, but safe, yet I still couldn't force myself to move. My mind was clogged in a fear so all-encompassing that I could almost taste it. Through that fear I peered across the perfectly tidy living room. No longer were there flowers strewn across the wood floors, the small magazine table beside the couch sat upright, the magazines stacked neatly atop it. The kitchen beyond looked just as it should—empty. My vodka, sitting in the glass door cabinet on the wall, was demanding me to get my pathetic ass over that threshold and possess it. Sensing my obvious distress, Charlie stepped into my line of vision. His smile was gentle, opposing the fierce warrior that I knew lurked underneath. He took my hand and raised it to his lips, kissing my fingertips, his eyes never leaving mine. I couldn't draw my gaze away from his if you paid me.

"Breathe, Betty Boop," he murmured.

I wasn't even aware that my lungs were full, holding precious air in. They say the first step is the hardest, they seriously have no idea. Hard didn't even begin to express the difficulty I was having taking that first step.

"You know, if you don't come in here soon, I'm going to go looking through that drawer next to your bed, the one that you told me to stay out of." Charlie's eyes sparkled with mischief.

I knew which drawer he was referring to, the very drawer I nervously asked him not to look in the night he packed a bag for me following my attack. The drawer where Big Red lived. I immediately stepped across the threshold.

Charlie laughed. "Damn, now I'm going to be thinking all sorts of wicked things."

I blushed like a schoolgirl and pretended to ignore his eyes full of playfulness. As I walked further into the room, the easier I found it. My house was just as it should have been: quiet and clean. I walked around the living area, taking in every little detail, looking for anything out of place, and nothing was. I moved to the kitchen and did the same thing, my eyes and hands moving across everything familiar, everything safe. Eventually I came to stand at the narrow hall that led to my bedroom and I froze. During my entire exploration thus far, Charlie followed behind me quietly, not pushing, not teasing. There were no questions about what the hell I was doing. Somehow I think he understood. I was forcing myself to see what was in front of me: my home and my things, untouched and safe. There was that word again—safe. It felt foreign. Again, Charlie didn't push, he just simply stood at my back, the warmth of his body drawing me against the solid wall of his chest. I leaned against him and his arms came around me, holding me tight. Charlie's earlier confession whispered through my mind, calming me, giving me a new focus and a break from my fears. He promised that he wasn't going to let me go again, and as possessive as his words had been, I held them dear to my heart. It didn't matter if I couldn't be with him intimately, he still wanted me. His staunch determination and his unyielding promise made me feel truly cherished for the first time in my life. I clung to him a little tighter and he didn't hesitate to squeeze me back. My token jealous streak caused my heart to ache at the thought of the other women he's been with, both before me and after our interlude, over a year ago. The warmth of his body by mine, his breath tickling my ear, and his declaration of propriety helped lessen that ache though. I wanted him, I always have. Suddenly the only thing that mattered was that he was mine now. The past was just that—the past—it couldn't be altered, it couldn't be reshaped, and with time the memories would fade. Right now and tomorrow was where my heart and focus needed to be.

"What's goin' through that head of yours, Betty Boop? I can hear the wheels turning."

"I'm glad you're here with me." There was no need to explain further, those few words summed it all up. I felt the deep rise and fall of Charlie's chest, as if a heavy sigh had silently escaped his lips.

"There is nowhere else I would rather be," he murmured. We stood like that a little longer. Charlie's arms were wrapped tightly around my shoulders, my back pressed hard against his front.

"This is freakin' crazy. I mean, I know there is no one down that damn hall, you're right here, and I'm completely safe, but I'm still scared. Maybe those bumps to the head dislodged something," I whispered.

Charlie's head dipped down and his lips brushed against the gentle curve of my neck, causing something in my body to hum with unspoken desire. My eyelids fluttered shut and a small sigh escaped my lips. In that moment, I was filled with two thoughts. Number one, I didn't think my body would respond to a man's touch ever again, so this was kinda awesome. Number two…number two? Charlie's lips moved to the delicate shell of my ear. Oh hell, thought number two was gone along with every other cognizant thought.

"There is nothing wrong with your head. After what you have been through, being scared is perfectly normal. It can do strange things to the mind. The first step in healing is to acknowledge your fears, and you've done that. The next step is to defeat them." Charlie's arms slipped from me and I instantly missed the contact. He slid by me and stood halfway down the hall, facing me with a cheeky grin that made his roguish good looks suddenly more boyish. "How about we make this interesting?"

It took a moment for his words to sink in and I shook my head. "What the hell are you talking about, Charlie?" I wondered out loud. Was my all-consuming fear not interesting enough for him?

"Well, if you can make it to..." he glanced around and took two more steps away from me, "here, I will give you a reward."

From the sexy grin on his face, I had an idea as to what my reward might be, and my body responded appropriately. My mind, however, was still nervous as hell. He had to be no more than ten feet away, a few steps, easy. I almost snorted, a few steps down my own God damn hallway should be more than easy; they should be thoughtless! One deep breath later, my shoulders back, head held high, I stepped down the hall. You'd think I was descending into the depths of hell from the way my heart was pounding with irrational fear. I kept my eyes on Charlie though and he reached out his hand out as I drew closer. I automatically grabbed for it as if his touch alone could save me from falling into an abyss from which there might be no return. Charlie pulled me roughly into his chest and his mouth crushed against mine in a brutally passionate kiss. By the time he pulled away, I was breathless. My fingers lingered over what I was sure were kiss-swollen lips. Charlie's forehead leaned against mine, a position we seemed to find ourselves in often.

"Do you realize how fucking incredible you taste." He sighed. "I could never forget that taste, not in a million lifetimes."

My heart tripped over his words as he began to pull away from me. I stood there, feeling dazed, thrilled, and thoughtless! Fearless! I smiled a little. Charlie now stood level with my bedroom door and all of a sudden that fear was back.

Charlie glanced into my bedroom. "Empty, Betty Boop. Nothing but your things. Go take a look and I'll give you another reward."

I eyed the doorway to my bedroom nervously before looking back at Charlie. My breathing sped up and my heart was beating furiously, but no longer from excitement, now it was out of fear. I closed my eyes trying to block out the images that flashed through my mind. Images of him, images of that night.

"No, Rebecca!" Charlie demanded. I opened my eyes immediately. "You keep those pretty blue eyes open and you keep them on me. It's just you and me here, and I don't want you to forget that."

I nodded and bit my lip nervously. Less than ten feet this time—I could do this. Hell, I just wanted another one of those blazing hot Cole kisses. Charlie raised his hand, and without another thought I took the four quick steps forward, practically throwing myself into his strong body. I held on tight, and in return, Charlie held on to me just as tight. I was breathing hard and fast, my head pressed against his chest, my eyes squeezed shut again. The loud beat of his heart was right under my ear and I focused on its steady rhythm, letting it lull me into some resemblance of calm. Finally, I was able to open my eyes and though my hands shook and my knees felt weak, I was okay.

Charlie took my face in his big palms and looked down at me with a look that I could only describe as pride. "Good girl," he murmured before pressing a slow, soft kiss to my lips.

This was different to the last kiss, which had been full of a fiery craving. This kiss was slow, full of adoration, respect and tenderness. When Charlie finally pulled away, I felt nothing but cherished under his hard body and piercing gaze. I wanted to beat my fears not only for me, but also for Charlie. To see him look at me like that filled me with a self-worth that I only now realized I'd been missing. Pressing my forehead against his hard chest, I took another long, deep cleansing breath and I turned my head, my gaze now falling on my bedroom. Just as Charlie had assured me, it was empty apart from my belongings. The curtains were pulled back, allowing light to fill the space. It wasn't so scary, yet I still felt anxious about going in there.

"Someone made my bed," I whispered. I felt Charlie press a kiss to the top of my head.

"Mercy," he confirmed.

Clean sheets, but not that clean. I could still picture him holding me down, touching me, tainting me. His hands had ripped away my confidence and left a stain in its place, a mark that I feared might never disappear.

"I need a drink," I groaned after a moment of silence. I promptly turned and made my way back into the kitchen where I grabbed a glass from the cabinet and filled it with a nip of vodka, actually it was a little more than a nip, but I think I earned it. Charlie followed me and began going through my fridge, pouring the sour milk down the sink and throwing the spoiled food into a plastic garbage bag. I threw back the vodka and coughed as the liquid burned a trail down my throat and into my chest.

"I'm out of practice," I wheezed.

"You should probably take it easy. I'm sure your doctor would not approve mixing alcohol with your medication."

I poured another shot as Charlie continued to fumble through my kitchen. "I'm not mixing anything. This is straight up vodka all by its lonesome. And hopefully, if I keep this up, I won't need any sleeping pills tonight."

"Well, how about I'm worried. If you get drunk you might try and take advantage of me." Charlie gave me a serious look and I found myself frowning. He didn't want me to take advantage of him? Could I take advantage of him? A smile cracked through his serious façade. "On second thought," he murmured. I hid a smile and threw back a second shot of the burning liquid that was leaving my chest warm and my head a little fuzzy. Charlie carefully poured some water into my Clitoria, the green leafy plant whose vibrant deep blue flowers resembled, well, a clitoris. I couldn't stop the giggle that bubbled from my chest as he carefully moved the flowers aside to make sure the water reached the soil. "What?" he asked, his brow furrowed with worry.

"You look like you've done that before. You are very gentle," I noted, trying not to laugh.

He shrugged. "I don't want to be too rough and damage the flowers."

"Oh, those flowers are pretty hardy. They can handle quite a pounding." Charlie stared at me, his faced etched with confusion. The shots had obviously found their mark and my giggles turned into hysterical laughter.

"Am I missing something here?" He regarded me, leaning casually against the kitchen counter.

"That is my Clitoria," I managed to say between bouts of laughter.

Charlie looked back at the plant, a horrified expression on his face. "Say again?" he asked for confirmation.

"Clitoria ternatea, named so because of its clitoris shaped flowers. It actually grows better as a vine, but I don't want to put it outside because the snow will kill it." Charlie's intense stare made me hesitate. The look wasn't humor, nor was it anger. It was something else, something more.

"You of all people should know how careful I am with such an exquisite bud," he said earnestly.

I choked on the mouthful of vodka that had just passed my lips. Cheeks aflame, I turned my attention away from the far too sexy man standing so casually in my kitchen, talking about my plant. At least I thought we were talking about my plant. Maybe our conversation had shifted to something far more personal and a whole lot more erotic.

My eyes settled on a piece of paper that was lying on the hardwood floors just in front of the back door. I considered it for a moment before moving across the room to retrieve it. A small gasp escaped my lips when I recognized the handwriting immediately.

"Rebecca?" Charlie asked from the kitchen. My eyes darted over the few words once, twice then a third time as I tried to make sense of the note.

"Who's B, and who's Em?" Charlie murmured from over my shoulder.

"I'm B, when Emily was little she couldn't say Rebecca so she started calling me B. It stuck and Em? Well Em is my sister, Emily," I whispered.

"I thought Emily left Claymont years ago?" asked Charlie. I nodded woodenly. "And what is she making right?" he continued, reading the note from behind me.

I shrugged as I read the letter again.

B, I'm so sorry. I promise I will make this right. Love, Em.

"Betty Boop, what is this about?" Charlie asked suspiciously.

"I have no idea," I replied honestly. "I was still a teenager when she left Claymont and I haven't seen her since. I would be completely oblivious to her existence if it weren't for the occasional phone call or letter, and up until recently I thought maybe she had forgotten I existed altogether. It had been almost two years since I last heard from her. But over the last month, I've heard from her no less than five times."

"What did she want?"

"She wanted me to sell the house. I got the impression she needed the money, but I refused to sell." Charlie took the piece of paper from me and read it over himself, his hand rubbing the rough hair on his chin. It had obviously been a few days since he last shaved.

"I saw her," I breathed. Charlie's gaze settled on me. His face betrayed no emotion as he patiently waited for me to continue. "Outside the store this morning. At the time I wasn't sure, it's been such a long time since I've seen her, and she looked so different. Then after everything that happened today, I completely forgot about it."

"How can you be sure it was her then?"

"The last time I saw her she was sixteen, she was still a child really. Her hair was slightly darker than mine, long, down to her waist. She had full cheeks and a curvy figure. She was gorgeous. The Emily I saw this morning was different. Her hair was short, like pixie short, and jet black. She was really thin, she looked tired, and was far too pale. Her eyes were the same though, eyes never change. Emily's eyes are blue like mine, only a little paler. She hated them, but I always found them beautiful, intriguing. When I saw her this morning, I saw those eyes and I thought right away that it had to be Emily, but the woman looked so different in every other way."

Charlie began pacing around the room and it made me nervous. He suddenly seemed agitated. "Why would she be back in Claymont? And if she is back here and was right in front of your shop, why didn't she come in to see you?"

I shook my head, I had no idea. "Bouquets isn't called Bouquets anymore, its Mercy's Angels and Bouquets and you can't see my part of the shop by looking through the glass. Mostly you just notice the chairs and tables for Annie's coffee shop through the windows. She wouldn't have even realized I was there, and as for why she is back, I have no idea. She was never fond of Claymont, she hated it. Em wanted the city, the lights and all the excitement that goes with it." Charlie rubbed a hand through his messy hair. "There were men with her—two men—and they were huge, like, intimidating bouncer huge. They looked like they were forcing her into a car." My heart started to hammer with panic. "What if she's in some sort of trouble?" Charlie glanced back down at the letter. I grabbed my cell phone off the counter and scrolled through my contacts until I found the last number she called me from. I dialed it and tapped my fingers on the counter beside me with impatience.

"The number you have dialed is no longer in service," the monotone recording echoed through my ear. I scrolled through to another number and pressed call. Again, I was greeted with the same recording. There was only one other number that Emily called from recently, and somehow I knew I would get the same result. I sighed with disappointment when the same recording picked up. I stared at the phone, willing it to ring, willing it to be Emily on the other end.

"Can I keep this? I want to show Dillon and Braiden." Charlie held the note in front of me.

"What on earth for?" I startled, his question snapped my attention from my phone and the empty, useless recording.

"Rebecca, you were attacked less than a month ago, and there is no suspect. Then suddenly your sister, who is hard up for cash, shows up in town with some questionable looking people?"

I just stared at him, taking in what he was saying. "You think she had something to do with my attack?" I finally stammered. That he was even suggesting it pissed me off. My sister would never do anything to hurt me. We may not have seen each other in nearly ten years, but we were blood, we grew up together. My sister would never hurt me.

"Maybe your attack had nothing to do with your sister, but it wouldn't hurt to have Dillon and Braiden poke around and make sure she's okay. I'm sure you would feel better knowing she is alright." Okay, that made sense. I nodded as I looked around my home, which now felt so cold and empty.

"I don't want to stay here," I quietly confessed. Charlie took the short few steps to me and wrapped his arms around my shoulders, pulling me into the safety of his chest.

"You don't have to, Betty Boop. We'll grab anything you need and you can come stay with me. We'll get the rest of your things from Jax and Ella's tomorrow. On the way to my place, we can stop by Dillon's office and show him the letter."

My head throbbed, my few carefree moments of vodka induced happiness had slipped away, and now, all I wanted was a hot shower and a full night's sleep. The shower wouldn't be a problem, the sleep definitely would be.

* * *

"This is the most recent photo you have of her?" Dillon Montgomery asked.

I sensed he knew what my answer would be, but perhaps he was hoping, by some miracle, I could produce a more recent one. It was one of Emily and me on Christmas morning, eight years ago. Emily looked so young, her hair in a long braid, a carefree grin on her lips. I stood beside her, two fingers peeking above her head from behind in a childish taunt. We looked so similar, apart from me being a good few inches taller and slightly more womanly. I began to develop my curves early, but Emily at sixteen, although she had a healthy curvy figure, was still flat chested, and her cheeks still held their child-like roundness. It was our last Christmas together. Two months later, Emily left Claymont, only a note explaining her need to see the world. I shook off the sorrow that threatened to consume me and nodded.

The office of Montgomery Securities was unusually comfortable. It was big and spacious, with high tech looking computers, combined with massive computer screens. A big comfy leather couch sat at the front of the room in front of a wide coffee table and a large clutter-free counter. There were framed photos on the walls, one of Dillon in his army fatigues, surrounded by a group of laughing children. The others were of foreign cities and landscapes; they were beautiful, exotic, and serene. I wondered if perhaps Dillon or Braiden had taken them. Off the reception area was a short corridor with three doorways. I knew one was Dillon's office and the other Braiden's. My mind raced with the idea that the third doorway led to some secret underground warehouse full of James Bond like weaponry and spy equipment. Okay, I really needed to stop watching so many movies. We were spread out around the reception area—Dillon was leaning against the neat counter; Braiden was kicked back in a chair, his big boots resting on the coffee table in front of us; and Charlie and I were sitting on the leather couch.

"We could dig around, look for police reports, driver's licenses, and arrest records. Might turn up a more recent photo there?" suggested Braiden.

That was the most I have ever heard Braiden speak. Six months ago, he bought a house in one of the brand new luxury estates on my side of town, and since Dillon was living with Braiden for now, it wasn't uncommon for him to tag along with Dillon to grab an occasional dinner or drink. He had always been quiet and a little reclusive, speaking only a few words and smiling less. It wasn't like he went around scowling in that dark and dangerous way you would expect, but instead he seemed to quietly consider everything that was going on around him. Ella told me Braiden had been an officer for NYPD's Emergency Service Unit before mysteriously leaving to do his own thing as a PI. When Dillon ditched the military to open his own security firm, Braiden had jumped straight in with him. Together they not only ran a successful and rapidly growing business, but were lusted after by every single woman in Claymont. Dillon, with his tall and athletic body, held himself with a confidence that oozed sex appeal. His hair was in a military buzz cut, and his eyes were a curious shade of green that were fanned with lashes that I was envious of! Yes, the Montgomery cousins were impressive.

"Is it possible that she goes under a different name now?" Dillon asked.

"I don't know. She's always just been Em, and I've always been B." I sighed, rubbing my throbbing head. The vodka shots were not my friends right now.

"Has she ever given any indication she was in some sort of trouble?" came Braiden's next question.

"No, I mean, other than seeming a little desperate for cash recently, no. I just assumed she was behind on her rent or something."

"Is she married? Boyfriend?" it was Dillon's turn to ask. I was beginning to feel like I was a spectator in a Montgomery tennis match.

"Not married, at least not that I know of. I'm sure she would have told me something like that. Boyfriend? I have no idea." I really didn't feel like I was giving them much to go on, and for the first time, I actually realized how little I really knew about my sister, my own flesh and blood. It was depressing.

"So, what we have is Emily Grace Donovan, twenty-five, short dark hair, light blue eyes, approximately five feet, two inches, slim build, in the company of two men driving a fancy black sedan." Dillon glanced at me for confirmation.

"Two fucking big men," I murmured. He nodded and I assumed at this point he would mock the lack of information—I felt like I was contributing so little. She was my little sister for Christ's sake, I should know more about her. I should have cared enough to at least look for her, check in on her. I had just let her walk away from me, from Claymont when she was nothing more than a wild teenage girl. Guilt rested heavy on my shoulders.

"Okay, that's a start. Do you have the last cell phone number she called from?"

"Yes, but I've already tried all three of them and they've been disconnected." Braiden grinned and I almost slipped off the couch. His smile was breathtaking—not too cocky, not too boyish—it was sexy, confident masculinity at its best. As handsome as he was though, as jaw dropping as that smile had been, he had nothing on Charlie. It was his cheeky arrogant grin that really melted my panties.

"That doesn't surprise me, but you would be shocked at the sort of trail a phone number can leave behind," Braiden said.

I left the last three numbers I had in my phone for Emily and finally found myself climbing back into Charlie's truck. He engaged in a quick private conversation with Dillon and Braiden in front of the office before joining me. In a despondent haze of aching head, tired limbs and worry, I leaned my head against the window of Charlie's truck and fell asleep instantly.

CHAPTER 12

Charlie

Rebecca was out before my truck left the parking lot. It had been a big day for her, so I wasn't at all surprised, especially after the way she knocked back those three shots of vodka earlier this afternoon. The curious note from her sister had left an uncomfortable feeling in my gut, and, as I expected, Dillon and Braiden had the same opinion. It was too big of a coincidence that Emily was sniffing around for money only weeks prior to Rebecca's attack. For the first time since her attack, I was beginning to think Luke Hollywell may in fact be innocent of the assault. Of being a fuckwit, not so much. For Rebecca's sake, I hoped to God her sister had nothing to do with it. But my gut told me she did. Rebecca's house on its own wasn't worth much, but the land it sat on was worth quite a lot, and she said that Emily seemed desperate for cash. It wasn't hard to reach a sinister conclusion.

Rebecca woke as I tried to carefully unbuckle her seatbelt, then she mumbled and cussed like a trooper as I steered her up the stairs, to my apartment which sat over Carter Constructions' office. Rebecca didn't like having her sleep interrupted. I wasn't even sure if her eyes opened as I led her through the small studio apartment. I pulled the sheets back and she sank into my bed, falling quickly back into a deep and restful sleep. I tucked her in and then grabbed her bag from the truck before taking advantage of the quiet moment to shower. Under the burning hot water, it was difficult not to let my thoughts stray to the beautiful woman who was laying in my bed. In fact, she was the first woman to lay in it. I decided a long time ago that it was easier to remove myself from a woman's home than it was to remove a woman from mine. For the first time in my adult life, I wanted this particular woman in my home. I wanted her clothes strewn about my bedroom floor. I wanted her vanilla scented shampoo in my shower. I swore I would never settle for the love of one woman, but Rebecca had opened my eyes to the warming notion. Rebecca and Rebecca only, forever? Hell yeah! As my thoughts began to stray to the erotic adventures I might play with this beautiful woman one day, I had to turn the hot water down and to douse my libido, yet again, with ice cold water.

In the kitchen, I turned the TV on to the evening news and set the volume down low, while I threw together some spaghetti bolognaise. I almost missed the soft groans coming from the bed on the other side of the apartment. I took the spaghetti off the burner and quietly made my way to Rebecca, who was beginning to toss and turn. She was still having nightmares and my fists clenched at the injustice of it. I fought the urge to climb into bed beside her and pull her into my arms. The mattress sank as I sat down, which caused Rebecca to roll towards me. I ran a hand through her soft blonde hair and whispered words that I thought might help. Her body seemed to lean into my touch. The tautness in her shoulders disappeared and eventually her eyelids fluttered open. I tensed, expecting her to freak out, but she surprised me when a shy smile touched her lips.

"Hey," I murmured, relishing the fact that she hadn't pulled away from me.

"Hey," she whispered back, "I think the smell of food woke me up."

I wasn't about to suggest a bad dream may have had something to do with it. She seemed so languidly content right now, I didn't want to spoil the moment. She was obviously hungry, so I would feed her. I hoped she liked spaghetti. Crap, what if she was a vegetarian? The thought made me realize just how little I knew about Rebecca, the woman I wanted forever with.

"What's that look for?" she asked, obviously noticing my inner monologue playing out on my face.

"What's your favorite food?" I found myself asking her.

"I have a soft spot of chili, how about you?"

"Italian, big time, like hard-on style big time." She laughed and the sound almost created one aforementioned hard-on.

"You get a hard-on for food?"

I shrugged. "Depends on whose cooking it and if it's any good. Take Mary's chocolate chip muffins for example, hard-on worthy and not because of Mary, but because they taste that damn good!"

Rebecca scrunched up her nose. "Okay, well, that's kind of weird, but luckily for you I can deal with weird."

I was reluctant to pull my hand from her hair, but when an awkward silence fell upon us, I forced myself to move. "Why don't you hop up and have something to eat, then you can take a shower and climb back into bed. We're having movie night." Rebecca slipped out from under the covers and followed me across to the kitchen.

"What movies are playing?"

I signaled to the wall of DVDs behind us. "Take your pick." Her mouth dropped open with astonishment. Yeah, I had a lot of movies. Not that I found myself watching them often, but I had somehow garnered a little bit of an addiction for buying them, especially the old school stuff like Cool Hand Luke and Rebel Without a Cause. I had accumulated over five hundred now. Rebecca strolled across the room to the massive shelving unit and began searching. I made two plates of spaghetti and by the time I sat at the small table, Rebecca made her choice and joined me. My eyebrows rose with surprise as she placed two DVDs down in front of me, Clerks and Clerks II.

"What?" she asked.

"Just didn't take you for a Clerks kinda girl." Rebecca's eyes sparkled with mischief.

"You know how every girl's parents put a pussy troll in them when the girls are young, to keep them from having premarital sex?" she said with a smile. The Clerks II quote made me laugh in disbelief.

"Myra's is named Pillow Pants. And so even though she totally wants to have sex with me, Myra says if I put my thing in her, Pillow Pants will bite it off." I practically knew every word in both of these movies—Jax and I have watched them like a thousand fucking times. I laughed loudly. "Do you have any idea how hot it is that you not only like that movie, but you can quote it?" She shrugged as she began to eat.

"What can I say, I have lived a repressed life thus far and quoting movies is a talent."

"Not your only talent," I murmured, recalling the night we spent together a year ago. Rebecca blushed and the color in her cheeks was fucking cute! "So, tell me about your family, about Emily," I suggested, moving the conversation along to perhaps an equally dangerous topic.

"Not much to tell. My mom and dad passed away in a car accident when I was nine, Emily was six. Our grandma took us in. Emily was the reckless one, the spontaneous one, even more so after our parents' death." That surprised me, after all, Rebecca has always seemed pretty damn spontaneous to me. She chuckled. "I know—the way I dress, my attitude—people assume I live life on the edge. I don't." She gave me a pointed glance. "I like things orderly. I like to prepare, know what I'm getting into. Emily didn't stop, it's like she had one speed: full throttle." Rebecca shook her head, a smile teasing the corners of her lips. "Claymont was too slow for a spark of life like Em. She left a few months after our grandma passed away, and it's been just me since then."

"No extended family?" I wondered out loud. She shook her head.

"What about you? Ella tells me your family is," she seemed to be struggling to find the right word, "unusual?"

I couldn't hold back the laughter. I'm sure Ella had an entirely different word for my family. I tagged along with Ella and Jax to the Claymont summer fair the previous year and Ella had had the misfortune of meeting my crazy-ass, right-wing mother.

"That's one word for them. Fanatical, eccentric, bigoted, domineering are probably more accurate." My temper threatened to spill at just the thought of my ultra-conservative family. One look at Rebecca's solemn gaze grounded me though. I sighed and rubbed a hand over my head which always throbbed in protest at the thought of my parents. "I was an only child and my folks are rather fanatical when it comes to religion. Don't get me wrong, I don't have a problem with people having faith in something. What are one person's beliefs might not be another's, and that is fine with me, to each their own and all that hoo-haa. But my family takes their beliefs and interpretations of the Bible a step further than most. Fuck, they take it a hundred damned steps further. They forbid the most basic of human wants and desires: music, television, brand name fucking clothing. Their way of demonstrating their faith is extreme. As far as I'm concerned, they pushed too hard, you know?" I peeked up at Rebecca. I wasn't sure what I expected to see in her face, but the gentle understanding in her eyes drained the fight out of me. Any anger that had built under the thoughts of my family disappeared. "I believe if you can't simply have a pure, strong, yet simple faith, if you have to force it or bend it, then maybe you don't have it in the first place. Inventing your own interpretation of the bible, or your own ideas of what God wants for us or doesn't want, makes you fanatical. They pushed it on me, tried to force me to accept their manifestation of what they thought was right and wrong. Hell, they even handpicked a girl that they believed was worthy of marriage when I was fourteen for Christ's sake." I laughed bitterly.

"The girl you scared away by cutting the cheese?" My smile was now genuine. Rebecca had been listening the night of her attack as I rambled on about everything and nothing on the other side of her bathroom door.

"The one and only." Our conversation came to a lull.

"So, I have no family and you have a crazy one," Rebecca noted.

"You have Emily," I reminded her. Her eyes became distant and anxious.

"I hope I do," she murmured.

We finished the meal in companionable silence, and I quickly cleaned up, while Rebecca moved quietly around the apartment, taking in photos and mementos from the few vacations I have taken over the years. With the lights off, we set up in front of my large screen TV and put the first movie on. When we both started quoting lines, we laughed loudly at our mutual talent. I was comfortable with Rebecca at my side and even manned-up enough to pull her close, my arm resting comfortably over her shoulders. She smelled too damn good. She felt too damn good—a perfect warm fit next to me as she nuzzled into my body. I didn't want to move, I could have lain here with her in my arms all night, but I was worried if she woke up in unfamiliar surroundings, and in the arms of a man, she might get terrified. Once I felt her breathing deepen and her body relax, I carefully moved her to my bed. Again a primal roar of satisfaction reared its macho head. Having Rebecca in my bed, in my home was nothing short of a sweet caress to my soul. I fought the need to climb into bed with her and took the couch, ignoring the throbbing want in my shorts. The thought of functioning without Rebecca in my life was impossible. She made me want more. A home, a family. Hell, kids! I liked kids. I've looked after Annie's boy, Eli, a few of times, and I liked goofing off with him. I liked taking him to the park and tossing the ball around. The thought of doing something like that with my own son or daughter made my head spin and heart hammer with furious longing. However much I liked kids, I never once thought I would be a father, my own childhood far too dismal to imagine me at the helm of my own family. Now I wanted it all. If ever a time came when Rebecca didn't want me in her life, it would break my fucking heart, and that scared the shit out of me.

CHAPTER 13

Rebecca

My eyes fluttered open. My body heavy and lethargic as I took in my unfamiliar surroundings. It was dark, the shadows in the room were causing my heart to pound heavily. Charlie's apartment, I remembered with a relieved sigh. I licked my lips, my mouth felt sandy and dry. I needed a drink like the desert needed rain. I started to get up and found that my body refused to cooperate, my limbs were frozen. Panic and uncertainty filled my veins as I tried to move again. It was then that I noticed the dark figure looming over me at the foot of the bed. All I could see of the figure were the whites of those dark, angry eyes. He had found me! Charlie! I tried to scream, but nothing more than a weak whimper escaped my lips. I felt the bed dip as the frightening figure knelt on the mattress.

"Hi, sweetheart, I told you we would finish this," he purred. I tried to scream again, but no sound would come. What the hell had he done to me? Had I been drugged? Where was Charlie? My eyes darted around the room looking for him. "It's just you and me, sweetheart." His hand found my leg, his palm was rough on my skin.

"No," I barely managed to breathe through my lips, but inside the frozen cocoon of my body, I was fighting with a fury unlike any other.

"Yes, sweetheart, it's time to finish this." He crept up my body and tears escaped the corners of my eyes, my breathing became rapid and out of control. His hands continued to explore my body, though they missed the tenderness of a lover—they were hard and aggressive, taking something I was not willing to give him.

"Noooooo!" I screamed, my voice finally returning. As my scream pierced the quiet night, I sat upright in bed, kicking with manic fury trying to back away from my attacker. Suddenly Charlie's apartment was no longer in darkness, the large room was bright. I was alone in the bed and at the realization, my back slammed painfully against the headboard.

"Rebecca?" Charlie's voice came from the doorway. His eyes looked wild and worried.

I searched for the intruder only to find he wasn't here. A nightmare, another fucking nightmare! A sob broke from my chest as I launched myself from the bed and ran straight into Charlie's arms. I hit him hard but he didn't budge as I wrapped myself around him, trying desperately to find the safety only he seemed able to bring.

"Shhhh, settle down, baby, deep breaths," Charlie murmured as he walked us back towards the bed. I shook my head furiously, I didn't want to be there, not so soon after the nightmare.

"N...Not the b...b...bed," I stammered. He moved us to the living area instead and sat with my legs wrapped around his hips, my arms tight around his neck. I began taking big gulping breaths, trying to rein in the panic. Charlie held me tight until I finally began to settle, and even once I had calmed down, he still didn't let me go.

"You scared me," he quietly confessed, which caused another stupid tear to fall.

"I'm sorry."

He shushed me and held me close. "This nightmare was different, wasn't it?" I nodded. "How?"

It took a while before I was brave enough to recollect the vivid imagery of the nightmare. "I couldn't move, I couldn't fight. He was here, in the apartment, and I didn't know where you were and I couldn't speak so I couldn't call out for you. He touched me and I couldn't do a fucking thing about it."

Charlie was quiet for the longest time. My heart began to slow to a steady rhythm and Charlie eventually moved, lying back with me still wrapped around his body.

"Am I too heavy?" I whispered. Charlie's chest rose and fell with a quiet chuckle.

"No, Betty Boop, you are no heavier than a very warm and pretty blanket. Are you comfortable?" I nodded. We laid like that for the longest time, me sprawled over Charlie, his fingers stroking my hair and down my back.

"I hate this," I finally said, the fear replaced with anger. "I can't get rid of that memory, it's like I'm trapped and can't move forward. I'm stuck with this stupid fear." Charlie shifted to his side and just like that we were face to face. He pushed my hair away from my face, as if he wanted nothing obstructing his view of my puffy eyes, red nose and blotchy skin.

"Then we replace that memory with a better memory." His words seemed like a logical solution. I arched an eyebrow, skeptical. Did he really believe it would be so easy? "Someone took something from you, they took control from you and forced you to give a part of yourself that you weren't offering. You need to take that control back." I wasn't sold on his idea, but I was definitely intrigued.

"How?" I finally whispered. Charlie licked his lips and I couldn't help but zero in on them. Remembering how he kissed me the previous day with such possession, my central loving station was instantly throbbing.

"Do you want to kiss me?" he murmured, a cheeky grin on his way too adorable face. My eyes darted back to his, and ordinarily a snappy retort would have been followed, but I was too curious to let my quip fly. And I really did want to kiss him. "You're in charge here, Betty Boop, if you want it, take it." I adored his nickname for me though I would never tell him that. Somehow I think he already knew. He wanted me to take charge, to make the first move. I had never been that girl, the forward one. In life, yes, I was independent, successful and I didn't get that way being all meek and mild. But when it came to men, relationships, the bedroom, I preferred a man who took charge of me. Fuck it, Rebecca Donovan didn't back down from a challenge. Closing the breath of space that separated us, I pressed my lips against his. The kiss was chaste, no tongue, I explored the soft, subtle tenderness that was Charlie Cole. When I pulled away, I couldn't pull my gaze away from those damn lips—I was ravenous for them. "More?" he asked, his voice low and rough. My answer was to lean in and kiss him again, this time slipping my tongue inside his mouth to gently caress his. I needed more though, this was too gentle, too restrained. What I needed was for Charlie to take control. Again I pulled away and sighed in frustration. I was so confused. A man had forced himself on me, so it made sense that I needed to be in charge of this situation, but I found myself needing more. Something I couldn't reach or claim on my own. Charlie groaned and the next thing I knew he was pinning me down and kissing the living daylights out of me. And I loved it. My leg automatically hooked around his waist and he slid one big hand down to hold it in place while he continued to devour me. This kiss was the something more that I needed. This kiss was something other than raw need pulling at us. This kiss was Charlie marking me, owning me, and it didn't for one moment frighten me. Only the need to take a breath finally separated us. Charlie lowered his body a little until his chest was pressed against mine. This position, closed in like this, made my body become rigid immediately. Charlie's eyes pinned mine with a look that demanded that I stay focused on him, which I did. As I relaxed again, little by little, my hands moved from the vice like grip on his biceps, to leisurely explore his body. I felt Charlie's sharp intake of breath and couldn't miss the hardening under his shorts, but I kept my eyes on him, reminding myself that I was safe, I was cherished and this could end the moment I wanted it to.

"I don't understand this," I finally whispered. Charlie pulled away a little so he could see me better. "You and me. I don't understand what we are, or aren't. Friends? Friends with benefits? I mean, I know Charlie Cole doesn't date or do monogamy, but I do and I'm prone to moments of insecurities and insane jealousy, which I can't help and wouldn't if I could—I don't like to share. I don't know what you want from me, Charlie, but if my little jealousy issue is going to cause problems, then I think we should stop now, before things go any further." I knew I was rambling, it was something I did when I was anxious.

Charlie grinned. "I guess I should make myself perfectly clear then. You're not sure what this is? It's us, you and me, Rebecca and Charlie, Betty Boop, and Caveman Cole. Friends? Always, but this is more, Rebecca. And you should know, I don't like to share what's mine, so monogamy has just become my new best friend. The fact that you have a jealous streak makes me ridiculously happy, I like to know that I'm yours. You should also know that only boys make their woman jealous of other women. A real man makes other women jealous of his woman. I intend to make every other woman on the face of this earth insanely jealous of you." I think I stopped breathing like some cliché book damsel and I smiled.

"So, we're, like, boyfriend and girlfriend?" I asked with a smirk. Charlie laughed and it was the most breathtaking sound I've ever heard.

"Hell no, that sounds like we're back in high school. I prefer to think of us as soul mates that just lost their way for a moment."

Holy shit, Charlie Cole was romantic. I sighed, and Charlie's grin turned a little too cocky. I shoved at his chest.

"Don't go getting all smug, Cole, it takes more than sweet words to win my heart. You haven't even taken me on a single date."

"That sounds like a challenge," Charlie murmured.

"Move," I shoved at his chest again, and this time he rolled away, straight off the couch, landing with a loud thump on the floor. "Holy shit, are you okay?" I gasped.

Charlie laughed. "I think I bruised my butt, wanna kiss it and make it better?" His eyes sparkled mischievously and I grabbed the closest cushion and struck him over the head with it.

"You will never see me kissing your ass, Cole," I growled, hiding the small smile that only this idiot is capable of pulling from me, following a horrifying nightmare.

The chilling sound of breaking glass from somewhere close by caught our attention. We both sat for a moment stunned, before hearing more glass shattering, quickly followed by the recognizable sound of squealing tires. Charlie raced for the front of the apartment and pushed the curtains aside.

"Fuck!" He spun around and grabbed his jeans. "We gotta move, Betty Boop." He pulled his shorts down and I was caught in shock at the sudden urgency in which he was moving, and the fact that his beautiful body was on full display in front of me. It was quickly hidden behind frayed, worn denim as he pulled his jeans up. Charlie grabbed his phone and held it between his shoulder and ear as he moved with fast efficiency around the room, throwing things into a backpack. Finally he noticed my paralyzed state and pulled the phone away. "You need to move that adorable little ass of yours, babe. Fire."

Fire was apparently the magic word because suddenly I was moving, grabbing my bag that hadn't been unpacked. I pulled on my sneakers and raced towards the door.

"Wait!" Charlie screamed, running across the room and all but pushed me aside. He pressed me back against the wall and opened the door slowly, too damn slowly for a situation as serious as a fire. His cell was back between his shoulder and ear.

"Dillon, we got a situation at Carter's—a hot one." He was quiet for a moment as he peered down the stairwell that led to the back of Carter Constructions' office. I wanted to push him down those damn steps, not at all keen to hang around a room that sat directly above a fire. "I've already called them. Call Jax and get here fast. A car beat it out of here pretty fucking quickly, but I don't know if anyone stayed behind to watch the show." The call ended with a grunt. He shoved the phone in the back pocket of his jeans and turned to face me. "Do exactly as I say and stay glued to me, got it?" he ordered.

The urgency of the situation had me ignoring the fact that he didn't say please. Charlie grabbed my wrist and pulled me behind him, slowly descending the stairs. I could see the angry, flickering orange flames through a small high window that looked into the office below Charlie's apartment, and they made me want to move faster. Charlie's cautiously slow pace was quickly pushing me toward the point of panic. Finally we hit the ground and the heat coming from the building was licking at my skin. I wanted to move away, far away, but Charlie kept us close as his sharp eyes looked around the small parking lot, watching the dark shadows that stretched to the large buildings around back that housed lumber. Charlie pulled my arm and we edged our way around the office, heading toward the dark empty street out front. The sound of distant sirens immediately calmed my panic as Charlie continued to drag me cautiously to the front of the building. When we were at a safe distance on the opposite side of the road, I could see that the flames had already made it to Charlie's apartment above the office. This was a large industrial park, the warehouses and factories around us were quiet and empty this time of night. Charlie's eyes continued to comb our surroundings while my eyes were morbidly fixed on the destructive flames before us. The low rumbling sound, of what I assumed was a muscle car, caught my attention and I tensed up. Charlie must have noticed because he pulled me closer to his side. "Dillon," he said without further explanation. I didn't know much about cars, but as it pulled to an abrupt stop, I could tell you the exact make and model of this one—it was my dream car. It was a fully restored, glossy black 1969 Chevrolet Chevelle with chrome trim, chrome wheels, and dual exhaust. It was an American made beauty that was sexy as hell. He climbed from the car and I knew immediately that he was carrying a gun, which caused me to physically tremble. Guns, weapons and violence weren't my thing. Hell, this life I was suddenly cast into wasn't my thing.

"I think they're long gone," said Charlie as Dillon approached. As the sound of sirens filled the quiet industrial neighborhood, I noticed Dillon discreetly tuck his weapon into the back of his jeans, under his shirt.

"I've got a license for it, I just don't want to cause unnecessary panic," Dillon explained at my nervous glance. A small explosion from within the building caused me to jump, and Charlie pulled me further away from the flames as two fire trucks pulled directly in front of us.

"It was deliberately lit, bombs of some sort," Charlie murmured. An ugly feeling akin to guilt filled my stomach and I felt instantly queasy.

"Is this because of me?" I asked, horrified.

"I get the feeling someone is trying to scare you," Charlie replied easily.

"Strangely enough, it's working," I said nervously, watching the flames. "Oh shit, Jax's business, all your stuff!" My voice was steadily climbing to panic. "What about the computers, paper work, oh my God, Charlie, your DVDs." I was close to hysterics now. Charlie pulled me tight to his side and pressed a kiss to my head.

"Settle down, Betty Boop. The computers are backed up every night and kept at Jax's place. As for my stuff, it's just stuff. You're here beside me so I've got everything I need right here."

I leaned my head against the solid warmth of his chest as we watched the firemen in front of us begin emptying water onto the uncontrolled inferno. The whole picture before me was surreal and I felt strangely detached from it, like I was watching someone else's life unfold. But this was my life, this was my mess, and never have I wanted my cozy, boring life back so bad.

CHAPTER 14

Charlie

Fuck! My mind was having trouble processing anything beyond that simple monosyllabic word. Fuck! While Ella comforted Rebecca, Dillon and Braiden filled me and Jax in on what they have found out so far about Rebecca's unaccounted for sister, Emily. And it wasn't good. I rubbed a hand down my face and took a deep breath. My lungs were assaulted with the sharp, bitter scent of smoke that lingered on my clothing. Rebecca was fast asleep as I navigated the gentle curves of the mountain range. Much to Rebecca's protest, we were taking a short vacation to my cabin. She was worried about leaving behind her business, her home, and her missing sister. There were enough people to take care of her business and home, and Dillon assured her as soon as they had news on Emily that they would call. The higher we got into the mountains, the better I felt. There was still a cluster fuck of shit spinning in my mind, but the further we pulled away from town, the more I felt Rebecca would be safe, and in turn, it made me feel calmer. As I slowed the car and left the asphalt to the gravel drive, Rebecca woke.

"Wow," she whispered as I drove down a short driveway lined on both sides with forest. Pulling into the clearing, my log cabin sat overlooking the fog drenched mountains on one side, tall firs and pine forest at its back. "When you said cabin I was expecting some sort of hillbilly run down shack. This isn't a cabin, this is a chateau."

I couldn't help but grin. I loved this place and bringing Rebecca here was all kinds of right. It wasn't a small cabin, but it definitely wasn't a chateau either. It was a two story dwelling with a front porch that ran the length of the building, and yeah, it was as pretty as a picture. I pulled my truck into the large three-door garage attached to the side of the house, and turned the engine off. Rebecca was scrambling from the front seat before I even had my door open. I grabbed our bags, but left the groceries I bought before we left town. I'd come back for them once I showed Rebecca the house. I was pretty sure she wasn't willing to wait. Seeing her bounce around excitedly at the door that led from the garage into the house made me chuckle.

"Impatient much?" I asked, pushing the door open.

"Charlie, I've never been in a mountain lodge before and it's been years since I've had a vacation. Give me an hour or two and I will totally come down from my buzz."

"It isn't a lodge, it's a cabin," I said smiling, but I appreciated her enthusiasm for my happy place. Rebecca lunged through the door and into the open kitchen. It was clean as a whistle with brand-new stainless steel appliances and granite countertops surrounding a kitchen island, which could serve as a second preparation counter or dinner table. She glanced quickly out the large windows which overlooked the forest out back then scampered through the open space living area. A stone fireplace sat at one end surrounded by a horseshoe style leather couch and large rustic wood coffee table. A state-of-the-art stereo sat against one wall, but no TV. I came up here to get away from the world, but I still indulged in a few luxuries. Two massive bay windows provided unobstructed views of the mountains before us, and the front door led out to a wide sweeping porch.

"Fuck, Charlie, this is incredible," Rebecca said on a wistful sigh.

I grabbed her hand and led her up the staircase to the second floor. I could have easily fit three bedrooms on the second floor, but instead opted for two large bedrooms, with a large adjoining bathroom. My bedroom overlooked the mountains, the spare room overlooked the forest.

"That's my room, all my stuff is in there, but if you would prefer it, take it."

"The other room will be fine." Rebecca wandered into the spare room. It had a large bay window, a queen size bed and large walk-in closet. I placed her bag on the end of the bed before heading to my own room across the hall. It was much the same as the spare room, except I had a king size bed and a leather recliner sat in the corner beside a bookshelf full of paperbacks.

"You like to read?" asked Rebecca, a little surprised.

Perhaps I should have been insulted, but I wasn't. "Yep, help yourself to anything. I don't have a TV here, but I've got music and books." I threw my own bag on the bed as Rebecca explored the two way bathroom.

"Shit, you've got a Jacuzzi." She sighed.

I joined her in the bathroom. "Maybe you'd like to take a shower, wash your hair and get rid of the smoke smell."

Rebecca sniffed her clothes and grimaced. "Shower now, Jacuzzi later," she whispered, her eyes staring at the damn Jacuzzi.

That got a rise out of my cock—the thought of Rebecca in that tub, the thought of both of us in that tub. "Go ahead, there are fresh towels in the cabinet below the sink. I'm gonna go get the food out of the truck and turn the heat up." I escaped the far too tempting confines of my bathroom, with a soon to be naked Rebecca in it.

Once the food was put away, I locked up downstairs, and attempted to lock down my libido as I made my way back upstairs. Neither of us had had much sleep last night, and though the sun was up, my mind and body were screaming for a break. Luke Hollywell was looking less and less like the perpetrator of Rebecca's attack. Part of me wished it had been him. That would have been simple. I would beat the fucker to within an inch of his life, problem solved. The lack of evidence and lack of suspects was frustrating as hell. My eyes stung, my mouth was dry, my head throbbed, and I was exhausted, I noted as I sat at the end of my bed and threw my boots aside.

"Hey," Rebecca's sweet melodic voice pushed all the weepy, pitiful shit away, and in its place was raw desire. Holy hell, I wanted her. I wanted to pick her up, wrap those beautiful long legs around my waist and fuck her hard and fast against the wall. I looked up to see Rebecca standing in the bathroom doorway, a pair of cute yellow flannel pajamas covering her beautiful body. God she was gorgeous. She could wear anything—t-shirts, skin tight fifties style dresses, sneakers, sexy as hell pumps, fucking pajamas—it made no difference to me. I'd want her anyway I could have her. She looked nervous and I remembered why we were here. This wasn't a romantic getaway; my motivation for bringing Rebecca to my cabin was to keep her safe. I couldn't feel like more of a shit head if you paid me. Here I was imagining my cock buried in her body while she was struggling with thoughts of intimacy. I jumped up quickly, which took her by surprise, but she didn't step away.

"Shower," I explained, placing a quick chaste kiss to her forehead. Under the hot spray, I washed away the smell of smoke. I grabbed Rebecca's shampoo to wash my hair and the familiar vanilla scent gave me an instant hard-on. I groaned and decided to do something I hadn't done in a long time. I clenched my fist around my thick, hard length and began to work myself to some form of release. I thought back to that one night I had spent in Rebecca's bed, how the light sheen of sweat on her pale skin looked almost like glistening diamonds. How her eyes fluttered shut with overwhelming pleasure as I thrust into her beautiful body. My hand clenched harder at the memory of her hot pussy wrapped around my cock. I didn't even hear the door open, my pleasure and imagination fully occupied.

"Charlie?"

Fuck! "Yeah," I somehow managed to say without my voice cracking.

"Uh, this is probably stupid, but—" She was quiet for a moment, standing on the other side of the frosted glass door while I stood under the water with my hand on my dick.

"Babe?" And now my voice cracked like a pussy.

"Can I just sit in here? I mean, I'm not going to watch you shower like a weirdo or anything. I'm just nervous being out there alone. I'll just sit at the door here until you're done."

Oh God. I somehow pried my fingers from around myself and took a few long, deep calming breaths.

"Shit, how pathetic am I. I'm sorry, I'll just put my big girl panties on and wait outside," she muttered.

I pulled the frosted shower door open and peeked out, keeping my lower half covered. "Baby, just sit and chill, you don't even have to ask."

She looked at me for a moment uncertainly, then finally leaned back against the tile wall and sank to her cute little ass. I pulled the door back and started thinking of anything other than sex. I needed to get my raging hard-on under control. It seemed as though when in Rebecca's presence, my cock was in constant need of attention.

"Why don't you live here?" Rebecca asked. "Permanently, I mean. And FYI, I don't feel so bad getting your apartment burned down knowing you have this."

I laughed. "Too far from town, otherwise I would."

"Why did you build so far away?"

"I needed my own space, a place I could come to have a time-out of sorts. Sometimes I kinda lose my shit; I have anger issues in case you haven't noticed." Rebecca was quiet for a moment and I hoped my admission didn't frighten her.

"Charlie Cole has anger issues? You're telling me the man who filled Jax's shampoo bottle with blue food coloring and carries a whoopee cushion in his truck can't control his temper?"

I chuckled, the little minx had been snooping around my glove compartment. "I know, outrageous. But yeah, I kinda get spitting mad and sometimes it takes something pretty insignificant to set it off. I was worse as a teenager, but Mercy put me in line when she made me start working my summer vacations at the shelter." She went quiet again as I turned the water off.

"That's why you spoke to Dave," she whispered. Obviously Ella or Jax had been gossiping about me, but the fact that they hadn't told her much of anything confirmed the friendship I had with them was solid. They would never betray my confidence.

"He's a good man, and an even better listener. Maybe you should try it sometime."

"What did Dillon and Braiden have to say about Emily?" I didn't call her out on the obvious and evasive change of subject, but I didn't answer her right away either. "Charlie?" she growled. It was so cute I actually smiled.

"I'll tell you, just give me a sec." I pulled the frosted glass door open. Rebecca's eyes zeroed in on my groin, her cheeks flushed with embarrassment or desire, I don't know. I had no problem being nude and she's seen it all before anyway. "You keep staring at it like that, and he's gonna start demanding attention," I moaned as my dick twitched under her scrutiny. She surprised me with a wicked grin and finally looked up at my face.

"Perhaps you shouldn't put him right in front of my face then." She smirked. The thought of that face, those lips even closer made my dick start to rise. Rebecca's eyes were drawn back down as she reached above her head and pulled a towel off the rack. She threw it to me, still looking at my cock, that I just talked down from a hard-on only moments ago, and was now quickly growing stiff again.

"Perhaps you should mind your manners and turn around," I countered. Rebecca grinned and it was a beautiful smile. I wanted to pull her to me and devour her lips like I had done the evening before.

"Emily?" Rebecca reminded me.

Hard-on once again contained. Once I finished drying off, I wrapped the towel around my waist and offered Rebecca my hand. She took it without hesitation, and I pulled her to her feet. I led her toward the door that led into the guest bedroom and she hesitated.

"You want the other room?" I asked, more than willing to give her my bedroom. She looked up at me through her thick blond lashes and blushed. I really wasn't used to this nervous and shy Rebecca, but it was just as sexy as the independent and fiery Rebecca most people were used to.

"After the last couple of days, I'm kinda nervous about being on my own," she murmured, and I understood what she meant right away. My heart jumped at the thought. I simply turned around and led her back into my room. I pulled the quilt and sheets down, and as Rebecca climbed in, I pulled the curtains across the wide open bay window to dim the room a little. I grabbed a pair of boxers from a drawer and quickly changed, feeling every bit of Rebecca's heated gaze on me as I did. Once in bed, I pulled the blankets over us and didn't think twice about pulling her into my arms. After a short silence she started again. My Betty Boop, ever the tenacious woman.

"Emily." Her voice was level and calm, but I knew she was seconds away from losing her patience with me.

"Okay, but no interrupting. You can ask questions once I've finished." Rebecca made a show of zipping her lips shut and locking them closed with an imaginary key. I was tired as hell so I took a moment to gather my thoughts and recall everything Braiden told me earlier.

"Braiden called me with information about Emily—I'm not sure how he got it, I'm not even sure if I want to know how he got it. She doesn't go by Emily Donovan anymore, but Mrs. Emily Levier—"

"SHE'S MARRIED?" Rebecca screamed, which made me wince right before looking over at her and raising a brow. I knew she wouldn't be able to stay quiet for long. She breathed deeply and re-zipped her lips.

"Married to one William Levier whose father, Jonas Levier, is well known to every law enforcement agency in America. Jonas is suspected of killing three women in Vegas." Rebecca's eyes lit up with angst and fear. "Obviously Emily is fine because she is here in Claymont somewhere, but yeah, he's bad news, and we assume his son is, too. William has been in trouble with the police as well, but nothing like Jonas, just petty stuff—criminal mischief, small thefts, and public intoxication. At a glance, William's father comes across as a legit, rich and powerful business man, but the police have been after him for a while and know for a fact that he's involved in some seedy shit. Apparently he is a self-proclaimed dom with a dash of masochist tendencies thrown in, like full on Fifty Shades of Grey crazy shit." It was Rebecca's turn to raise a brow.

"You've read that?" she asked.

"Fuck no! I dated a girl who told me about it."

"You don't date," she said matter-of-factly. "And if I wandered over to that bookshelf, would I find a copy of Fifty Shades on it?"

"Zip it, Betty Boop, I am seconds away from passing out from exhaustion," I growled, giving her a gentle tap on the ass. I was worried I might have crossed some sort of line touching her like that, but she grinned, and once again zipped her lips and went to use that ridiculous invisible key. I grabbed her wrist and stopped her. "No point in locking it, your key doesn't seem to work." Rebecca settled her head back down on the pillow.

"So, my sister is into BDSM," Rebecca murmured.

"No idea, just because William's father is into it, doesn't mean he or Emily are into it as well. Anyway, Jonas owns a whole bunch of fetish clubs in Vegas that, on the outside come across as your regular skanky BDSM fuck lounges, but allegedly, these clubs are a front for men and women with similar predilections as Jonas: sick fuckers who get off on their masochistic needs with underage girls and boys. Rebecca seemed to take a moment to digest this information.

"Maybe that's where Emily has been since she left Claymont?" she whispered.

"Maybe she met William in an ice cream parlor and knows nothing about all this shit, but I get the feeling that she is twisted up in some fucked up shit." I rubbed a hand down my tired face and grimaced when I realized how long it had been since I shaved. I was a hairy mother right now. "I dunno, babe, this is all kinda out of my league. I'm no detective and I'm certainly no expert on BDSM," I gave her a cheeky grin, unable to help myself, "but I'd be happy to explore certain aspects with you. Just say the word, baby. I'm all about self-discovery and exploration." Rebecca thumped me in the chest.

"How can you turn a serious conversation into something so sexy and dirty at the same time?"

"It's a gift." I winked. "Anyway, that's about as far as Braiden got. Your sister is married to the son of a sadistic S.O.B. and, Rebecca? There isn't a chance in hell I am sitting down and doing the whole meet the family dinner thing with them." Rebecca snorted and tried to hide a yawn. I pushed my arm under her head and pulled her in close. "Get some sleep, baby. Braiden and Dillon are doing their bad-ass shit out there on the streets; they're looking for your sister. All we can do is sit tight for now and keep you safe." Rebecca nuzzled her head into the sensitive crook of my neck, and her warm lips moved against my skin. My dick twitched with curiosity as Rebecca held herself there pressed up against me.

"Charlie, would you do something for me?" she whispered in a tone so soft I barely heard her.

"Anything," I murmured back.

"Will you touch me?" Her request had me freeze like a damn deer caught in the headlights. "I just want to know that I still can...you know...be touched...like that."

Every fiber of my being demanded I roll her over and touch her, but I was worried she might not be ready. "Rebecca, someone sexually assaulted you only a couple of weeks ago. You don't have to be ready to do this yet."

"I know," she sighed, "but I feel safe with you. In fact, I feel constantly damn horny when I'm with you, and I want you to touch me. I want to know that I can still have that. I like sex, a lot! Surely you remember that."

I grunted my acknowledgement. Not a day passed by where I didn't recall just how much Rebecca had blown my mind that night.

"It's been a long time for me and that's one of the reasons why I went on that stupid date with Luke. And then I was attacked, and now I'm scared shitless that I will never have another orgasm again."

"How long?" I asked, blatantly ignoring the mention of Luke Hollywell. My mood would be seriously compromised if I thought about Rebecca and him together.

"Since you," she breathed.

Well, that surprised the shit out of me. Rebecca was stunning, she was feisty, and yeah, she liked sex. To think she hadn't been with anyone since me was strangely satisfying, which only reinforced the idea that I had turned into a complete fucking caveman. I hesitated before rolling to my side and looking down at Rebecca. Damn she was beautiful—her eyes were so many different shades of blue without a hint of another color, her skin was flawless, and her full lips were soft and pink. I ran a hand over her hair that was so blonde it bordered on white. Her body was healthy, not stick thin but not heavy; she had womanly curves and a pair of exquisite breasts that filled my hands easily. From the rapid rise and fall of her chest, I don't know who was more nervous: me or her. I simply let my fingers whisper across her skin, over her cheeks, down her neck, but I faltered at the buttons of her pajama top. Charlie Cole never had trouble undressing a woman, but Charlie Cole was treading in unfamiliar waters right now. Rebecca obviously sensed my reluctance, and slipped the buttons open for me. Her eyes were determined; there was no sign of apprehension. Gently and slowly, I pushed open her top to expose her stunning breasts. I stared, like flat out stared, my mouth open and tongue ready to fall out.

"Not helping." Rebecca chuckled nervously.

My lip quirked in a smile as my fingers resumed their leisurely trail across her skin, purposefully ignoring those perfect breasts. I wanted her out of her mind, begging for my touch and she would not get it until the word 'please' escaped that sassy mouth of hers. I wanted her so desperate for my touch that it eclipsed all fear and wiped away the bad memories. My finger circled her little belly button and I found myself wanting to lean over and dip my tongue in it, but this moment was for Rebecca, not me. My fingers swept up close to the underside of her breasts, across her shoulders, over the elegant arch of her collarbone and along the invisible line that ran down the center of her body.

"Charlie," she panted.

"Yeah, Betty Boop?" My voice almost trembled.

"This isn't the touch I had in mind." Her eyes fluttered shut as I brushed closer to her breasts.

"No?" I asked, unable to stop my grin. She shook her head as my fingers moved away from the delectable rise of her breast.

"Charlie!" she groaned.

"I need you to tell me what you want, baby, I don't want there to be any misunderstandings, and, Rebecca?" She opened her eyes and looked up at me. "You say stop, and I stop."

Her gaze softened and she gave me a shy nod. "Touch my breasts, please."

My body sagged in relief and I wasted no time guiding my fingers up her chest and over the pale rise of one breast. My touch was a light caress as I gently teased her nipple. I moved to the neglected breast wishing I had both of my hands free to use on her, but one arm was currently holding my weight so I could get an unobstructed view of the beauty beside me. Soon her body was flush with obvious desire and Rebecca began to shift. I knew she was seeking relief from the lower part of her body. Hot on the tails of that thought, she grabbed my wrist and pushed my hand lower. I played with edge of her pajama bottoms refusing to go any further without verbal permission.

"Touch me, Charlie," she ground out in frustration.

"I am, baby." She shook her head. I was fairly sure I knew what she wanted, but I needed to hear it, it needed to be clear. I was nervous enough without presuming to know what was going through her head at the moment.

"If you don't touch my central loving station this instant, I'm going to kick your ass!" she ordered.

I laughed. "Your what?" I murmured. I knew several guys who had a name for their dick, but I have never once met a woman who had a name for her pussy, until now apparently.

"My vagina, my snatch, my mound, I don't care what you call it, but I call it my central loving station because...well...it's a central loving station." I grinned, damn she was adorable. "I used the words, Charlie." That she had.

"I prefer pussy, but central loving station works for me, too." I pushed my hand under the waist band of her pajama bottoms. My fingers continued their dance over the thin barrier of her panties. I explored her from behind the barrier until she was again squirming.

"More, please, Charlie."

Damn, she said please. I leaned over and kissed her. I kissed her hard, pretty much forcing my tongue into her mouth before finally peeling aside her panties to find her very wet central loving station. I noticed the change immediately. She stopped moving, her body became rigid. I didn't move my hand away, but I stopped moving my fingers and allowed my kiss to become less dominant, softer, safer.

"Rebecca?"

"Don't stop," she quietly begged.

My hand remained still where it was as my lips travelled down her chest until I could take one soft nipple into my mouth. I sucked and nipped at her until she was relaxed again, then I moved my fingers into her folds. I played and teased at the moist hot flesh between her legs for the longest time before I slowly slipped a finger inside her.

"Talk to me, Charlie, I need to hear your voice," she breathed.

"Open your eyes," I gently commanded. Her blue eyes shot open and watched me cautiously. "You feel so good, baby, just like I remembered." Her hips moved tentatively, as if almost testing the waters. "Fuck, I have thought about that night so many times. We fit together just right, Betty Boop, my cock inside you like it was made for you." I saw the heat flare in her eyes and a low moan escaped her lips. "I love your breasts." I leaned in and took a nipple into my mouth again just to prove how much. As I pushed a finger slowly in and out of her body, my thumb found her clit and I gently rubbed the little nub. "I love everything about you, you feel perfect. Inside..." I added another finger and pushed inside her with a little more force to emphasize my point. "And out." I sucked a nipple into my mouth, and maybe it was a little too forceful, but the loud groan accompanied with her clenching around my fingers told me she liked it. I didn't stop and I watched her face carefully for any signs of fear until her eyes began to flutter shut—just how I remembered—surrendering to her impending orgasm. When her pussy finally clenched around my fingers and her back arched with unrestrained desire, I swear I have never seen anything more beautiful. I gentled my touch as her dazed eyes found mine. A tear slipped loose and I withdrew my hand in a panic. Had I pushed her too hard, too fast?

"Oh shit, Rebecca," I whispered.

Her hands found my face and pulled me down for a kiss that seemed her way of claiming me. "Thank you," she finally said.

"Are you okay?" I asked, not yet sure if her tears were a good thing or a bad thing.

"I haven't been this good in a long time," she confessed.

Fuck, it had been almost too much for me—too much apprehension, too much emotion. I was exhausted and horny. I collapsed on my back, pulling Rebecca to my chest. After a short, silent moment, her fingers began to glide towards the edge of my boxers that were hanging loosely over my hips. I stopped her progress and brought her fingers to my mouth, pressing a kiss to the tips.

"This was about you, Betty Boop," I explained.

"You're not...uncomfortable?"

I laughed loudly. Hell yeah I was uncomfortable, but in a good way. "Perhaps this is my punishment for failing to relentlessly pursue you like I should have a year ago." Rebecca's arms clinched tight around me.

"Let's not talk about the past anymore," she murmured, her words accompanied with a yawn.

"Sounds good to me, baby. Get some sleep before I change my mind about this being all about you." Rebecca's shoulders shook on a silent chuckle before we both fell into a comfortable silence, followed by some much needed sleep.

CHAPTER 15

Rebecca

Last night I slept blissfully nightmare free. I had no idea why. Perhaps I was just too tired to dream, perhaps the amazing orgasm Charlie had gifted me with had wiped me out, or perhaps it was because I had slept in the protective and unyielding embrace of my strong and fearless warrior. Or maybe I had finally found my damn back bone. I don't know, I don't care, all I knew was I felt refreshed and coherent for the first time in weeks. And of course there was that amazing orgasm. Charlie touched me and although once or twice I came close to losing my nerve, I hadn't. His touch had been as mind blowing as I remembered. Just the thought of it made me shudder. I sighed like a love sick fool as I called Ella from the front porch of Charlie's chalet. I knew it wasn't a chalet or a lodge—it was a cabin—but it was a big damn cozy cabin!

"Hey, Betty Boop," Ella answered in a sing song voice.

"Hello to you, too, short stuff." I chuckled.

"So, how is the redneck inn?"

"Not so redneck," I acknowledged, taking in the beauty of the mountains before me.

"Uh-huh, told ya you'd like it."

"You've seen it?" I wondered out loud.

"Nope, but Jax told me all about it. Sounds pretty damn wicked. Does it really have a Jacuzzi? I want a Jacuzzi, but not before I get my fucking kitten," Ella growled, her curiosity morphing into a small temper tantrum. I laughed.

"Yeah, it has a Jacuzzi. I'm sure Jax would get you one. And why the hell are you waiting for him to get you the damn kitten? Just go out and buy one."

"But what if he is really allergic to them?" she asked, her tone gentling to worry.

"Ask Mercy."

"You really are the smartest woman I know," Ella joked.

"Well you really don't know all that many people, so it's not saying much." I chuckled.

"So, you sound remarkably calm for someone whose life has been flipped ass over tit." If I wasn't so used to tiny, angelic Ella's crude and upfront vocabulary, I would have been shocked. Ella spent four years on the run from her stepfather, four long years living in shelters, and occasionally on the street. She has lived a hard life, with hard people and was certainly no prude. But she has come out on the other side with her heart intact, and a back bone of steel. Over the past year, her confidence has only grown. Jax, Charlie, and I created a monster. "You sound like a woman who's indulged in some horizontal refreshments, perhaps," the monster went on.

"Ella, you know I don't drink while lying down. I drink till I fall down."

"That's not what I meant and you know it." I knew what she was talking about, but I wasn't going to give in that easily.

"I have no idea what you're talking about, Ella. You've been hanging around Lola too long. You both talk in riddles."

"You did the fuzzy bump!" Ella exclaimed.

I could not contain the laughter that spilled from my lips. "I did the what?"

"Fuzzy bump, you know, bumped uglies."

That only made me laugh harder. "Bumped nasties?" I offered.

"Slap and tickle?" Ella suggested, and I'm sure I was blushing, remembering the tickle fondly.

"A jiffy stiffy?" I carried on, and Ella snorted loudly through the phone. We played this game often and it usually ended with us laughing so hard that one of us would end up making a dash for the bathroom.

"You had yourself a shaboink, I can tell from the sound of your voice," Ella said, and I could just imagine the smirk on her face. Shaboink?

"There is nothing different about my voice," I said with a nervous chuckle.

"Oh, hell yeah there is. You sound all husky and sated." What the hell did that mean? "Boss, you sound very relaxed and very well fucked," Ella explained.

"Well, you are obviously off your game because I wasn't shaboinked and I'm not your boss anymore." Ella snorted again. "But I might have had an orgasm," I quickly added.

"Big Red?" Ella exclaimed. Damn giant red vibrator. I had once told Ella I refused to use an inanimate object to find release; however, curiosity had gotten the better of me and I had relented once or twice, or maybe a few times. Screw it, I've used it so many times I've lost count.

"No, not Big Red. Big Charlie helped, but there was no sex involved. I didn't think I could even handle being touched, but clearly I can." I grinned. Damn straight I could. Ella sighed.

"Of course you can. No asshole, brute of a man is ever going to keep you down. You're Rebecca Fucking Donovan, you kick ass," she said it so matter-of-factly that I couldn't help but smile. Charlie stepped out the front door, two beers in his hands.

"Hey, I gotta go, I'll call you tomorrow." I knew I was ditching her like yesterday's news, but Charlie, standing before me in jeans that hung low on his hips and a simple grey hoodie that clung to his chest, had me ready for orgasm number two.

"He's there isn't he?" Ella asked with a droll voice. "Put him on." I handed Charlie the phone and he passed me a beer.

"Hey, pocket rocket, what's going on?" His boyish grin made me want to climb up his body and kiss him senseless. As if feeling my heated gaze, he quirked an eyebrow in my direction before pulling me to my feet and taking my place in the chair. Before I had a chance to be outraged, he dragged me down to his lap. Oh yeah, this is where I wanted to be. "Ella, she's fine, I promise. Anyone who wants to hurt her is gonna have to move mountains first, then me. So as you can clearly see, she couldn't be any safer." I felt Charlie's chest rise in a silent chuckle. "Yes, ma'am, and tell Jax I'm sorry about the office, but he did burn down my tree house when we were fourteen. Perhaps it's just karma setting things right." Charlie sat back after disconnecting the phone.

"Why did Jax burn your tree house down?" I asked, amused.

"Because he caught me kissing Lisa Bell."

"Who is Lisa Bell?" I found myself asking.

"The girl Jax spent four weeks in the ninth grade trying to kiss. He didn't miss out on much." Charlie grinned taking a long pull on his beer. "So, Ella tells me I have to give you no less than two orgasms a day." Charlie wiggled his eyebrows. "I'm up for the challenge."

"Jax has turned that woman into an animal," I growled.

"I think she was always one, she just needed to be let out of her cage." Charlie smiled fondly and I knew he cared for Ella. I wasn't jealous because I knew the way he cared for her was the way a big brother cared for a little sister. I was happy Charlie had her, especially since he didn't have any siblings of his own. "You ever fired a gun before, Betty Boop?" I spun around to face Charlie, needing to know if he was serious. The grim look on his face told me he was.

"Hell no!" I growled. Charlie leaned his head back against the wall of the cabin behind him. After a moment of contemplative silence, he picked me up off his lap and disappeared inside. I stood staring at the door, mouth open, mind spinning. What the hell just happened? A moment later Charlie reappeared, holding a gun. I took a nervous step away. Guns freaked me the hell out. As he held it in his hand, I noted how innocuous and plastic looking it seemed. Perhaps this was some sort of sick and twisted joke. Maybe he would press the trigger and a small flame would pop out the muzzle. Then he would grin and say, 'gotcha'.

"This is a Glock Nineteen, 9mm semi-automatic pistol," he opened the chamber at the top, "not loaded." He wasn't joking.

"Where the hell did you get it?" I demanded.

"Jax." Say no more. Jax was a giant was a weapons freak. "I know you're not keen on the idea, but desperate times call for desperate measures. If handled correctly and if respectfully cared for, a gun could save your life." Charlie gave me a cocky look. "Ella knows how to use one, in fact, she's a damn good shot." He was goading me, and unfortunately it was working. I could never back down from a challenge. "Here, hold it, get a feel for it." He raised his hand, the gun carefully held with the muzzle pointing away from me, even though it was not loaded. It was lighter than I expected and felt a little chunky in my hand.

"It's a little bulky in the handle. You'd be more comfortable with a smaller gun, but this is a temporary situation so it will have to do." I ran my fingers over the weapon, marveling at how seemingly innocent this killing device actually was. "You want to fire it?" Charlie asked. I continued to simply stare at it. I couldn't believe this is what my life had been reduced to.

"I'm a fucking florist, Charlie, not a soldier," I whispered. His hand circled the back of my neck and he pulled me forward into his body.

"Rebecca, I'm not Jax or Dillon, or Braiden for that matter. I'm not military trained in any way. I'm just plain ol' Charlie who knows how to secure a good deal on lumber. I put up a good fight though and I know how to use one of these." He took the gun from my hand. "You are a hard-ass, tough as nails, sexy florist who needs to know how to protect herself, and I want to give you that, I can give you that."

I sighed. His words were the magic key that opened my inner Sarah Connor. I was ready to go all Terminator on someone's ass. I pushed my shoulders back, rolled my neck and gave Charlie a confident nod.

"Alright, plain ol' Charlie, show me how to empty some lead from that thing." Charlie's grin was contagious; his subtle dimples came out to play, making him look younger, more carefree. This was the Charlie Cole most people knew and saw. I liked that I was getting more insight into the real man, it made me feel closer to him, significant and perhaps a little territorial where Charlie was concerned. I would always hate the fact that so many women had shared something intimate with Charlie, but at the end of the day it was just sex—straight up sex without emotion. I, on the other hand, was getting something more meaningful from him, his heart. I wasn't lying when I told him I have a jealous streak. The few boyfriends I've had over the years found my green eyed tendencies more of an irritation than a cute display of affection. The more time I spent with Charlie, the more territorial I was feeling about him. If he decided once this was all over, that his feelings were nothing more than protective inclinations towards a mere friend, I would be screwed. It would surely shatter my heart. As much as I tried to protect myself from attachments, from caring too much, Charlie had become part of the special and selective group of people that I could not be without.

We set ourselves up far from the house. Charlie picked out a tree for target practice, which I felt bad about maiming. Geez, if I was already feeling sorry for shooting a tree, how the hell was I supposed to shoot a human being? Then my thoughts drifted to the asshole that attacked me, and if I were back in that moment, with this gun in my reach, I know I wouldn't have hesitated to use it. Charlie slipped a cartridge in, bringing me out of my morbid thoughts.

"Fifteen round mag," he explained. "The gun has three safety mechanisms, first being on the trigger." He pointed it out. "The other two internal safeties are released when you fire the weapon." Charlie put the loaded gun in my hand. Then he turned me to face the poor innocent tree who was about to be on the receiving end of a whole lot of whoop ass. The warmth of Charlie's body pressed against my back made this lesson in weaponry a whole lot more appealing. I subtly rubbed against him, and Charlie gave me a firm smack on the behind. My crazy body loved it, while my mind screamed at me to hit him back. "Behave," he growled, his lips close to my ear. He took my hands, and raised them and the gun in front of me. "Move this leg back a little," he corrected my stance. "This is your trigger finger and it sits right up here above the trigger until you are ready to pull it. This hand goes underneath to help hold it steady." I was knew I was tense so tried to relax into the stance. After a few short moments, I began to feel something close to confident, maybe even a touch bad ass. I had never considered myself a gun wielding sex goddess! I giggled like a moron. "Concentrate, Betty Boop. I don't want you shooting yourself, or me for that matter." The gentle reminder of what we were doing here helped ground me. "You've got your sights outlined in white. See?" I closed one eye and watched carefully through the guiding white box to the white dot at the end of the muzzle. "Now you're just going to pull the trigger nice and slow."

Charlie took a small step away from me and I was suddenly nervous without his warm presence at my back. I tried to concentrate on looking down the sight, narrowing my aim and locking the innocent tree into my view. I hesitated on the trigger until I felt Charlie's warmth at my back again. The confidence I gained at having him there helped me pull the trigger. The gun jarred in my hands, not uncontrollably, but I was unprepared for it. Charlie reached around to steady my hands. "Shit, I should have warned you about the recoil." I took a moment to catalogue what just happened. I was okay, I was steady, and I wasn't freaking out.

"It's okay, let me try again." Charlie lowered his arms and took a small step away. I closed one eye and looked down the sight. When I pulled the trigger this time, I was prepared for the recoil.

"Good girl," Charlie whispered from behind me. I pulled the trigger again, and again. Six times in all before I began to lower my arms. Charlie quickly grabbed my wrists. "Finger off the trigger, Betty Boop." I raised my finger and lowered the gun. I didn't know whether to be embarrassed by the rush I got from firing the weapon, or just go with it and dance around the forest like a crazy nymph. I was more than prepared to embrace my inner Resident Evil fem-fatale, Alice. I imagined myself in a slinky red dress, knee high boots and complimenting thigh holsters. Hell yeah, I was down with this. I smiled at my overactive imagination.

"Did I kill the tree?" I murmured. Charlie laughed from behind me.

"The tree is safe, I'm horny as hell, and you need to eat. I could hear your stomach growling over the gunfire."

Yeah, all this macho chick stuff was making me hungry and maybe a little horny, too.

As we made our way back to the cabin, I watched as Charlie took the cartridge from the gun, leaving it safely unloaded. He may not have been combat trained like Jax or Dillon, but he sure as hell looked every bit the hard and deadly warrior. As he led us through the tall firs, it made me wonder about the time he spent with Dave, learning how to overcome his anger. I have never seen Charlie lose his temper. I have seen him irritated, angry, seething in fact, but he has always managed to keep himself relatively contained around me.

"Did you ever hurt anyone when you lost your temper?" I found myself asking. The panicked look on Charlie's face made me regret my question. I wasn't sure how I felt about him hurting someone, especially if it had been a woman. His hand ran through his hair making it stick up in all directions. He didn't answer right away, and when I began to think he wasn't going to, he spoke, his voice low and rough.

"You gotta understand, Rebecca, I was in a bad place emotionally. I was only a teenager, I was fighting both inside and outside the ring. My parents had just about driven me certifiably insane, and I know that isn't an excuse, and that's not who I am now. Mercy pulled me out of that life and if it wasn't for her, I'd be dead, in prison, or worse—I could have hurt someone I really cared about."

I stopped walking, and when Charlie realized it, he turned around to face me. The pain in his eyes had me wanting to reach out and take him in my arms, but my heart was pounding furiously with angst. What had he done? He shoved the gun in the back of his jeans and rubbed his suddenly tired looking eyes.

"I was seventeen and had been matched up to fight another seventeen year old by the name of Michael Hayward. It was an evenly matched fight both physically and experience in the ring. It was a full contact fight with limited protective gear. There were eight, two minute rounds, so it was a pretty intense fight for semi-professionals. Michael was renowned for taunting his opponent, it's how he worked, making it more of a psychological battle, and even though I was prepared for it, I lost it." Charlie cast me a worried gaze. "He spent most of the fight insulting my parents." He shook his head, a grim smile on his lips. "He obviously didn't realize I could care less what he had to say about them. But he found my weakness when he verbally attacked Mercy. I just lost it. It was like everything else failed to exist and all I saw was Hayward clouded in a red haze. I went at him with everything I had and it took three officials and my coach to drag me off of him." Charlie kicked at a pine cone, his strong carefully constructed persona suddenly compromised with his guilt ridden admission. "I was covered in blood and Michael wasn't moving. I thought I'd killed him, and the fucked up thing was, I was still so high on anger, I didn't care. In fact, if he would have tried to sit up, I would have gone at him again. It wasn't until later, when I had calmed down, the realization of what I had done hit me. Michael never stood on his own two feet again, a fracture in his spinal cord had him stuck in a wheel chair, paralyzed from the hips down." I gasped and hated the sadness in Charlie's eyes when the sound passed my lips. "The only thing that prevented criminal charges was the fact that Michael had a pre-existing back injury that he and his team kept from officials. He wouldn't have been allowed to fight if they'd known about it."

The lost, distraught look on Charlie's face had me take the few steps to him. I wrapped my arms around his torso, burying my head in his chest. He was quick to return the embrace. "That's not on you, Charlie," I murmured, my voice somewhat muffled in his body. "You were just unlucky enough to be the poor schmuck who had to fight the ass. If it hadn't been you, it would have been someone else. Michael shouldn't have been fighting, his injury was obviously a ticking time bomb waiting to happen." Charlie's lips pressed against the top of my head.

"That's where you're wrong, Betty Boop. If I had kept my cool and fought the rest of that match like I had done the previous seven rounds, I would have won. I was ahead on points anyway and Michael's injury and the burden that lay with it may have eventually lain on someone else's shoulders. Hell, he might even still be walking." Charlie released me and stepped away, though his hand stayed on the back of my neck. "But it is my burden to bear and it's a reminder of what I am capable of. That memory helps keep my temper in check. I never fight in full-contact fights anymore;

only light-contact or sparring." He gave me a pointed look. "I promise you, I will never hurt you. I won't ever hurt anyone like that again." Then he grinned with malice. "Unless I get the opportunity to be in the same room with the son of a bitch that hurt you. That fucker is absolved from my no-hitting policy. I will tear him to shreds and not blink an eye while doing it." His declaration should have scared me, but it had the opposite effect. It made me love him just a little bit more. And love it was. This was no high school crush, no lust driven itch, no simple friendship. What I felt for Charlie Cole was pure, unmistakable, heart filling love.

CHAPTER 16

Charlie

Telling Rebecca about my fight with Hayward was like lifting a heavy weight off my shoulders. I would always carry the guilt over what happened to Michael, but with Rebecca knowing, I felt like there were no more secrets between us. We had passed through a relationship door of sorts—we had reached the point where we no longer had secrets, our hearts and souls were completely exposed and vulnerable—it was in this place our relationship could only flourish. My promise that I would never hurt her was the easiest declaration I have ever made. It would be simply impossible for me to harm a blonde hair on her beautiful head.

Watching Rebecca fire a weapon has seriously been the sexiest thing I have ever seen. I knew she'd been nervous, even a little repulsed by the idea of firing a gun, but by the time she finished, she had a new respect for firearms. The little spark in her eyes had been full of power. She'd missed the tree by a longshot, but damn if I wasn't impressed by her determination. We would practice every day to help build her confidence in handling a weapon. I hated that she had to do this; I hated that she needed protection. I wanted to give her back her cozy life in her cute little house, but I couldn't help but love all the one on one time I was getting with her. Yeah, I was a selfish prick through and through.

Later that day, I watched her flit around the kitchen like it had been made for her. She had quickly settled into my home; she fit here perfectly. I could absolutely get used to her being here permanently. Just doing normal stuff like cooking together, eating together, showering together—I wanted it all.

"Charlie, when are you supposed fight Luke?"

"Next week." Her question brought me from my Betty Crocker haze. I finished chopping the onions and put them in a bowl beside her, ready for her world's famous Donovan chili she was preparing.

"Well, since it seems as if Luke isn't the one who hurt me, maybe you don't have to fight him anymore. I don't want you to break your no-hitting rule because of me."

I leaned against the counter beside her, not wanting any space between us. "He might not have hurt you, but he was still an asshole who was disrespectful to you. He needs to be knocked down a peg or two. Besides, I'm in better control now than I was all those years ago. I'm not concerned that I'll lose control of myself. And this fight with Luke is a one time thing. I trust the General. He'll make sure it's a low contact fight with minimal risks." Rebecca looked up at me from under those long lashes. The little spark in her eye made me smile.

"You realize that's total bullshit, don't you?"

"Bullshit?" I raised a brow.

"You don't have to fight him just for being disrespectful. Shit, Charlie, do you have any idea how many men have spoken to me in a less than respectful way over the years? Are you going to fight them all?"

"There's a good chance," I said, shoving a few slices of carrot in my mouth. Rebecca sighed and shook her head.

"What if he says something about me and you lose your damn temper," she murmured.

I moved to stand behind her and didn't miss the tension that coiled through her body. It didn't last long, but it was still there. I wondered if it was because of my recent admission or her memories of the attack. "Rebecca?"

"I'm okay," she whispered. "Just bad memories."

I ran the tips of my fingers over the gentle slope of her shoulders. She was small, but not as small as Ella. Her blonde head sat under my chin as if she was made for me. My hands continued down her arms, eventually leaving to trace the line of her waist and eventually finish my exploration under the hem of her shirt, my hands resting on the slight roundness of her stomach.

"Just another bad memory we are going to replace with a good one." I nibbled her neck and smiled when she all but melted into my embrace.

"You're trying to distract me," she breathed.

"I've got my temper under control, Betty Boop. I'd rather fight Luke in the ring, under the watch of officials than confront him in the street."

Rebecca shook her head. "Freakin' Neanderthal," she muttered.

I laughed and brought my lips to the shell of her ear, pressing slow kisses down her neck, inhaling her soft vanilla scent. "You've got me torn in two, baby," I whispered. She tilted her head slightly so I could nuzzle closer.

"How so?" she whispered breathlessly, and I marveled that I could make her feel that way.

"On one hand, I want to put you on my arm and parade you around town like the treasure you are. I want everyone to know you're mine and I'm yours." I licked her neck and she shivered. "Then on the other hand, I want to keep you here, in my home, in my bed where no one else can touch you, where no one else can even fucking look at you." She reached up and grabbed a handful of my hair, pulling my lips to hers. I groaned and kissed her with everything I had. When we finally parted, her big beautiful eyes looked up at me with wanton desire. "Dinner first, dessert later," I murmured with a parting kiss to her nose.

"Damn tease," she growled.

I never brought women up here, so it was fair enough to say that I wasn't prepared for romantic candle lit dinners, but I found some candles hidden in the back of one of the drawers. I can't remember buying them or stuffing them in the bottom of that particular drawer, but I'm thankful for the forgotten decision to do so. I didn't have a lavish dining room, but I wiped down the island in the middle of the kitchen and lit the candles. I didn't have any wine, so beer would have to do.

After setting the table, I brought Rebecca to her seat and pulled out her chair, helping her climb up onto the stool. The genuine appreciation of my effort in Rebecca's eyes was enough to commit me to doing this regularly for her. The silence as we ate was comfortable, interrupted only by my possibly far too vocal moaning and enjoyment of Rebecca's famous chili. She arched one of those perfect eyebrows in my direction and I shrugged.

"I thought we covered this, I get a hard-on for food." She shook her head and took a swig of her beer.

"So," she began, "when we go back into town, I thought I might talk to Dave."

I was both surprised and pleased with her decision. "That's a great idea, and if you find yourself uncomfortable talking to him, he can recommend someone else, someone you can trust." Rebecca was swinging her legs back and forth and I realized it was out of nervousness.

"If you're not ready to talk to him, don't force it. Dave isn't going anywhere."

She pushed her empty plate forward a little, and fidgeted with her empty beer bottle. "He helped you, obviously."

I nodded in agreement. I owed my life to both Dave and Mercy. "He did. He helped me realize where my anger stemmed from. Once we knew where all that shit was buried, I was able to address it, deal with it. I was angry with my family and lashed out at not only them, but everyone around me. I had to let that anger go, I had to move forward. I still get pissed from time to time when I think about my childhood and some of the shit I went through, but I know that it all turned out okay. I'm good now. I have a good job, I'm fit, healthy." I caught her eye when she looked up at me. "I've got a beautiful woman in my life that completes me. Anger doesn't control me anymore."

She blushed and covered her reaction with a smart ass remark, "Except for Luke Hollywell."

"Except for Luke Hollywell, and the other asshole that hurt you. There is a special place on my shit list reserved for that asshole. You can't blame me though, they hurt what's mine, and don't get me wrong, I might not have realized it at the time, but you were mine." Rebecca slid down from her stool and began clearing the table. "You get nervous when I speak about my feelings for you," I observed.

She cast me a quick glance over her shoulder and shrugged. "I guess I'm not used to it. My parents died when I was young, and my grandmother brought me and Emily up. She was pretty old fashioned and had been raised by her own grandmother, who was pretty cold and impassive. My grandmother loved Emily and I, there was no doubt about it, but she didn't know how to express that love, she never said the words and I guess I never really needed to hear them."

I understood what it was like to grow up in a home that lacked love and affection. "My mother once told me she thought Satan had deposited me in her womb as punishment for her impure thoughts." Rebecca looked horrified and I laughed at the outraged look on her face. If my mother walked into the room right now, I think Rebecca might just get a little scrappy. "Mercy never let a day go by where she didn't tell me she loved me, that I was worthy and cherished. She wiped away all the crap my parents fed me, and helped me become the man I am today. Never doubt the power of words, Rebecca, they can help you heal, make you feel whole. Not a day will pass where you won't hear those kinds of words from me." She just stared at me as if searching for the truth and when she saw it, she took the three too far away steps towards me. I pulled her into my body and kissed the daylights out of her.

"I want you," she whispered, when I finally allowed her to breathe.

"Go upstairs and run yourself a bath. I'll clean up down here and lock up." I pressed a kiss to her forehead. "I won't be far behind you." Rebecca quickly disappeared upstairs and I found myself cleaning like a man possessed. I wanted to give her enough time to think this through. As much as I didn't want her to change her mind, I didn't want her doing something she wasn't ready for either. Once I secured the locks, then double checked them, I took the stairs two at a time. I followed a trail of clothes from the bedroom door to the bathroom, and chuckled as I picked them up. The bathroom was in a haze of steam, the Jacuzzi full of hot water, and Rebecca submerged to her neck in bubbles. "I have bubble bath?" I asked, a little surprised.

"Shampoo," she admitted without opening her eyes. Damn she was beautiful, her hair was in a messy bun on the top of her head, her face free of makeup. Her big blue eyes opened to settle on me staring at her from the doorway. "Are you doing laundry?" she asked, taking in my arm full of clothes.

"You know something," I asked, placing the clothes on the bathroom counter, "I think you are the most beautiful woman I have ever seen, in clothes and out of them. But I miss the pretty dresses and skirts you used to wear." She looked surprised and sat up a little straighter as I knelt by the tub.

"You don't think they were silly? Immature?" she asked.

It shocked me into silence. Rebecca Donovan radiated confidence. She never cared what anyone thought about the way she dressed. Her ability to hold her head high and disregard the curious looks she got by people who didn't know her was just one of the many things I admired about her. "Did you ever think they were silly?" She shook her head. "Then what does it matter what other people think." She looked away and I put my finger under her chin and brought her eyes back to mine. "I'm not going to let him take away your confidence, Betty Boop. It's not his to take. You are a strong, intelligent, sexy, spirited woman. You wear those hot as hell sexy outfits because that's who you are. You don't give a fuck what others think about you, and that's just one of the things I love about you." Her sharp intake of breath alerted me to what I had just said. I loved her? Fuck, I guess I did. If being in love was seeing yourself grow old with someone, seeing her belly grow with your child in it, kissing her lips at the end of every day and at the start of every morning from here until eternity, then hell yes, I was in love. "Don't you dare say it back, 'cause that will make me think you're only saying it because I did. Say it when you're ready, when it feels right."

I stood and began peeling off my clothes. Her eyes were glassy as I watched her gazing at me. Even though I was nervous about how she felt over that little chick-flick moment where I talked about my feelings for her, I will still as hard as steel. Not only my heart wanted her, my body did, too. My feelings for Rebecca had seeped deep into my body, right down into my heart. Every little thing about her was beautiful—her stubborn pride, fierce independence and strength, and the subtle fragility that I could see underneath all that passion and intensity. Surely those images of perfection would never disappear from my eyes. Loving Rebecca for the rest of my life would be the easiest thing I would ever do.

CHAPTER 17

Rebecca

He loved me. Charlie Cole loved me. Charlie Cole, who loved everything but love, loved me. I wanted to cry, but more than that, I wanted to return the beautiful sentiment to him. But he was right—I didn't want to say those sacred words just because he had. I knew I felt the same about him, but I wanted it to be perfect when I finally acknowledged it out loud. At this moment, I felt like the most powerful woman on the planet, and when he stood, stretching to his full six foot whatever height, and began peeling off his clothes, my eyes were riveted to the beautiful man and his stunning body. As he unbuttoned his jeans and lowered the fly, my eyes were drawn to his groin. As the worn denim left his hips, I moved aside, eager to have him in the water with me. He was a masterpiece, his muscles shaped to perfection, the rough shadow of hair on his chin gave him a handsomely rugged appearance. Charlie climbed into the Jacuzzi and moved me forward to position himself at my back. Feeling his skin against mine was comforting, and as his arms slipped around my waist, I felt protected in his firm hold.

"You always smell good," Charlie murmured.

I needed more. I needed his hands on me, I needed him in me. He was already in my heart, now I needed him marked on my soul. He was mine and I was his. Nothing would stand between us, especially some faceless monster. I grabbed Charlie's hands, which sat chastely on my stomach, and moved them to cup my breasts. The twitch of his cock at my back emboldened me, and I reached around to grasp the rigid length as he pinched my nipples.

"So damn pretty," he whispered. As he played with my breasts and kissed my neck, I grew restless quickly—this was still not enough—I couldn't get close enough. I turned in Charlie's arms, straddled his lap, and pressed my lips to his. He let me take control of the kiss. I explored his lips, his mouth. Sucking at his lower lip, I pulled away to look into his intense green eyes. I knew he was watching for any hesitation or fear.

"I want this, Charlie, I need you." One of his hands left my waist to slide down between my thighs. As his lips took possession of mine, his hand took possession of me more intimately. I found myself shamelessly riding his hand, and I didn't care how brazen my body had become. Charlie had that effect on me. I found myself comfortable with him, open and willing to be whatever it was that he needed me to be, to take whatever it was I needed from him. We were a perfect fit on every level. Soul mates that had lost their way for a short while, just like Charlie had said. I was quickly worked into a frenzy and found myself pushing Charlie's hand aside and gripping his cock, guiding it towards my hot core. Charlie didn't try and stop me, but his eyes never once left mine, watching me cautiously with unconcealed desire. My eyes fluttered shut as I began to slowly sink down onto him. He was big—damn!—how had I forgotten how big he was? I worked myself slowly down, becoming accustomed to his size as Charlie gripped my hips, thrusting gently into me. Once I was fully seated on his erection, I tentatively rocked forward, allowing myself to become reacquainted with Charlie's body. My hands traced his neck, shoulders, chest, arms, while he lovingly did the same to me.

"No condom, Betty Boop," Charlie whispered.

I didn't stop riding him at the leisurely pace I had found. "I'm on the pill and I'm clean," I murmured. "And I'm sure you wouldn't have let us get this far if you weren't."

He nodded, his cheeks flushed. "I would always protect you, even from myself." His words encouraged me to ride him harder, faster. The water in the Jacuzzi churned like a rough sea, the water slipping over the edge and to the tiled floor. One of Charlie's hands gripped the back of my neck, pulling me forward to his demanding kiss. His other hand slipped down to my clit and pressed with gentle yet determined strokes. Charlie growled with unbidden pleasure and that's all it took to set me off.

"Shit," I groaned as my orgasm teetered on the edge. Charlie pressed a little firmer at the bundle of nerves between my legs and I fell, my orgasm flooding my veins as my body soared with complete abandon. When conscious thought finally claimed me once again, I realized Charlie had also reached his own peak, his head resting against my shoulder. His cock twitched inside me and I inadvertently clenched around him.

"Damn, I could do that all night." He chuckled.

I sat up and smiled. "I wouldn't be opposed to it."

"You are a dream come true," he said with a hint of mockery, but the sincerity in his eyes told me he meant every word of it. "Come on, it's getting cold in here." Charlie lifted me and I climbed from the tub. We dried off and when I attempted to pull my pajamas on, Charlie pushed my hands away and dragged me naked to his bed. "You've got me to keep you warm, you don't need them." With Charlie spooned against my back, his arms wrapped around me, legs thrown over mine, I did feel warm, inside and out. Charlie's soft kiss to the back of my neck was the last thing I remembered as I drifted off to sleep.

* * *

I don't know how I had managed to disentangle myself from Charlie without waking him up, but I did. I wanted him to sleep in. Twice during the night, I woke up screaming from dreams of dark, ugly, tainted memories. In the end, Charlie had left the bedside lamp on and soothed me back to sleep, and now I felt guilty. Charlie shouldn't have to deal with my drama. Why the hell couldn't I just get over it and move on? When I was awake, I could acknowledge my fear had somewhat diminished in Charlie's presence. I wasn't as nervous and jumpy during the daylight hours, but as soon as darkness descended, so did the nightmares. After my attack I feel like I've lost so much—my identity, my strength, my self-confidence—and Charlie was helping me get that back. But there were still many deep-rooted fears that had taken up residence in my heart: fear of being overpowered, of not being able to defend myself; fear that someone could so easily invade the safety of my home and hurt me. A fear I had never experienced before the attack and sometimes felt so thick and strong I thought it would suffocate me. I didn't know to fix that.

Sipping my coffee in front of one of the large bay windows in the living room, I stared at the snowy mountains before me. Damn it was gorgeous up here; I couldn't believe this was Charlie's. The bachelor pad above Carter Constructions was more like the Charlie I knew before; this cozy and welcoming cottage was more like the Charlie I knew now. The thought of Charlie's burned down apartment and Jax's burned out office made me cringe. My fault, I solemnly thought. A warm kiss pressed to my neck made me jump.

"Sorry, Betty Boop, didn't mean to scare you," Charlie said, kissing me gently on the top of my head again. When I turned to face him, I did a quick perusal of his fine form. He was wearing sweats that sat low on his hips and a tight fitted shirt, and his light brown hair had that just fucked look that he wore so well. Charlie smirked.

"You hungry? Cause you look like you wanna eat me." I snorted, but didn't say anything, because quite frankly, he was right. "Come on, we're going to work-out together."

I took his outstretched hand, but paused at the mention of working out. "Ummmm...say again?"

Charlie laughed. "Really, scared of a little exercise, Betty Boop?"

It was my turn to laugh. "No, not scared, I just prefer my exercise to be done on a bed, horizontally." I wiggled my eyebrows suggestively at him. "Or vertically, against a wall, whatever works for you."

"Damn, woman. Why does it suddenly feel like I'm the chick in this relationship and you're the dude?"

I stood up and cupped him intimately. "You don't feel like a chick to me." I smiled seductively.

"Fuck me," Charlie growled, before slamming his lips down on mine. He pulled away abruptly. "Fine, we exercise your way first, then my way." He spun me around and pushed my chest over the back of the couch. His firm hands pulled my pajama bottoms down my hips and I carefully stepped out of them. "You have the sexiest ass, baby." He stood behind me and took his time exploring my flesh, which was covered in goose-pimples, and not from the cold. It didn't take long before I was wriggling with impatience. Charlie gave me a gentle slap on the ass, but my protest was feeble because I did actually enjoy it. "Stop moving," he murmured as his hand pressed firmly against my spine, pushing me down even further. I could hear his pants slide down his legs as his feet moved between mine to kick my legs further apart. His fingers teased me, caressing me so close to where I wanted them, but not close enough. I wiggled with impatience and Charlie chuckled. Without warning his fingers were in me, pushing in and out and my head fell forward as I let all my worries slip away and simply allowed myself to feel. Charlie removed his hand and suddenly the rigid texture of his fingers was replaced by the warm wet heat of his tongue. The thought of him going down on me like this made me self-conscious, but then his lips sucked hard on my clit and he groaned a deep growl of satisfaction and I no longer cared. Instead, I pushed back a little, encouraging him and moaned low and long as he lavished me like a starved man. Just when I thought I couldn't take any more, that my legs would crumble under the pressure of a hard orgasm, he was gone.

"Charlie!" I hissed furiously, so close to climaxing.

"Fuck, you make me so hard, baby."

He ignored my protest and pressed the solid length of his cock against the cleft of my ass as if to show me proof. His fingers were once again in my pussy and I almost purred out loud like a happy kitten. When his fingers left me this time, they were replaced with his cock, and as he entered me, we both groaned at the intimate contact. Charlie pulled back, his cock almost pulling all the way out, then he smoothly pushed forward again, riding me at a leisurely pace. His hands massaged my ass cheeks as I hung awkwardly over the back of the couch. His pace slowly became more frantic, and suddenly he pulled away from me—again! I was about to protest the loss, but before I could say a word, he nudged me toward one of the bay window seats and pushed me down on my knees. His hands found my wet core once more and I pushed back on his greedy fingers. They were quickly replaced with his hard cock as he slammed home—hard—almost pushing my head against the clear glass in front of me. I barely noticed the breathtaking snow-capped mountains as Charlie took my breath away with his greedy, long, sure strokes. I felt the solid heat of his chest as he leaned over me, licking and kissing a trail up my spine to my neck.

"You feel so fucking incredible Rebecca—so hot and wet—I can barely stop myself from coming the minute I get inside you."

His words sparked a light within me that pushed me towards orgasm. He gripped my shoulders and pulled me back to meet his hips that that were now thrusting harder, faster.

"Sexiest fucking woman I have ever seen. I can barely keep my fucking hands off you."

"Charlieeeee," I moaned loudly.

"Yeah, baby, I'm right there with you."

He reached around and cupped my breasts, squeezing and pinching my nipples before his hand ran the length of my body to find its way between my legs. He began to stroke my clit. His chest pressed against my back as his free hand wrapped itself possessively around my neck. There was no pressure in his hold, nothing for me to be scared of—it was covetous and tender, and it made me feel like the most treasured woman alive. He began to thrust even harder, but he didn't break our close contact, and when he finally growled loudly on a hard urgent thrust, I screamed his name wantonly. There was no one around to hear the sounds of our desperate love making, so I could scream until the rafters collapsed. I suddenly found myself wanting to go again, just so I could.

Charlie lifted himself from my back and slowly pulled away, his hands still caressing my body as if he was reluctant to part with me. I stood on shaky legs and turned to face him. His cheeks were flushed with the exertion of our lovemaking and sweat glistened on his perfectly sculpted chest and abs.

"I like working out your way," he murmured as he leaned down to kiss me hard.

"We could just do this all day rather than try your idea of exercise," I suggested.

Charlie grinned. "How about we do a little exercise my way, then I can lay you over the bench press and fuck you till you can't walk anymore?"

I considered that for a moment. "There are some parts to that plan that I am very much on board with, however, your version of exercise worries me a little. I'm not sure I can keep up."

Charlie spun me around to face the stairs. "I promise to easy on you, for the exercise part anyway," he patted me on the ass. "Go get dressed and get back down here. I am but a mere man, I need a few minutes to recover before I can have you screaming my name again. A good run should have me ready to go in no time."

Dressed, sated, and looking a little well-fucked, as Ella would say, I met Charlie in the kitchen.

"Right, now that we got that out of our system, let's see if you can kick my ass."

In the basement, that I didn't know existed, Charlie had the ample space decked out like a small gym. A weight bench sat on one side of the room, a punching bag was in the center, and a treadmill was on the other side. Taking pity on my out-of-shape condition, Charlie situated me on the treadmill, starting me out at a steady walk that eventually moved into a steady jog. When I say steady, I mean flat-out trying to kill me. By the time the machine slowed back to a walk, then eventually stopped, I was breathing like a woman with an unhealthy does of emphysema and losing more moisture than a shower stall. Charlie led me through some basic self-defense maneuvers and eventually I gave him a ruthless shove and collapsed on the ground. We had been working away in his make-shift gym for almost two hours and I was done. This was officially a record for Rebecca Donovan: the only exercise I have ever allowed to continue this long was sex. Laying in a boneless heap on the floor, Charlie laughed as he wiped his face down with a towel.

"You did good, Betty Boop. Long way away from kicking my ass, but you made a valiant effort which deserves a reward." I pulled my limp, jelly arms away from my face, and looked up at the wicked man that stood above me.

"Reward?" I smiled and his lazy grin became sinfully hot.

"Shame I can't move." I breathed heavily.

Charlie winked. "You don't need to move."

A trickle of sweat fell down my forehead, reminding me that I was a stinky, perspiring mess right now. "You're not touching me till I've showered," I said sternly. Shit, the determined look on Charlie's face had me both slightly worried and a little excited. "Uh-huh, no way. I can barely stand the smell of myself and you're all sweaty."

"You know, this is the second time you've suggested you have a problem with my perspiration. Let me get this straight, it's okay if it's in the bedroom, but not in the gym?" He raised a brow.

"Not just in the bedroom. The living room is okay, too, or the bathroom, laundry room, maybe the kitchen, but not on the table, island, or counter because that's just unsanitary. But, yeah, sex sweat is okay, gym sweat is gross."

Charlie laughed loudly. "You do know it comes from the same place within our body, right?" he teased, with that wicked grin of his. Just when I had my snappy retort ready, our playfulness was interrupted by the sound of my cell phone. Worried it might be Emily, I scrambled to get it. The caller ID showed an unknown number, which meant it could very well be my sister.

"Hello?" I asked, having regained some composure following Charlie's mischievous smile.

"Sweetheart," a man's voice drawled, "have you missed me?" An immediate chill swept through my body. I opened my mouth to answer, but nothing came out. The room around me narrowed and my heart echoed loudly in my ears. "I've missed you and that hot cunt of yours. Emily is pretty fucking tasty, but she's a little too used for my liking. You're fresh meat. Hot, juicy, fresh pussy." He smacked his lips together and I lurched forward, holding the wall to steady myself.

"Who the fuck are you?" My voice didn't waver and my fear was quickly replaced with anger. "And where the fuck is my sister?"

CHAPTER 18

Charlie

One more minute, that's all I would have needed, and Rebecca would have been stripped bare and beneath me. I was surprised her phone actually worked out here; coverage at the cabin was patchy at best. As I began putting away the few light weights we had used, I glanced in Rebecca's direction. Her face was pale and sickly looking and she seemed to waver for a moment. I stood slowly, watching her carefully as she held the phone to her ear. When she demanded to know who was calling and where her sister was, I knew immediately who was on the other end. I was by her side in a second and snatched the phone from her hand. Rebecca's eyes flamed with fury, and when she tried to wrestle the phone back from me, I caught her hand and pressed it against my chest, leaning in close so she could hear, too.

"You are either really brave, or really fucking stupid to call this number," I said with more composure than I felt. My words were met with a low snicker.

"Charlie Cole," an unfamiliar voice crooned with amusement. I was surprised the fucker knew my name, but I played it cool, not wanting him to know he had caught me unawares.

"A little unfair that you know my name and I don't know yours, don't you think?" I knew who it was. The air of arrogance and entitlement in his voice assured me that it was William Levier. I couldn't imagine Jonas Levier stooping so low as to make threatening phone calls. I'm sure he would have minions do shit like that for him. William, on the other hand, was an insignificant piece of shit with daddy issues, trying to make his own way in the world, and was failing miserably. He didn't offer me his name as he rambled on with a voice full of conceit.

"I would have forgotten all about this little situation and be happily at home, balls deep in some whore if it weren't for your dogs."

I wasn't exactly sure what the fucker was talking about, but I assumed my dogs were Dillon and Braiden, so I decided to take a chance and play along. "You shouldn't have touched Rebecca. Then you wouldn't have had to worry about my dogs."

The asshole chuckled again. "Well, then I wouldn't have had the enjoyment of being buried knuckle deep in your woman."

Only the tensing of Rebecca in front of me kept me sane. I gripped her hand a little tighter over my heart. "I'm going to give you fair warning now, fucker. Get out of Claymont. I won't ask you again. If you don't leave in the next twenty-four hours and stay the fuck away from my woman, you will be hunted and gutted, just like the worthless piece of shit you are." He laughed again and I wanted nothing more than to have the asshole in front of me. I wanted to wrap my hands around his neck until the fucking thing snapped off.

"Firstly, Mr. Cole, you do not want to threaten me. If your dogs have done their work, then they know who I am, which means they know who my father is. Secondly, I have no intention of staying in this hell hole of a town, but I'm not leaving till I have what I came for." Rebecca's head rested against my chest and I held her close. "Half a million. I know property value, Mr. Cole, and I know your woman's property is worth at least that, so transferring the deed over to me will cover it. I will have someone call back at this number within the next hour for a time and location to meet with me and my lawyer. If I don't get what I want, I will take Rebecca as payment and put her to work in one of my father's clubs—even though she's much older than we like our girls, I'm sure she'll put up a good fight for one of our clients—and she can earn me every fucking cent of that money. You would be surprised at the number of men that like a girl who fights back—I have no doubt a red hot innocent like your girl would make a fortune chained, gagged and flogged."

Rebecca whimpered and the sound made me see red. "You better hope you can find a hole deep enough to hide in fucker, because when I find you, I am going to rip your heart out and shove it down your throat, and, Mr. Levier?" I let his name hang for a moment, giving him fair chance to correct me if I was wrong—he didn't. "That's a promise, not a threat." I hung up before the prick could hang up on me.

Rebecca's eyes flew up to mine and she began to shake. Then she started hitting my chest and screamed, "Why did you do that? You hung up on him and it'll make him mad!"

I grabbed her fists easily. "Betty Boop!" Her frightened eyes looked at me straight on. "I want the fucker mad. Mad means easily distracted, on edge, not thinking clearly. People make mistakes when they're mad." A tear ran down her cheek.

"He might hurt Emily," she sobbed. I straightened a little at her words. It hadn't even occurred to me that Emily could now possibly bear the brunt of his anger. I dragged Rebecca quickly up the stairs, and dialed out using the landline. Braiden answered on the first ring.

"Rebecca just got a phone call from William Levier," I growled. Braiden was quiet for a moment, and I imagined him sitting silently at his desk, mulling over what I just said. Braiden was a thinker, a deep thinker. He watched, listened, and seemed to see all. Anyone that quiet had to have dark secrets lurking beneath their cool exterior, and I had no doubt Braiden had plenty, but I still trusted him explicitly.

"What did Levier Junior have to say?" he finally asked.

"He wants cash and he'll take it in the form of the deed to Rebecca and Emily's property."

"Or what?" Braiden asked calmly, too calmly.

"Or he'll take Rebecca and put her to work in one of his father's clubs."

"You know he won't get his hands on Rebecca," Braiden said matter-of-factly.

"Yeah, but she can't live the rest of her life looking over her shoulder."

"She won't have to and we will. Head back into town, I don't like the idea of you guys out there on your own. You can stay with me and Dillon. Between the three of us, we can keep Rebecca safe. Don't use Rebecca's phone until I've had a chance to look over it. The call will most likely be untraceable, but I've got a guy that can check it out anyway. Keep your weapon handy, too, Charlie," Braiden spoke. His efficient composure impressed the shit out of me.

"Braiden, we need to find Emily."

"On it." Braiden hung up. Rebecca was still crying a flood of tears as she stood helplessly across the room, staring at me. I wanted to hold her, soothe her fears and tell her everything would be okay. But I couldn't lie to her; I had no idea if everything would be okay. And I was feeling guilty as shit about stirring William Levier up when he might have Emily within his reach. She needed to hold it together, we had to be strong and smart if we were going to defeat this fucker.

"Pull it together, baby, we need to stay sharp. We are going to get your sister back and these mother fuckers are gonna wish they were never born. You know Dillon and Braiden will find Emily, this is what they do. Hell, Jax told me they've handled more than a dozen missing person cases over the last couple of years, and their success rate is better than most." She took a few long, deep breaths and her tears finally slowed to a trickle. "I'm sorry I antagonized him, I shouldn't have done that," I added. Rebecca came to me easily, wrapping her arms tightly around my waist.

"What do we do now?" she whispered.

"I need you to go upstairs and pack our stuff. We're heading to Dillon and Braiden's. I'll lock up everything down here."

Driving back through town sucked. The cabin was my happy place, and it was where Rebecca had been free to let go of the shit that had been drowning her. Now, as I made my way through the darkened streets of Claymont, Rebecca's knees bobbed up and down in a nervous cadence, and her lip was caught in a stressed pinch between her teeth. The dark rings under her eyes were absent, but I knew they would return in the near future. Part of me was pissed as hell at Emily for bringing this shit into her sister's life. Another part of me wanted to mete out vengeance on the Levier men for their grievances on Rebecca's own flesh and blood. None of us knew exactly what part Emily had played in this fiasco. Hell, she was married to William Fucking Levier, but the little shit had made it loud and clear that Emily had been put to work in his father's clubs against her will. The idea made me sick to my stomach. The fact that he suggested the same would happen to Rebecca made my calm façade almost melt away under the blistering heat of anger. My hands were locked in a tight grip on the steering wheel, my jaw clamped down stiffly—I was on the razor's edge. One of Levier's men had called a while ago with instructions for a rendezvous in two days, at a hotel back in town. It would give Rebecca ample time to organize the necessary paperwork to transfer the deed to her property over to William. Rebecca begged me to be calm during the conversation and to ask if they had Emily, and if so, if she could speak to her. I couldn't deny her a single damn thing, so I tried. There had been no idle chit chat though, just the bare essential information with a decisive click and end dial tone. The devastated look on her face broke my heart. This was the closest I've come to losing my shit in years, but there was no one here to take it out on. Going into a rage was pointless and would get us nowhere. Finding that calm place within my soul was a difficult task, but I followed the exercises Dave taught me years ago. But the long deep breaths with the slow repeated mantra of, keep calm playing over and over in my mind wasn't really helping. I used the technique of imagery, and that almost had the desired effect. Imagining my cabin with Rebecca in it, laughing, carefree and happy had my heart rate lowering somewhat, but I was still teetering on the edge of madness.

"Charlie?" Her voice was almost like a faraway echo of tranquil calm cutting through a storm of emotion. "You need to pull it together, you need to stay sharp," she whispered my very own words back at me. "I need you to keep it together, because if you lose it, I'll be right behind you." I released the tight grip on the steering wheel and flexed my fingers before reaching across to take her hand.

"I'm good, Betty Boop," I murmured. She centered me and kept me focused with nothing more than a few simple words. She needed me to be strong for her; therefore, I would be. There was no other choice.

* * *

Dillon and Braiden's home was the ultimate man cave. These guys had their pad down! It was a brand new house in one of the few upscale gated communities in Claymont. It was a short drive from Rebecca's exclusive neighborhood, so I knew it was in an affluent part of town. Obviously the Montgomery Security business was doing exceptionally well. The single story home was located on a large block that backed onto the base of the Claymont Mountain Ranges. The wide open glass doors at the back of the house overlooked a heated pool that was layered in a thick layer of steam as the heat met with frigid air. Beneath the water, the pool was lit with a sparkling array of twinkling lights. A large hammock hung on the small wooden deck of an ostentatious pool house at the back of the property. Back inside the living, dining and kitchen area was a massive open plan design decorated in contemporary black and white furnishings. On the wall hung photographs, much like the ones that adorned the office of Montgomery Securities. The place was spotlessly tidy, so much so I was afraid to take another step before removing my dirty-ass boots.

"Eli hangs out here with you?" Rebecca asked, astonished. Yeah, their house didn't really have a child friendly vibe about it—it was too neat and orderly.

Dillon laughed. "Yep, if you look closely, you'll see the stains as proof. Just don't point them out to Braiden, he's the neat freak. I don't really care, houses are meant to be lived in and Eli loves the pool. It's a bit cold for it this time of year though." Dillon showed us to a spare room at the back of the house. It was huge.

"Holy shit. I could fit my entire house in here." Rebecca admired the open space.

"REBECCA!" came a familiar voice, screaming from the living room. We dumped our bags and made our way back out. Ella hit her at full speed and I stood firmly at Rebecca's back to prevent her from falling over.

"Fuck, squirt, take it easy," I huffed.

Ella punched me in the arm—hard. "Don't call me that!" she protested.

Jax stood in the doorway, actually he more like filled the doorway—I'm fairly certain he's still growing. In one hand was a bottle of vodka, in the other was Rebecca's Clitoria.

I smirked and nodded to the innocuous looking plant. "You look awkward with that in your hands."

"Fuck you," Jax growled.

Behind him came Annie and Eli, followed by Mercy and Dave, then, surprisingly, Lola.

"Who the hell is watching Mercy's tonight?" I wondered out loud.

"Beth and Blue have got it covered," said Mercy, bypassing me and heading straight for Rebecca.

I turned and held my arms open. "Where's my love?" I growled.

Mercy scrunched up her nose. "From what I hear, you've been getting plenty of love lately." I blushed—I fucking blushed—and it silenced the entire room as my eyes settled on Ella.

She raised her hands in self-defense. "I only told Jax," she said, looking slightly nervous.

My gaze moved to Jax. "I only told Mercy."

I arched an eyebrow at Mercy, and she shrugged. "I only confided in Annie."

Annie at least had the good grace to look a little ashamed. "I only told Dillon," she whispered, and I groaned.

"No one told me, but I guessed as much," said Lola.

Bunch of fucking gossips. I rolled my eyes. "Glad our love life keeps you all entertained."

Ella and Mercy made their way to the kitchen and started pouring drinks. Rebecca moved to my side and I wrapped my arm around her.

"I don't know if I really feel like celebrating," she whispered, which Ella heard loud and clear.

"Remember when my life turned into a circus and Jax and Dillon went all macho He-Man on me and we had drinks at your place? You filled me with alcohol, and even though at the time I wasn't sure I wanted it, I really did need it. I'm repaying the favor." Ella strolled towards Rebecca with a full glass in hand. She held it out and Rebecca took it without hesitation. "And I owe you more hangovers than I care to remember." Rebecca seemed to sigh in defeat, and I noted that she really didn't put up much of a fight. Either she knew these women were relentless when it came to protecting and taking care of their own, or she knew she really did need something to take her mind off the situation we couldn't do anything about right now. Dillon had already notified Frank, Braiden had taken Rebecca's phone and was out doing his thing. We just had to sit tight and wait.

"How you holding up?" asked Jax, when he caught me alone in the kitchen. The women were giggling from the large white couch in the living room. Dillon had set up the Xbox in his bedroom for Eli, and for now, things almost felt normal.

"I'm good." Jax passed me a beer.

"Uh-huh. That why you look like you wanna kill someone?"

"I do want to kill someone," I admitted easily. Jax smirked and held out his beer. I clinked my own bottle against his.

"These pricks who fuck with our women need to know exactly who they're dealing with. No one threatens what's ours. I'm with you on this, if you need anything," he gave me a pointed look, "anything at all, you ask."

This was one of the reasons Jax Carter was my best friend. The dude had my back, always, and even though he struggled with memories of blood and death, he would take up arms again in a heartbeat for me. I gave him a quick nod.

"Ella has turned you into a pussy, you know," I said a little gruffly, and Jax laughed.

"Yep, I'm whipped and proud of it." He patted me hard on the back as we made our way back to the gaggle of women. It wasn't long before

Rebecca's eyes were looking a little glassy, and the lazy smile on her face told me she was quickly reaching the contented point of no return.

"You know, the jeans and shit are all good and well, but it's still weird seeing you in them," Ella said, pushing her way under Jax's arm.

Rebecca glanced down at herself then back to Ella. "They kinda feel weird," she admitted, and it surprised me.

"Then why are you wearing them?" Ella asked in a challenging tone. I smiled because I knew the little tiger was baiting Rebecca. My damn Betty Boop couldn't back down from a challenge, she was too feisty and independent.

"I have no idea. I guess I felt silly in my other clothes, but to be honest, now I kinda feel silly in this." She glanced down at her clothes once more then suddenly stood up. For a split second I thought she was going to give Ella one hell of an ear full, until she smiled.

"Be right back." She disappeared down the long wide hall and into the monstrous room we had been settled into. Fifteen minutes later, she sauntered back into the living room wearing a light pink dress that hugged her breasts and fell into a full skirt. Her hair was pulled up into a high pony tail, her feet bare. It was a familiar sight that made my dick instantly hard. She collapsed gracefully and unabashedly into my lap. "That feels better," she whispered. Nobody questioned her wardrobe change, they didn't need to. Old Rebecca had somehow found her way back. I didn't care what she wore, but this did make me insanely happy. It felt right, it felt like she had taken a final step in healing. I knew she still had rough seas ahead, we still had shit to deal with, but right now Rebecca had slipped back into the woman she was before her attack, and I wasn't referring to just her clothes. Her heart had once again found its strength and determination. She glanced around the room, her eyes taking in the people who conversed amongst themselves—her friends, her family. I couldn't drag my eyes away from her to save myself.

I leaned forward and whispered in her ear, "You are beautiful, you know that, right?" The goose bumps that prickled her skin made me grin. The back of her dress dipped down so low, I knew there was no way she was wearing a bra. I wished we were alone so I could slip my hands under the fabric and see if her nipples had hardened under my whispered caress. Rebecca leaned back into me and I held her against my chest.

"Calendar," she murmured after a short while, and Lola, who was sitting beside us, gave her a curious look. "It passed through my mind the other day, just as a joke, but I think we could do this," Rebecca went on, not really explaining what the hell she was talking about. Everyone was watching her expectantly now. "We could have a Mercy's Angel's calendar and fill it with the gorgeous men of Claymont, proceeds going to Mercy's

Shelter," she spoke fast, her voice full of excitement. The girls suddenly grinned, but all the guys, myself included, became rigid with fear. "Charlie can be January, because you know, what a way to start the year." Her fingers laced with mine and I gave them a gentle squeeze.

"Dillon can be July because with that military cut, he has that all-American, Fourth of July look," Ella said, playing along.

"And Braiden has to be one of the winter months, because he's so dark and mysterious," Lola suggested.

"Jax is December." Ella smirked. Jax raised a horrified brow in her direction. "You've got Christmas down, babe," she smiled, "you're like one giant Christmas present."

Mercy laughed loudly. "I don't know about that. A few years ago, Jax and Charlie went out on Christmas Eve and indulged in just a little too much Christmas festivity. The next morning when we came downstairs to open presents, Charlie was asleep under the tree wearing nothing but a pair of red boxers and a red bow tie around his neck."

It was Dave's turn to laugh. "That's right. It was a disturbing way to greet Christmas Day."

Mercy's eyes twinkled with excitement. "David is April, because that's the month we met."

Dave's smile vanished instantly. "Honey, I think I'm a little too old for this calendar business."

"Oh no, you're not!" demanded Ella.

"Dave, you really have that distinguished Richard Gere look going on. You'll make a perfect April," Annie said thoughtfully, only encouraging the women further. I looked around at the guys in the room who were all looking a little ill.

"You only have five guys. That's not nearly enough for a calendar. Damn shame," Dillon growled.

"Brent, from the gym, he's hot, and I know he's definitely confident enough to do something crazy like this." At the mention of Brent, I became a little stiff. Rebecca had noticed the pretty boy and it didn't sit well with me. She turned in my arms and pressed a kiss to my lips, chaste but forceful. "God knows none of them have anything on you," she whispered. Okay, I was an absolute caveman and my cavewoman knew just how to soothe me. Just like Jax, I was whipped.

"And Blue from the shelter, he has that cute skater look that some girls go for," Ella continued on. I groaned loudly, along with the other three men in the room. However, even though the thought of modeling for a calendar scared me, I couldn't refute the fact it was a good idea, and it was for a very worthy cause. And if Rebecca asked me to do it, there was no way I would be able to refuse her.

"Well, I can totally rock Christmas," Jax finally said with a big shit eating grin on his face. "I mean, I look pretty damn good in red."

"I don't see it, your fucking ego is in the way," I joked. The rest of the night played out much like that. The guys giving each other shit, the girls rattling on about their damn calendar. It was finally brought to an end around eleven o'clock when Rebecca promptly passed out in my lap. I carried her to our room and looked down at her splayed out across the bed. Her dress looked too nice to sleep in so I carefully rolled her to her side and unclipped the button at her neck and unzipped the zipper at her waist. Under her protesting moans, I slid the dress down her body then stood, brazenly staring at her beautiful, nearly naked form. She was wearing nothing but a pair of lacey white panties, her breasts bare as I had assumed earlier. Her skin was milky white and smooth, her curves feminine and soft. She wasn't a waif like some men preferred, she was all female, shapely like a woman should be.

"You just gonna stand there all night and stare at me, or are you gonna make me come?" Rebecca's eyes fluttered open and her sexy grin hit me hard in the chest. I did want to make her come, over and over, but she was drunk and I wasn't taking advantage of that.

"You're in no condition tonight, maybe in the morning, if your head can handle it." I pulled my shirt over my head and felt Rebecca's eyes on my chest.

"No way, Charlie," she sat up, "that," she pointed a finger in my direction, "is all mine, and I want a taste, now!"

Arrrggghhh, fuck. My willpower where this woman was concerned was non-existent. I lowered myself over her and kissed her hard, forcing my tongue in her mouth. She tasted like vodka and orange juice, the perfect combination of bitter and sweet. She wriggled beneath me and I somehow managed to remove my mouth from hers and moved to take her breasts in my hands. After kissing and teasing her pale pink nipples for a short while, I realized she had stilled under my sexual attack. Lifting my head I noticed her eyes were closed.

"Way to make a man feel two feet tall." I chuckled. She had fallen asleep under my hands. I knew it was the alcohol—not my lack of expertise—but I was silently thankful. I couldn't refuse her, yet I knew I shouldn't have been taking her in this state. I pushed myself up onto my forearms and simply took in her beauty. A low snore escaped her nose and it was too fucking adorable. I rolled off of her and proceeded to take off my jeans and climb into the bed, pulling her small body slightly under my much larger one. I was probably squashing her—but this is where she ended up the last few nights we slept together—partly buried beneath me where I could keep her safe—and this is where I needed her now. She hadn't complained then, so I assumed she's just as happy with the position now. The night had ended with laughter and ease, but I knew tomorrow reality would return. Rebecca's worry would carry in her delicate features and my anger would once again simmer. Yeah, right now life was a bitch, but I was going to fix it. William Levier was going to wish he'd never been born.

CHAPTER 19

Rebecca

Charlie stood at my back, Dillon not far behind us. We were at the firing range close to the house, practicing with the gun Charlie taught me to shoot a couple of days ago. I was terrible—my aim was off by a long shot—pun intended. I was actually worried about the few people who stood alongside me, firing their own weapons.

"She's holding her breath," Dillon noted.

"You have to breathe, Betty Boop, and relax, you're all tense."

My head was pounding like a mother fucker. I was grouchy, hung-over, tired, and ready to shoot both of these men any second. I woke up way too early this morning and was unable to go back to sleep after having another nightmare. I walked around Dillon and Braiden's pristine home, wishing I could return to my own house. I missed it, I missed my stuff. Almost every night my eyes fluttered shut, after sleep took me into its cool embrace, I was confronted with nightmares. That bastard controlled my nights and it felt like some kind of failure on my part, like I was somehow allowing him to manipulate me. And then there was the fact that he and his father had hurt my sister—may still be hurting my sister. They were going down for that—I had no idea how—but I wouldn't rest until they did. That thought alone had fueled me enough to get me to the firing range, but now I was stuck in a well of self-pity. I needed a bucket of ice cream, pronto.

"Her right foot needs to be forward a little more," observed Dillon patiently. His calm comments were making me not so calm. Charlie tried to physically move my leg, and I stepped quickly out of his reach. Enough was enough.

"Okay, I've had it!" I yelled. Charlie was quick to take the loaded gun from my hand, probably realizing if he didn't, I would be too tempted to use it on one of them. "My head hurts, I'm tired and I'm just not good at shooting. I'm a florist for God's sake, I make bouquets and they are fucking impressive and perfect, because that's what I do. You are the soldier," I pointed at Dillon, "and you are a kick-ass fighter that won't let me out of his sight, so how about you guys do the Rambo gun bullshit and leave me to fucking worry about my sister." I took a deep breath, feeling somewhat lighter after my tantrum. "I want ice cream," I growled to no one in particular, then walked away from our booth at the firing range. Of course the guys didn't let me get too far ahead, carefully maneuvering me between their hulking mass of bodies.

The drive back to the house was quiet. My heart began to hammer when I saw Braiden's car as we pulled into the long driveway. He'd been gone since last evening when he took my phone and left without a word. It was already afternoon again and we only had a little over twenty-four hours to organize the paperwork that would transfer the ownership of my house to William Levier. Dillon and Charlie had no intention of allowing me to do such a thing. As far as they were concerned, it wouldn't be necessary, but I yearned to have the deed in my hands, ready to go, just in case. I had always sworn there wasn't a single thing that would convince me to give up my family home. I was wrong, dead wrong. The safety of both me and Emily was worth more than that. At the end of the day, the house was simply a house, a material object.

We found Braiden seated in front of a massive computer screen in a sharp looking office. He was dressed in an expensive looking black suit, his black hair hung over his eyes in an almost wild carefree way. His jaw had a two day growth, and his dark eyes looked a little tired, but still intense. I wondered what the hell he was up to last night. He looked spruced up enough that I wondered if he had been on a date—he'd been gone almost twenty-four hours without so much as a call, and now he looked as though he had stepped from the pages of GQ magazine—when he had clearly stated he would be looking into 'things'. Braiden didn't look up or acknowledge us in any way. Charlie and Dillon sat lazily in chairs, just watching him, I, on the other hand, paced nervously around the room, wanting to ask him what the hell he'd found out. Watching him sit so still at that damn computer, completely oblivious to my panic and anticipation had me wanting to shake the shit out of him. Just when I thought I might start screaming like a crazy woman, Braiden swung the computer screen around to face us. An image of a tall, lean blonde haired man with cold blue eyes and a deep olive complexion filled the screen. He had that educated, upper-class, pretty boy look, but at the same time, he appeared cold and cruel.

"William Levier, your brother-in-law," Braiden said, glancing at me. He flicked to another picture—this one was an older man with similar blue eyes, his hair a little darker, but peppered with grey. He was handsome for an older man, but he also looked ruthless and calculating. While perfectly groomed into the rich and powerful businessman he portrayed on the outside, you could clearly see his callous and hard exterior went further than skin deep. The gleam in his eyes, the hard line of his jaw, he looked like the human personification of Lucifer. "Jonas Levier, William's father." Braiden skipped to the next picture.

I gasped and tears immediately filled my eyes. Emily. She was dressed in an elegant, knee length wrap dress, standing tall and proud in expensive heels. Her short pixie style hair was fashionable and sleek, and her makeup was flawless, accentuating her crystal blue eyes. But it was in her gaze that I could see the truth clearly—she looked defeated, her eyes were hollow and empty—the spark of life that had once filled them was gone. Charlie pulled me down to his lap and I went willingly.

"Last night I took a quick trip out of town." Braiden glanced a little nervously at Dillon. It was unusual to see Braiden show any visible signs of discomfort. "I visited one of Jonas Levier's smaller clubs—one of the legal ones. I didn't expect to find anything in such a short amount of time, but I met a woman there." Braiden sat back in the black leather chair and linked his hands behind his head, any signs of worry gone. He looked cool and aloof once again. "Her name was Madison and she knows of your sister." I forced my tears away as I listened to Braiden, ignoring the picture of the elegant, yet broken girl on the screen. "She is well known amongst the staff of Jonas's establishments, she's been in his employ for a long time now. She used to be one of his most sought after women that had a price tag that would make you shudder." Braiden's eyes flickered with something I that couldn't identify and his hands left the casual embrace behind his head as he leaned forward. "She fought, and many of the men that frequent Jonas's clubs like that in a woman." My hand held fast over my mouth in an attempt to hold back the vomit rising in my throat, while my body shivered uncontrollably. Charlie wrapped his arms around me, pulling me closer to the comforting heat of his body. "Apparently, a couple of years ago she stopped fighting, became compliant, and the only reason Jonas kept her around was because she still looked sixteen. When she turned twenty, she started to look her age and found herself with a whole new cliental. Still men with dominant predilections, but they weren't masochistic; they didn't hurt her like the others did. Madison seemed to be under the impression that Emily had been very happy in her new place of employment. She was basically a kept woman, one of Jonas's favorites."

"How did she end up married to William?" Dillon asked, his voice low, murderous. He was angry and I got that. As soon as the horror fled my body, anger would be left in its wake, too.

"Madison isn't on the inside, she only knows what she knows because of rumors. According to said gossip, Jonas gave Emily to William as a gift of sorts. William had wanted Emily for a long time and the rumor is Emily did something to embarrass Jonas. Being handed off to William was part of her punishment."

"Part of it?" I asked through trembling lips. Braiden looked at me for a long time before answering.

"Dominant men like Jonas have certain ways of delivering punishment to a sub depending on the severity of the misconduct. Madison seemed to think Emily did something quite terrible that may or may not have left a client more than a little uncomfortable in the region of his genitals." One corner of Braiden's mouth lifted in a half grin, but it was gone as fast as it appeared.

"What sort of punishment, other than being forced on William, did Emily endure?" I persisted. I needed to know, and it would more than likely make me sick to my stomach, but I needed to know what she had gone through. As if knowing was a form of punishment for allowing her to walk away from Claymont. She had been nothing more than a child, I should have filed a missing persons report, or I could have tried to tracked her down and drag her home until she was eighteen, by which time she might have settled down a little. Braiden's gaze went from Dillon's to Charlie's, then back to mine. "She is my sister, Braiden, not theirs. Tell me!"

"As I said, Madison isn't privy to the inside world of Jonas, it's mostly rumors," he hedged.

"JUST TEL ME!" I screamed, my patience finally gone.

Braiden didn't flinch or show emotion of any sort. "It is said that he scarred her body in a way that makes her worthless now." I held my breath, waiting for him to explain. Braiden's eyes flared for a moment with fury. "He whipped her. Some dom's use a whip in sexual play—Jonas is renowned for his execution with such equipment—but on this occasion he used it to break the skin and left marks. In the upper class world of Jonas Levier, such marks make a woman worthless; hence, she was given to his son." I felt numb. I couldn't comprehend the world Emily was living in; I couldn't comprehend the life that was suddenly drowning me. "William has been shunned by his father. He acquired himself a taste for heroin and got himself in a sticky situation with one of the local city gangs—he owes them money, a lot of money. Jonas has officially wiped his hands of William and word is he is currently looking for his property—he wants Emily back."

"What does that have to do with Rebecca? Why are they here?" Charlie asked.

"From what I gathered, William found out about Emily and Rebecca's property here in Claymont. William has accumulated a lot of property, but the majority of it is tied up in his father's businesses. Rebecca's home is worth a bit of money and with William's connections in property, he would be able to find a buyer quickly for it. It would be an effortless way to get himself out of his current financial quandary. My guess is he tried to get Emily to convince Rebecca to sell, and when that didn't work he thought he might be able to scare her out of the house."

"So he attacked her," Dillon surmised.

Braiden nodded. "Didn't go to plan though, so now he's grasping at straws, throwing around his father's name in hopes that people will bow down out of fear and give him what he wants. For William this is about money, nothing more, nothing less."

"And Emily is just piece of property stuck in the middle." I stiffened at Charlie's description of my sister and stood up from his lap.

"She's not a piece of property, she's a fucking human being, Charlie, she's my damn sister, my flesh and blood and they hurt her. They forced her to do things she didn't want to do!" I found myself screaming at him. Horror now replaced with anger.

"I know baby, I didn't mean any disrespect. You know that's not how I feel."

"Do I? I know you blame her for my attack. You've blamed her for it the moment you saw that piece of paper on the floor in my kitchen. What the hell am I supposed to think?" Charlie stood and I saw the rage in his eyes. My heart raced, and my head pounded, but not with fear, this was all anger.

"If she hadn't run away all those years ago, neither of you would be in this predicament now." It felt like he slapped me, I actually flinched. Braiden stood along with Dillon.

"We can't change what happened; choices were made and we can't hold that against anyone. If you want to play that game, we could go back and pile hate on the women who birthed both Jonas and William Levier. The blame could be endless. The only people who should hold our anger and hatred right now are the Levier men. They are the monsters here, they are the reason behind Emily and Rebecca's situation." Braiden sounded so calm, he almost doused the fire burning in my veins—almost. I still wanted to smack Charlie, hard. Before I could do anything irrational and crazy, I turned and stormed out of the office—no one followed me. I slammed the door closed on mine and Charlie's room. I stood there, seething, anger coursing through my body. I picked up the closest thing to me—Charlie's shoe—and threw it hard. It slid across the top of a dresser, knocking an expensive looking art deco sculpture off the top of it, which broke when it hit the carpet. But it didn't made a sound when it landed and it frustrated me. I wanted destruction, I wanted noise, I wanted to break shit. I picked up and threw the other shoe, then began throwing clothes around the room, pillows, my make-up, anything I could get my hand on, until I finally ran out of objects to throw. I sank to my knees as big ugly sobs fell from my lips. I cried for my sister. I cried for the injustice those demons inflicted on her small body, I cried for the damage that such abuse would have inflicted on her soul, because in that picture of Emily, that's what I saw. A broken girl and it would haunt me for the rest of my life.

I barely noticed the large hands that picked me up off the floor. I knew instantly it was Charlie, and I was still angry with him, but I couldn't find the energy to escape his embrace. He sank to the floor, his back against the bed, me in his lap.

"I'm sorry, Betty Boop, I didn't mean to belittle your sister or what she's been through. Seeing her in that picture though, hearing Braiden's story, it destroyed a small piece of my heart. I was furious and I didn't know how to deal with that, still don't."

I wrapped my arms around him and held him close. "I failed her—I shouldn't have let her go, I should have looked for her when she left, I should have asked her to come home—but I never did, not once. Those rare phone calls she made to me, I was so indifferent and angry at her for leaving. And she was being raped, held against her will. How can I ever forgive myself for that, I'm her big sister for fuck's sake." I was pressed so hard against Charlie's chest, I was sure when he finally released me I'd have bruises, but at the moment I didn't care.

"No, Rebecca, this is not your fault. Like Braiden said, the only ones to blame are Jonas and William Levier. We can't change what happened, all we can do is fix it." We sat like that for the longest time, Charlie's steady breathing under my ear cooling the flames of anger and despair. He and Braiden were right, Jonas and William were the only ones to blame.

"What now?" I finally sniffled, my eyes heavy with the familiar feeling of sorrow. I had cried so much over the last month, I was surprised I wasn't suffering from dehydration.

"Well, Dillon and Braiden left, they're meeting Frank and going to do a sweep over Claymont. This isn't that big of a town, and a rich, drug addicted city boy hanging out with hired muscle shouldn't be that hard to find. In the meantime, I believe you requested ice cream." I somehow managed to chuckle. "I need to tell you something and I probably shouldn't, it's not really our business. But in retrospect of what's going on...Jonas and his clubs and what Emily has been through..." Charlie took a deep breath and I pulled away so I could see him better. "Braiden is pretty invested in finding Emily. Dillon says he's never seen Braiden this emotionally involved in finding someone."

I almost snorted. The cool, calm and collected exterior of the dark and mysterious Montgomery cousin had me doubting Charlie's words. "I don't know what you see when you look at Braiden, but I haven't noticed much in the way of emotion. He's so calm, it's actually a little unnerving."

Charlie swept a strand of loose hair behind my ear. "Believe it or not, Braiden is pretty fucking torn up over all this. He's barely slept more than a few hours each night since he started looking for Emily, and last night he didn't sleep a wink. Dillon said he's kind of obsessed." Charlie hesitated.

"That's a good thing, right?" I wondered out loud.

"Yeah, I guess. But his interest in Emily seems to go beyond simply finding a client. And the reason Braiden has been able to find out so much about Jonas Levier and Emily is because Braiden has similar tastes…sexually."

My eyes widened and my stomach coiled with disgust. "He rapes women?" I almost screamed.

"Fuck no, of course not. He's a diehard protector, he'd never hurt a woman. But he likes things a little rough in the bedroom. He's visited clubs like Jonas's, not hard core ones full of unwilling women, but gentler versions, if you can call them that. He was even in a dom/sub relationship once."

Oh, wow. He was like a real life Christian Grey! I realized why Charlie was concerned. "Emily doesn't need that, Charlie, after everything she's been through, she doesn't need to come home to that kind of attention."

Charlie silenced me with a finger over my lips. "Braiden isn't an idiot, he's actually pretty damn smart. He's good in those relationships because he is good at knowing exactly what women need, what they want. He's pretty intense, if you haven't noticed. He likes to just sit back and take things in. I trust that he will know exactly what Emily does and doesn't need. He won't hurt her, I trust him with her and you can, too."

I actually found myself thinking Braiden might be good for Emily. If he understands the world she's been living in, if he's willing to put her needs before his own, he just might be able to help her.

"Alright, let's get you that ice cream, then we can slouch around this mansion and watch their giant TV. Have you noticed how everything is so big and oversized in this house? I think Braiden is overcompensating for something."

And just like that Charlie had made me smile again.

CHAPTER 20

Charlie

Night had once again fallen, and as the clocked ticked by, I grew increasingly nervous. I hadn't heard from Dillon or Braiden in a few hours, and with tomorrow being the day we were supposed to meet with William, I was beginning to feel stressed. There wasn't a chance in hell William Levier would get his hands on Rebecca, but since he had her sister he would no doubt try to use her as leverage. Rebecca was on the phone in the office talking to Lola. Bouquets was beginning to feel the strain of Rebecca's absence. Orders needed to be filled and accounts needed to be paid, but I didn't feel comfortable letting Rebecca go there, so she was on a conference call with Lola trying to sort it all out from here. I needed to run, fuck, or fight this hostility that was coursing through my veins, but none of them were an option right now. So, that's when I found myself searching through Dillon's drawers for a pair of swim trunks, I figured swimming laps would be just as good in trying to get some of this aggression out. The dude better not be a speedo man, no way was I wrapping my junk in that shit. Bingo! I stripped bare and pulled on a pair of black swim trunks, which were a little too tight, but I didn't give a fuck right now. I needed to blow off some steam—now. I walked out the back sliding glass door, the cold air outside hitting me so hard I almost screamed like a girl. I moved a little faster for the pool which was steaming with warmth. I dived in, the warmth embracing me like a blanket. It wasn't as warm as my Jacuzzi, but it beat the outdoor temperature hands down. I began swimming laps and when I stopped for a break, I found a cute pair of bare feet directly in front of me. Her toenails were painted a soft shade of pink that I hadn't noticed before. I reached out and gently grasped her ankle, allowing my hand to travel up her calf. She wore a warm, bulky bathrobe, and as my hand travelled higher, I suspected that she was naked underneath it. I glanced up at the amused look on her face.

"Warm in there?" she asked, her voice a gentle feminine stroke to my dick. I nodded. Her eyes never left mine as she shrugged out of the bathrobe, revealing her spectacular naked body beneath. "Shit, it's not out here." She shivered, climbing into the water beside me.

"I should warn you, if Braiden and Dillon drop by and see you like this, I might have to kill them." She smiled and began to move away from me. Fuck, I needed her, now. I pulled off the too tight shorts and began to stalk her through the warm water.

"We needed to have make up sex, that's the best part about fighting and we missed it." She backed herself against the side of the pool and I moved in.

"I've never had make up sex," I admitted.

"I've never had it with someone I loved," she said, blushing.

She finally said it—the L word. I had already confessed my love to her and I knew she cared for me, a lot, but I didn't expect to hear it from her so soon. It stopped me in my tracks and I could see her become visibly nervous.

"So," she said awkwardly, "we should move right on to the sex part."

I swam forward and pressed myself against her, kissing her hard, allowing my tongue to delve deep into her mouth. My hands got busy, stroking and caressing her body, and when her little hand wrapped around my dick I nearly came from the sheer beauty of it. I encouraged her to wrap her legs around my hips and I guided myself into her hot core. Nothing felt better than this—being with Rebecca like this. Her unyielding love and unbreakable desire was like heaven.

"I didn't hear it, say it again," I murmured against her ear, slowly moving in and out of her.

"If you didn't hear it, how do you know what you missed," she whispered back a little breathlessly.

I stilled my hips and she tried to move like the greedy little vixen she is, but I held her steady. "Say it," I said as I kissed her neck and palmed her breast. Not moving within her was excruciating, but I knew it would be worth the wait just to hear those words again.

"Move," she panted desperately.

"Not until you say it," I argued. She grabbed my face with both hands, and raised my gaze from her breasts. She kissed me like a dying woman, and I was about to say, to hell with it, and fuck her senseless, when she looked right into my eyes and whispered, "I love you."

That did it, I fucked her senseless. Panting, bodies pulsing with the lingering effects of our orgasm, I pulled her from the pool and we made a dash for the house. We warmed up in a hot shower where we once again lost ourselves to lust and when we finally made it to the couch in front of the overcompensating TV, I fell into a deep and easy sleep.

Rebecca

Charlie looked younger when he was asleep. His face relaxed, the lines around his eyes were all but gone. He pulled off the goofball persona well, but I knew him better than that now. He laughed, he played, and he could seduce a woman better than Don Juan himself. But he also struggled, he fought with his emotions and he wrestled with anger constantly. The fact that he had found a way to manage it, contain it even, was impressive as hell. He had my respect for that and for his honesty and steadfast devotion, he also had my love. I loved him and I had told him as such. My entire body seemed to relax as soon as I had said it. I might still have some emotional stuff to deal with following my attack, but loving Charlie was one thing I didn't have to worry about. I knew that with his love and help I would eventually move past the demons that plagued my dreams, and I also knew that between Charlie, Dillon and Braiden, I would have Emily home soon. Once we had the situation with Emily under control, I would face my fears of returning home. There was no way in hell was I letting that fucker William Levier keep me from my family home, and now that Charlie was essentially homeless, maybe I would ask him to move in with me. Mind you, having Emily and Charlie living under my matchbox roof would be more than a little cozy. We would figure it out though. Maybe I could borrow money on the equity of my house and have Carter Constructions add a room or two. I never once, in all my years, dreamed of my future playing out the way it was right now, with Charlie Cole no less. God, how I have lusted over this man for so long. Even before our one night of passion over a year ago, I had seen Charlie around town, and spent many carefree hours dreaming up possible scenarios for the two of us. When Charlie came home with me that night, I didn't fool myself into believing it would be more than one night of unrestrained sex. Like a lovesick fool, I had hoped though. The past year without his smiles, without his touch left me feeling hollow and empty. Now he was mine and he wanted me, he loved me. I pinched myself and looked down at his sexy sleeping form. Nope, not a dream. This was real, my dreams had become my reality. A future with Charlie. Maybe we would get married, maybe we would have children together. My hand fell to my stomach at the thought of Charlie and I as parents to a sweet little girl with blonde curls and blue eyes, or a handsome little boy with light brown hair and Charlie's subtle dimples. I've seen Charlie with Eli only once, but he was wonderful with the little boy. He'd be the perfect father who wouldn't rest until his children were laughing hysterically. I wondered if Charlie even wanted children after his sorrowful family history. It didn't matter to me if he didn't. I didn't want to be anywhere other than by his side.

The sound of my cell phone ringing broke my idealistic thoughts and I jumped up and raced for it. It was still sitting in Braiden's office where I had left it following my earlier temper tantrum.

Unknown flashed across the screen, and with shaky hands, I answered, "This is Rebecca."

"Ahhhh, there is my sweetheart."

His voice didn't make me recoil with fear this time. I replied with pure unadulterated anger, "Where is my sister, you sick fuck?" He snickered and it just made me angrier. "You know what?" His laughter died down. "You are nothing but a spoiled little shit with daddy issues. Get over it and let Emily go." That got his attention.

"You don't know shit about my father and if you did, you wouldn't throw him into this equation so easily. He would search and find every person who ever meant anything to you, then put a bullet in their head without thinking twice. He would leave you for last, just so you could watch him destroy everyone you love."

I snorted with unladylike grace. "Yeah, well, from what I hear you should be scared of daddy, too, because apparently your little drug habit doesn't fly with him, and your financial burdens are nothing but an embarrassment to the Levier name. Perhaps I should call him and let him know what you've been up to. Let him know you're in Claymont and that you have Emily?"

"So fucking brave," he growled with unrestrained hostility. "Here I was prepared to make you a deal and you have me second guessing myself. Maybe I should just kill Emily now and be done with it." I didn't know how to answer that; I didn't want to beg, but I didn't want him to hurt Emily either, so I remained quiet. "So, now that I seem to have your attention, this is a one-time only offer, sweetheart. I know your man Mr. Cole and his security dogs have encouraged you not to proceed with handing me over the deed to your property. I know the Montgomery boys are currently searching Claymont for me, and I can guarantee you they will not find me. Therefore, I am giving you the option to save your sister. I have a lawyer ready and waiting, all you have to do is meet me, sign over the deed to your home, and I leave. I get the money I need out of your property, and you'll get your precious sister. But you come alone. You ditch Jean Claude and get your fine ass into a car and start driving east on the main highway, out of town. Fifty-five miles outside of town, you'll see an exit for Mountain Range Road, it shouldn't take you more than an hour to get there. Pull off on the side of the road, sit there and wait for my next call. What do you say, Ms. Donovan? You brave enough to rescue your sister or are you as soft as that warm pussy of yours?"

I glanced out the study doorway. Charlie was still fast asleep on the couch, his truck parked in the driveway. I could do this. I loved my home, but I loved my sister more. If all it took to keep her safe was to give up our house, I could do it without hesitation. "Why would I trust you to not hurt me or Emily?"

He laughed. "If you have even half a clue as to who I am, then you know I can't be trusted, but, sweetheart, you don't have a choice because I will put a bullet in your sister's head and not think twice about it."

"I'm on my way," I said with more determination than I felt.

"Remember, sweetheart, you come alone. If I catch wind of anyone else with you, I will kill Emily."

I hung up, not wanting to hear another word from that asshole's mouth about killing my own flesh and blood. I tiptoed out of the office and quickly dressed in warm cargo pants, a t-shirt and hoodie. I hesitated at getting the gun that Charlie had secured in a drawer beside the bed. So I couldn't shoot straight, but maybe, if I got close enough I could hit something vital. I shoved it down the back of my pants like I've seen Charlie do it, and found it incredibly uncomfortable, so instead I chose to stick it in the pocket in the front of my hoodie. Not very hip or gangsta, but as much as I was a creature of style, I was also a creature of comfort. Standing over Charlie, watching the gentle rise and fall of his chest, I couldn't bring myself to simply leave him without an explanation. He would freak out and if the situation was reversed, I would go ballistic. When he eventually woke, I had no doubt he would search the house high and low for me. So I scribbled him a quick note letting him know William's directions and left it on one of the pillows on the bed, hoping he wouldn't miss it. I wasn't stupid, I didn't trust William, and I wasn't about to put my life completely in his hands.

Climbing into Charlie's big truck, I started it up. I held my breath with the ridiculous notion that it would somehow keep the noise down and get me away from the house without waking Charlie up. Idiot. As I drove off down the street, the front door to Dillon and Braiden's home remained closed.

I wished I was still back in there, securely wrapped in Charlie's arms.

CHAPTER 21

Charlie

The slamming of the front door woke me with a start. For a brief moment, I had forgotten where I was, and stared at the unfamiliar surroundings in a daze. My senses returned as Braiden stormed into the living area, an exhausted, pissed off scowl on his face. Yeah, this boy's cool persona was cracking. He was emotionally involved in this case on a whole other level.

"Everything okay?" I asked sleepily.

"No," Braiden honestly confirmed, flicking on the coffee pot in the state-of-the-art kitchen.

"You care about her." It was a statement, not a question.

Braiden grunted. "I don't even know her. I care about her situation, it feels personal."

I knew he was referring to his extra-curricular activities in the bedroom, but I didn't really want to open that can of worms. If the dude wanted to get personal about his sex life, he'd have to find another dude to hash it out with. Sure, I had swapped bedtime stories with Jax back in the day, but now it just felt perverted and dirty. A wave of protectiveness washed over me, and I felt compelled know exactly what Braiden's intentions were where Emily was concerned.

"If and when we get her back, she doesn't need another dom taking control of her life."

Braiden raised a brow at my announcement. "I don't know whether to admire your devotion to Rebecca's kin, or punch you in the face for insulting me," he admitted.

I rubbed my face thoughtfully and grinned at him. "You can try to punch me in the face."

Braiden smiled, something he rarely did. "I'm not much for Dr. Phil moments, Charlie, so I will say this once and only once: I can't even begin to understand the horror Emily has endured: being raped, being forced into the BDSM lifestyle, especially at her age. For any woman that sort of degradation would be shattering, for an innocent girl barely seventeen years of age..." Braiden's eyes flared with anger and he shook his head as if trying to clear the thoughts that were consuming him in that moment. "What I can understand, to a certain extent, is what is involved in a dominant/submissive relationship. Jonas was Emily's master, he would have trained her to behave a certain way. For example, he may have made her kneel at his feet, possibly have her speak only on command. She will be used to a life filled with a strict regime which is common in that lifestyle. When we get her back, she is going to need help separating her life as a captive slave to a free woman. Long ago I decided that life wasn't for me, but when I did explore it, I learned to read women well, to know what they wanted and needed before they knew themselves. I think I can help Emily and I can do so while understanding the needs she might have that others wouldn't understand. The need for command, the need for someone to control her; she will most likely be afraid to act without it for fear of reprisal. I have never and would never hurt a woman or give her something she wasn't ready for. Emily is going to need to be treated with kid gloves for a long time. She will need extensive counseling and family and friends she can rely on and trust implicitly. But she may also need something no one else can provide. I have no plans to become her dom or anything like that, but I will be prepared to listen if she needs to talk about something no one else understands. And unless you have been hiding a deep dark secret about a predilection for restraints, floggers, and butt plugs, I'm assuming you wouldn't have a clue."

I'm pretty sure my eyes were the size of saucers by the time Braiden had finished. Firstly, this was the longest conversation we've ever had. Second, it was a glimpse into the world of BDSM that he apparently lived and breathed once upon a time.

I grinned. "Who was the butt plugs for, you or her?"

Braiden's lips twitched in an attempt not to smile. "You asking because you are intrigued about my ass Cole?"

"Not fucking likely, just wondering exactly how kinky that shit got."

"You'll have to keep wondering, I'm done discussing my sex life with you."

Speaking of sex life, where the hell was Rebecca?

"I'm gonna change, I've been wearing these clothes for forty-eight hours straight, then I'm gonna head back out. Did you put your car in the garage?" I gave Braiden a questioning look and realization hit us at the same time.

"Rebecca?" I yelled out, jumping from the couch and racing through the house. Braiden was slamming doors behind me as I reached our bedroom. The light was on and the clothes that had been strewn all over the floor in her fit of anger earlier that day were still lying there.

"Where the fuck would she have gone?" I asked, the urgency in my voice no doubt alerting Braiden to the fact I was moments away from a panic attack.

"Bed," Braiden said with a nod.

I followed his gaze and saw the paper lying on the pillow.

My heart hammered with fear. Was she still pissed off about the fight? She couldn't have been, we had make up sex and she had told me she loved me. I picked the paper up and it shook in my nervous grip.

"Oh fuck," I whispered. Braiden read it quickly from beside me and was already dialing Dillon as we moved out of the house. There was no need for words, both of us knew what needed to be done. Braiden's sleek black Corvette Stingray sat in the driveway under the moonlit night.

"Dillon's in town but headed out that way now with backup, I need you to put your thinking cap on, Charlie, you know this town better than me. William would be holed up somewhere secluded. A house, a shed, warehouse, anything you can think of will help us find them. He won't be out in the open, it's too fucking cold out. If he's lawyered up and holding Emily, he'll want shelter."

My mind ran over the possibilities. There was only one main highway that led out of town. At the Mountain Range Road exit, there were two directions: west that led towards the mountains or east that led through eighty miles of thick forest before hitting the next small town. My hands grabbed roughly at my hair as I tried to think of a place like Braiden was describing.

"Talk to me, tell me what you're thinking."

"Mountain Range Road exit...he could have headed up the mountain—"

"That would be unlikely. Less exit strategies and he's unfamiliar with the terrain. He would keep it close to the main highway, but far enough from the road that you couldn't see lights."

I mulled over the possibilities as Braiden spoke. "Old Morris's shack," I murmured. "It's the only place I can think of that fits that description. Take the Mountain Range Road exit. The shack's about fifteen miles past the exit and the turnoff for the road it's on is barely noticeable. The shack's been abandoned for years over a family dispute. It sits on a hundred acres of secluded forest. It doesn't have electricity though, do you think that would matter?"

"I doubt it, especially if there's not much else around. William would make do, it's temporary after all. It's a start though so let Dillon know, and if you can think of anywhere else they might be, tell Dillon to check them out, too."

Braiden drove fast, like fucking fast, and although I was grateful, it didn't mean he wasn't making me nervous. I gripped the arm rest a little tighter when I noticed the speedometer clipped one hundred miles per hour. The black Stingray cut through the forest roads like an inky bullet.

"Just warning you, I might just plain out kill this fucker when I see him," I said, in an attempt to take my mind off the excessive speed, slick roads and the shadows passing too quickly outside my window.

"Just try and contain yourself until we're sure the girls are safe. Our first priority here is the girls, Levier Junior is second priority, but I do agree, the prick needs to go down. To be honest, I think his father would probably thank us for taking care of the pain in his ass."

We reached Mountain Range Road faster than I have ever made the trip and slowed to a stop when we noticed my truck pulled off to the side of the road. It was empty and the engine was cool. Rebecca had left it here some time ago. My gut churned with sickness at the thought that she could have been in the hands of William Levier for such a long length of time—enough time to do as he pleased with her. If he had so much as laid a finger on her, I would cut out his heart and set it on fire. Without making a sound, we were back on the highway and the next few miles passed in a haze of bloody images of William. Apparently I was a sick bastard because I had entertained some pretty fucked up ways to torture and maim William Levier. In my bloodied vapor ridden thoughts, I missed the turn off for the road to Morris's shack. Although the winter snow, which was slowly receding, had flattened most the grass on the roadsides, the tall firs and forest that surrounded the long winding driveway to the dilapidated hovel had thickened a lot since I had last been out this way. As I quietly berated myself for wasting such precious time, Braiden subtly redeemed my self-discrimination.

"This is good. If any noise from passing traffic makes it to the shack, they would only think it was a car passing by. We can back track more carefully now and move in quietly. Trust me if they are here, a surprise attack will definitely be to our advantage." It was only a five minute drive back along the quiet stretch of highway before I noticed the barely discernible mail box sitting deep within the overgrown brush. Braiden pulled the car a safe distance off the road, and quietly exited the vehicle, nudging the door closed with care. With the crumbling cabin sitting an easy mile away from the road, I didn't think stealth was called for at this point, but I followed his lead anyway, slipping silently from the car. Braiden was at the open trunk, clicking back the lock on a long, large and heavy looking box that took up most the space. As he lifted the lid, my eyes bulged with unsuppressed surprise.

"Fuck me, you planning on going to war sometime soon?" I admired the clean, orderly, and extensive array of weapons displayed in the three tiered, custom built steel box. Braiden moved quickly and efficiently, grabbing guns, loading cartridges and pocketing extra ammunition in the side pockets of his cargo pants. He handed me a gun, which I loaded, and slipped extra ammo in my back pocket.

"Call me old fashioned, but I always like to be prepared," Braiden murmured, shoving a bad mother fucking looking knife in a sheath anchored securely around his leg.

"You were NYPD with SWAT training then a PI, right?" I asked him in disbelief. As far as I was concerned, Braiden was far too equipped for an ex-police officer let alone a private investigator. His weaponry and the way he moved, the way he carefully thought of everything and planned ahead was something more in line with Jax and Dillon, maybe on a special ops scale. Braiden lowered the trunk's lid and it shut tight with a quiet snick.

"Yep," he answered vaguely.

When he turned toward the dark forest before us, I would have stormed off like a noisy pissed off man, ready for battle. Braiden, however, pulled me back with a pointed glare. "Stay behind me, try and follow in my footsteps. Make sure your phone is on silent. We know this prick has at least two on his security detail who are more than likely patrolling the perimeter right now. Don't speak unless you absolutely have to. With a bit of luck this is our target, if the place is deserted we fall back and contact Dillon ASAP."

Frustrated at the slow progress we were making, I knew that Braiden was right. Storming in like a herd of elephants wasn't really going to achieve anything but get Rebecca and most likely Emily killed. I didn't know shit about this kind of shit. I threw a mean half-hook, a pretty damn cool roundhouse kick, and I managed a construction company. This was Braiden's life and I would follow the set rules he had just dished out like a boy fucking scout. Walking through a soggy forest quietly wasn't as easy as it seemed. Where Braiden moved like the wind, I moved more like a lazy cow. Even though it was a cloudless night, under the thick firs the radiant moon barely broke through, so to say it was dark was an understatement. It was pitch fucking black and following in Braiden's footsteps was a joke. For every silent swift step he took, I took one long clumsy stride that seemed to snap every twig in the vicinity. Braiden came to an abrupt stop and glanced back over his shoulder.

"Wait here," he commanded quietly.

I stood motionless, knowing I was impeding this whole stealthy ninja attack. My heart was pounding furiously, demanding that my feet move forward to the old shack that stood no more than half a yard in front of us. Every now and again I thought I saw a distant light break through the trees, but I was beginning to think that it was perhaps no more than my hopeful imagination. My body felt wired and jittery, much like I felt before and after a fight. I needed to run, or beat the shit out of something, but I could do neither. Rebecca's life depended on me holding it together right now, and for her I could do anything, even the seemingly impossible.

A sturdy hand on my shoulder had me turning with my gun raised, finger inching towards the trigger. A rigid hand gripped my wrist and pushed the weapon to the side. Right before I could morph into attack mode, Braiden's shadowy face got up close and personal. "Don't fucking shoot me or I will hit you," he growled in a low voice.

I almost laughed as relief filled my veins. I thought I was about to get my moves on with some badass fucker from the city. A pissed off Braiden I could deal with. At that moment, the moonlight found a clear pocket in the canopy of trees and reflected off the wicked knife now in Braiden's hand. It shimmered with a red sticky substance as he wiped it on his pant leg, then shoved it carefully back in its sheath. I guess that meant Levier was here, which meant Rebecca was, too.

"One down. Keep moving forward, quietly if you can manage it at all." He gave me a pointed look and I raised my hands in self-defense.

"This covert shit is not my deal, man, I just like to hit things."

"I'm going to make my way around to the east and circle the perimeter to see if we have anyone else out here patrolling. Dillon is in route, he's fifteen minutes out and bringing backup, but I don't feel comfortable waiting. We don't know how long Rebecca has been here or what's going on in that cabin. I've cleared the way to the front door for you. When you get there stay low and see if you can get a visual on what's going on inside. Whatever you do, don't fucking panic—no matter what you see—you gotta keep that raging head of yours calm. If Rebecca is in there, we need to know where she is, what room she is in, same goes for Emily. See if you can make out how many people are in there, focus on weapons and points of entry. We gotta do this smart or bad guy blood won't be the only blood spilled tonight." I took long deep breaths and knew this was important. I had to keep my temper in check. "Don't go in without me," were Braiden's final words as he slipped away into the darkness, as sleek and swift as his fancy fucking car.

I rubbed a hand down my face and rolled my tight neck and shoulders, then turned to cautiously move the rest of the way to the old shack.

CHAPTER 22

Rebecca

My eyes felt like lead weights and my mind was fuzzy, vague. I had no recollection of the bender I must have had the previous night, but my body was telling me it had been a big one. As I began to blink away my blurry vision, I realized the room I was in was unfamiliar. Then reality slammed into me full force. I lurched forward, sitting up in a strange bed that squeaked and moaned beneath me. I met one of William's huge, scary-ass men on the side of the road at the Mountain Range Road exit and he had swiftly patted me down and taken my gun. I actually expected it; I hadn't been able to come up with a plan to hide the weapon anywhere else. Nor had I thought up a plan to obtain any other sort of weapon. I had walked into Morris Poreman's dirty old shack defenseless and desperate. The flickering light from several lanterns lit up the room as I came face to face with William Levier. His cultivated good looks hadn't surprised me, I already knew what he looked like, but his size certainly took me unawares. He was easily as tall as Charlie and equally as wide. He didn't look like a drug addict; he looked like a freakin' body builder. His snide smile and angry eyes had perused my body in a way that had my throat filling with bile. I pushed it down and pressed my shoulders back. I was here for two things: to sign a fucking piece of paper and get my sister back.

"You look tired, sweetheart, did you have a difficult week?" William had asked me with a smirk on that evil face of his.

"We can skip the petty remarks and witty banter, William. I want to see my sister or I won't sign a thing for you." My voice was strong even though my hands shook so badly, I had to force them behind my body in an attempt to hide my weakness. William nodded to another mountain of a man, who resembled a pro-wrestler rather than a body guard for a spoiled rich boy, standing next to a door on the other side of the room. He opened the door promptly and from the dim light within, I could clearly see my sister, and gasped at her appearance. Her wrists had been tethered and she was hanging from a rickety looking beam which ran across the ceiling. Her feet were barely touching the floor and her naked body was bruised and battered. Her head hung limply, and for a moment, I thought she was dead.

"She fought, therefore, she was punished, but that feisty heart of hers is still beating. We should probably move this along though so you can get her to a hospital." William's lawyer, a coward of a man who could not even bring himself to look me in the eye, seemed efficient and organized with his paperwork, but as for the character of the man himself, he was shit residue scraping the very bottom of the barrel. I think I hated him almost as much as I hated William. It was pathetically weak people like this who enabled the

Levier men to live the evil lives they lived. As soon as the paperwork had been signed, William had stood tall with a shit-eating grin on his face. I had demanded he give me my sister then—BAM!—the world went dark.

Now, sitting on a dirty mattress in a room that smelled like week old feces, I felt the painful drum in my head. I tried to reach up to check for damage only to find my hands tied behind my back.

"B?" a soft voice murmured from the other side of the room.

I spun so fast the world tilted, and I feared I was going to pass out again. I sat still for a moment until the room righted itself and took in the sight of my sister. Cuts marred her body, so many I couldn't discern one from another. Her ribs were black and blue, blood dripped from, well, everywhere. My eyes widened at the sight of her until they finally reached her face, also bruised and bloodied.

"It looks worse than it is," she whispered. A sob escaped my lips at the sound of her voice. "Don't cry, B, I made this bed, and now I have to lie in it."

I couldn't hold back the tears that fought their way up my throat. "What the hell is that supposed to mean?" I demanded, not caring if anyone outside the closed door heard me.

"Can you get your hands in front of you?" she asked, clearly ignoring me.

"Why?" I wondered out loud as the tears continued to fall.

"Because you can fight easier with your hands in front of you," she calmly explained.

I shook my head at the absurdity of such a thought. "Who am I going to fight?"

"B, William will be back any minute. He's just waiting for you to regain consciousness. If you're not under the age of seventeen, he gets off on the struggle. It's no fun fucking a girl who doesn't fight back." Her words were not spoken in anger or fear. It was a statement from the lips of a girl who knew, but they were whispered with a control and nonchalance that made me a little nervous.

"Em, what happened to you?"

She didn't flinch, she didn't look away; her face was passive and emotionless. "Can you get your hands underneath you and over your legs?"

I stared at her for a moment before deciding that now was not the time for a family reunion. I shuffled my hands under my ass and around my legs, and when they finally popped over my feet, I rolled my stiff shoulders. Standing, I examined the ropes that held Emily in place.

"I'm going to need a knife to cut through that," I murmured.

Emily shook her head. "No knife and no time. The windows will more than likely be jammed, but try them anyway. If you break one, it'll alert William and he will be here before you'd have a chance to get through"

I checked the two windows in the room, and just as Emily thought, they wouldn't budge.

"Look around for something to use as a weapon, check under the bed."

I began searching the tiny room—it didn't take long—although the room was quite large, there were little furnishings with only a bedside table, and rickety bed with its questionable looking mattress. The bed was made from a steel frame construction, held together with nuts and bolts. If I could get one of the legs off, it would make a great weapon. The first two nuts I tried to get loose were rusted on tight, the third began to unscrew with a few curse words and a lot of grunting.

"Hurry up, I can hear someone out there." My sister's tone was suddenly nervous, which made me even more nervous. I fumbled with the second nut that was slowly coming loose. I too could hear the heavy footsteps outside the door and my breathing became frantic as my fingers worked to twist the nut off. My wrists were bound so movement was difficult. As the door knob twisted, the steel leg came loose and fell away from me, trapped between the bed and the wall. I whimpered with frustration as I stood up, hands empty and turned to face William.

"Hmmmm," he hummed with a thoughtful grin, taking in my hands still secure, but now in front of me. "Have you girls been catching up?" he asked. "How's your head, sweetheart?" William walked further into the room, completely ignoring Emily's presence, his sights set on me.

"You have our property. It would be wise if you would now fuck off now, before those dogs of mine track you down," I said with false bravado.

"As I mentioned earlier, your dogs are busy scouring Claymont. No one knows you're here. We have a little time for some fun before I leave." His eyes roamed over my body and I shivered. Please let Charlie have found my note, I silently prayed. William took another step toward me and instinctively I took a step away, my legs hitting the bed behind me.

"Leave her be, William, you won't enjoy her, I can promise you that," came Emily's calm voice.

He snickered, his eyes still watching me like a hungry lion. "Are you jealous, Mrs. Levier?" he crooned. "Because I've already had a small taste, and I thoroughly enjoyed it."

I chanced a quick glance over his shoulder at Emily. Although her face had remained impassive so far, at the mention of her married name, she grimaced. William reached out and nudged me back onto the bed. It tilted slightly to the side where I had removed the leg and I scrambled back to avoid William's hands.

"Leave her be, you fucker," growled Emily.

William reached out again, this time getting a firm hold on both my ankles as I attempted to kick him. He laughed, holding me easily.

"I like a fighter," he purred. Yanking hard on my legs, he pulled me closer to him. I hated his touch, I hated his scent, I hated him so much my heart beat an urgent rhythm in protest and I struggled not to scream hysterically. Screaming wouldn't do me any good, especially with no one around to hear me.

"Fuck you," I ground out as I continued to push his body away with my bound hands. With my lower half now pinned under his body, William grabbed the ropes around my wrists and pulled my hands above my head. He had me restrained and I could feel his cock thickening through his pants at my core—my fighting was getting him off—I needed to stop, I needed to calm myself. Easier said than done when you were about to be raped. Somehow I forced my body to comply and relax. William looked down at me with an edge of triumph in his eyes.

"You limp dick, cock sucking, fucker," Emily cursed from behind him. William paid her no attention though. I, unfortunately, had his full, undivided attention. "You will never be him," she continued to scream. "You are a pussy compared to your father." William's body became rigid and still. Oh shit, little sister had touched a nerve. "He's more successful than you. He created his own empire from nothing," she spat, and William backed off a little, glancing over his shoulder in Emily's direction. "Yeah, you piece of shit husband, I'm talking to you," Emily growled.

William turned back to look at me and pressed his lips to mine. I ground my jaw down tight, not allowing him access to my mouth. William sat back and gave me a quick wink. "One minute, sweetheart, let me take care of this first."

Panic filled my body, I knew he was going to hurt Emily. "No!" I yelled, trying to scramble up off the bed. William simply pushed me back down, like he was swatting a bothersome fly.

"B, I got this." Emily smirked, her hate filled eyes never leaving William's. The power and strength I saw in my sister amazed me. I had thought of her as a broken doll, as beaten and defeated, but clearly she was far from that. She hung before William, nude and bloodied, but she still looked like a beautiful avenging angel. As they glared at one another, I pulled my gaze away and took in the slumped side of the bed. With William's attention off of me, I had a chance at grabbing the steel leg from behind the bed. William must have heard my movement and when he began to turn back towards me, Emily launched into her verbal attack again.

"Jonas doesn't have to buy his loyalty, people fear him for more than his name." I was once again forgotten as William moved towards Emily. "He

155

hits harder than you, he looks better than you, and you know what else?" William was close enough to touch her, his fists clenched, his body wound tighter than a bow string. "He fucks better than you, too," she snarled.

William moved so fast I barely noticed. His fist buried into her stomach and Emily coughed out a painful wheeze. A whimper broke from my lips and a tear slipped down my cheek at the sight. With William's attention otherwise occupied, I leaned over the bed and peered between it and the wall. I could just make out the steel bed post lying on the hardwood floor.

"Fucking pussy," Emily chuckled painfully, "that was a love tap compared to what your father can dish out."

The slap of skin behind me had me reaching down behind the bed, my fingertips brushing the cool metal. The leg post threatened to roll away in my awkward double handed reach, but desperation had me wrapping my hands around the makeshift weapon.

Emily laughed, though it wasn't humor that forced out the sound. "After six fucking years with Jonas, do you honestly think that there is anything you can do that could compare to his torture?" she screamed hysterically.

I pulled myself around and slipped off the bed, the bar held tightly in my bound hands.

"Did he rape and beat your sister while you watched?" William roared.

That made me pause for a moment, the horror of what he was planning to do sitting uncomfortably raw in my stomach. Emily didn't answer, she didn't have to. But now it was my turn to bring some Donovan hate down on this prick. I swung the steel bed post hard. It was nothing like in the movies. I mean, I expected a big loud thump and William to crumple to the floor in a heavy heap. Instead, the sturdy, yet thin bed post merely bounced off William's shoulder. He turned to face me, his eyes full of barely restrained rage. As William moved to lunge forward, Emily's legs wrapped around his waist from behind, slowing his progress and I swung the steel again, this time connecting with the side of his face. Though stunned, he still didn't go down and I swung again, and again, cursing the fact I didn't have that damn kick-ass gun of Charlie's. Thunderous footsteps filled the room and I glanced up to see one of the insanely huge body guards enter the room.

"Shit," I whispered as Emily continued to struggle with William, who was at least moving a little slower following my beating. The big man grinned at me and I knew we were seriously fucked now.

CHAPTER 23

Charlie

Glancing through the filthy windows of the decrepit old shack, my heart hammered as I took in the empty room. I moved along the house until I reached the next window and found a dark room which, as far as I could tell, was also empty. Patience was clearly not my forte and I struggled to keep my composure and remain calm. Edging around the side of the shack, I found what I assumed was once the kitchen, and in it stood William, looking out the windows into the forest beyond. He was on his phone, his attention distracted as I stayed down low for fear of being caught.

"Tell him I'll have the cash within the week, I already have a buyer and my lawyer left less than an hour ago to prepare the paperwork." His voice, though somewhat muffled through the closed windows, was confident and smug. Rebecca was here, and if I didn't find her alive, this fucker was going to die in the most painful way possible. I heard William's footsteps retreat from the window at the same time that Braiden appeared out of nowhere beside me. Dude was a damn ninja, I swear.

"Third guy just entered through the front door. Second has been taken out and I think that's all. We do this now. Dillon will be here any minute but I don't want to wait." Braiden chanced a glance through the kitchen window then kneeled back down beside me. "They are in the back room, only room with the windows covered. We go through the front. First priority, take out Big Guy, then Levier. And we do it with no harm to the girls, agreed?"

I nodded, because I really couldn't find fault in his plan. How exactly we would execute it was a little out of my grasp though. I followed Braiden back around to the front of the building where we glanced through a grimy window to see if anyone occupied the room beyond the door. Empty. Braiden turned the handle on the door and pushed it open. My body tensed, expecting a loud and obnoxious creak on such old hinges, but there was nothing. Braiden glanced my way and indicated he would go first. Expertly, and with far too much stealth and badass-ness than any average Joe should possess, Braiden moved forward into the building, his gun raised and ready to fire. Trying to mimic his movement, I followed. I could hear a female's voice at the back of the house, but it wasn't Rebecca. We followed, clearing the rooms we passed, looking for any sign of Big Guy. As we rounded a corner in the small dilapidated shack, we found Big Guy, who was, in fact, fucking huge, just like Rebecca said. He filled the doorway, just standing there, hands on his hips. Braiden didn't hesitate, his gun held steady and high, he fired. Big Guy went down hard and we moved quickly down the hall.

"Noooooo!" screamed a woman's voice, still not Rebecca's. Braiden entered the room first, and I followed behind. The room was large, lit with a bright lantern sitting on a small wooden bedside table. There was a twin bed slumped to one side. Following Braiden's gaze, I was struck fair in the chest with fear. William Levier stood in the center of the room, Rebecca held firmly to his chest, a gun shoved under her chin. Hanging behind them, looking barely conscious was Emily, her naked body limp like a rag doll. My eyes sought out Rebecca's, and she watched me, panic and fear consuming her blue depths.

"Weapons down or I decorate the ceiling with her pretty little head," growled William. "And drop the fucking stick, Ms. Donovan." A metal bar fell from Rebecca's hand and hit the ground with a resounding twang.

My finger sat on the trigger of my weapon, trained on William and Rebecca. I glanced over to Braiden looking for clues as to what the ninja had up his sleeve next. Without hesitation, he raised one hand off his gun and withdrew his finger from the trigger, and threw it to the floor. Fuck, not what I had in mind, Braiden. I didn't drop my weapon, I simply couldn't. William's gaze zeroed in on me and he pushed the gun a little harder into the skin under Rebecca's chin, making her whimper. Closing my eyes briefly and conceding defeat, for now, I lowered my weapon and threw it on the ground. I raised my hands and linked them behind my head in a sign of submission.

William smirked. "Wise choice, Cole." He began to pull Rebecca to the doorway.

I took a few hesitant steps backwards trying to block his only exit, praying I didn't spook the fucker, causing him to accidentally blow Rebecca's head off. He seemed a little frantic and twitchy. His plans had obviously been thrown into chaos. He was also a man with a small heroin problem, most likely needing another fix. As he edged around me, his back to the doorway, a shadow in the background caught my eye. Dillon, thank fuck! Never have I ever kissed a man, nor have I ever wanted to, but in that split second, I would've laid a wet one on the former GI Joe or perhaps offered him my first born child. I lowered my hands and took a bold step towards William and Rebecca.

"The only way you're leaving here with her is if you shoot me, so you had better fucking do it now." Rebecca's eyes widened and William paused as if considering his options.

"I'm not an idiot, Cole, I take the gun off her to shoot you, and he'll shoot me." He nodded to Braiden.

"Kick your weapon under the bed, Braiden, and do the same with your backup." Braiden did so, pulling the second gun from the back of his cargos, making sure they both slid under the bed. "Now, you mother fucker, you got the balls to shoot me, or do you leave the hard stuff for your daddy to handle?" I heard Emily snicker from behind me and was pleased to hear she was alive. I saw the fire in William's eyes as his gun shifted and he extended his arm. He was already a good six inches taller than Rebecca, add that to the fact that he now had his body turned slightly to take me out, Dillon had a clear shot—his gun was only a matter of feet from the back of William's head, he wouldn't miss. The loud bang that cracked through the stiff, quiet standoff seemed almost surreal. William immediately slumped to the ground, taking Rebecca with him, his brains splattering all over the room. Rebecca screamed as Braiden lunged forward to pull her free from her tormentor. Seeing her body flail so helplessly broke my heart. I mean, seriously broke it, painfully. Too much pain and not really in my heart, more in my shoulder. I glanced down to see a small red stain quickly bleed out into my shirt. Holy shit, he fucking shot me! Rebecca flew across the room, screaming and sobbing as my knees went weak. I wasn't dying. Well, I didn't feel like I was dying, but the thought that I'd been shot was making me feel a little woozy. Damn I was a pussy. The room quickly filled with Dillon, Frank, and Jax.

"Lay down, brother," Jax commanded and I obeyed without protest. Like I said—pussy.

"You fucking asshole! You let him shoot you. How could you do that to me?" Rebecca demanded a little hysterically.

I laughed. "Sorry, Betty Boop, promise I won't let it happen again." I winced as Jax pressed something hard against my shoulder and rolled me slightly to check the other side.

"Clean exit," he said, to whom exactly I have no idea. I glanced up to see Braiden carefully cutting Emily down.

"Baby, I'm good. Go check on your sister." Rebecca's eyes left mine for a moment as she too watched Braiden tenderly wrap Emily in a blanket. He carried her tiny body closer and knelt down beside us, his movements slow and cautious as if he were carrying a wild animal. Emily was watching Braiden, her eyes big and scared. "He won't hurt you," I whispered. She somehow dragged her eyes away from him and looked me over.

"He shot you," she breathed, her face beaten in a way that reminded me too much of the night Rebecca was attacked.

"Just a scratch," I replied, and at that moment Jax pressed down a little harder on my shoulder. I sucked in a breath. "Fuck me, quit doing that would you!" Jax laughed and I nearly decked him right there and then.

"Suck it up, princess." He smirked.

"I'm sorry." The room went quiet at Emily's soft apology. Rebecca scrambled to reach across me and take her sister's limp hand.

"You have nothing to be sorry for, this is on him, not you!" She said it in that stubborn tone of hers that broke no argument. Emily watched her through tired, weary eyes.

"This is all on me, B. The moment I walked out of Claymont with a far too big chip on my shoulder, I created this mess. You will never know just how truly ashamed of myself I am for doing that, for bringing this down on you." Rebecca sucked in a surprised breath. Emily stared back with solemn guilt and shame etched into her features. I knew this wasn't something that could be erased from Emily's heart with a few words. This girl had seen evil, she had lived it, tasted it, and inadvertently brought it to her sister's doorstep.

"You did everything you could to protect me, that's why you stopped writing, stopped calling, right?" Rebecca insisted. Emily's eyes were downcast and she seemed to melt further into Braiden's embrace, which pretty much amazed me. "You insulted William just now in an attempt to get him to leave me alone. You put yourself in danger to protect me, and he hurt you. This isn't on you, Em." Emily's body seemed to become limp, which freaked Rebecca out more.

Braiden carefully checked her pulse. "She's just passed out, Rebecca, which is probably for the best, she's in a lot of pain." The look of inconsolable grief on Rebecca's face was pissing me off. I wanted to hold her, comfort her. Without thought, I reached for her with the arm that just had a bullet put through its shoulder. I groaned when the pain shot through my body.

"Keep still, you dumb shit," Jax murmured. Rebecca wacked him on the arm and I gave her my best happy face.

"Thanks, babe."

"Ambulance is five minutes out. Be nice if you boys would stop getting yourselves into these shit-storms," Frank said quite bluntly from above us.

"Last shit-storm was all on Jax, Frank. I had nothing to do with that one," I said with a little too much grouchiness in my voice.

"And I didn't get here on time to partake in that one. I did try my best though. Nothing like a good shit-storm to spike up adrenaline levels," Braiden said thoughtfully.

"Did he just try and crack a joke?" Jax asked.

"Not sure. He's been doing that shit a lot lately and I don't get it. Maybe he doesn't have the whole humor thing down yet," I admitted. Braiden gave us the royal finger before standing with Emily in his arms and walking out of the room. "She'll be fine, Braiden's got her." Rebecca's worried gaze returned to mine, and one of what I assumed would be many tears escaped.

"I want to go home," she admitted.

Her request melted my heart. Her last step to moving past all of this was her going home.

"Then let's get me patched up so I can take you there."

CHAPTER 24

Rebecca

The last two days moved by like a full blown hurricane. Police interviews, media reports, doctors, nurses—I was bombarded left, right, and center. To top it off I had to spend more time in a hospital than I ever cared to, my eyes wide open, seeing it all. It made me queasy and anxious, but for the two people I loved most in this world, I would do anything. I still needed a time out though, badly! For the last two hours, Ella has been stoically by my side getting on anyone who dared approach me like a rabid dog. I couldn't help but grin and turned to pat her head as she sat with her nose buried in a comic book. She looked like she was twelve damn years old.

She looked up and smiled at me. "Why are you patting my head?" she asked.

I shrugged. "You're a good guard dog, the best." She snickered as her eyes dropped back to the book. Charlie finally exited the bathroom, dressed in a sexy pair of low rise jeans and a black long sleeved t-shirt. His arm was in a sling, much to his distress. Jax told him only pussies needed a sling, but Dillon assured him that anyone with a gunshot wound to their shoulder needed one. The moment I had seen him go down in Morris's shack, my world tilted. A world without Charlie Cole in it, was a world I didn't want to live in. It would have destroyed me if I had to bury someone else I love. When he had laid there, joking with Jax, and trying to soothe me with blood gushing out of his shoulder, I had broken down. My capacity to deal with what Frank called a shit-storm had reached its toll. I couldn't go with Charlie in the ambulance because they needed to transport both Emily and Charlie together. Instead I rode with Jax, who explained to me how he had to follow Ella's ambulance from Frank's squad car when she had been attacked by her stepfather twelve months ago. He admitted how crazy it had made him and he hadn't known whether to cry or punch something. He told me it was okay to do either, and I opted for crying. He placed his giant of a hand over mind to offer what support he could. Two days, later the circus that surrounded our ordeal with William Levier and his subsequent death was in full swing. While the media had pounced on the news, Dillon, Braiden, Jax and Charlie all sat on the razor's edge, concerned about retaliation by the business mogul, Jonas Levier. No one had heard a peep from him; he hadn't even made a statement to the media. He was more than tight-lipped, it was as if he had vanished and it was making everyone nervous.

Emily was healing slowly. She had required more than eighty stitches to cuts spread at different intervals over her entire body. She had three broken ribs and I had a slight measure of understanding about that sort of pain—bruises were excruciating, broken would be intolerable. Her shoulder was dislocated from hanging for so long from that fucking rope and her wrists were bloodied and bruised. A fractured cheek bone and concussion rounded out her list of injuries. What broke my heart: she didn't complain once. She didn't even look to be in the slightest amount of discomfort, and since she has become lucid, she refuses any pain medication. The doctors confirmed Braiden's story by bringing to our attention the scars on her back. She had been whipped to the point of bloodshed and her entire back was laced with permanent scars. The concern the doctors have at this point though were the scars on her soul. They ran deep and were the sort of scars that never fully healed. I tried to talk to her, but she refused to acknowledge me, her eyes set on the ceiling of her hospital room, her mind quite possibly a million miles from the safe haven of Claymont. I told her I loved her, that I didn't hold any of this against her, and however horrifying the circumstances of the last month were, they brought her back to me, which I was grateful for. She said nothing. Now as I watched Charlie pack his overnight bag that Jax delivered this morning, I was ready to blow this joint.

"So, you've advanced from first grade picture books to comic books? Good work, squirt," Charlie teased Ella.

She raised her middle finger without looking up from her book. "Eli gave it to me for Christmas, what did he give you?"

Charlie snorted. "The Dark Knight Rises, on Blu-ray."

Ella's eyes snapped up to meet Charlie's smug grin. "What the hell did you do to get that? You bribed him, didn't you?" she accused him playfully.

"Nope, he just likes me better." Charlie grinned and reached for my hand. When he went to lead us from the room, Ella pushed in front and Charlie smirked. "Really, pocket rocket, you're going to protect us from the hordes of media?"

"As if she needs protecting," Ella signaled my way, "she beat the shit out of Levier junior with a steel bed post. She's a fucking hero."

I couldn't help but laugh. "It was more along the lines of: tapped him repeatedly, causing little to no effect," I amended her impression of what happened.

"You fought the fucker because that's what you do," Charlie said, kissing my head. "You fight back because you are Rebecca Donovan," he declared proudly. "My baby has the courage of a lioness. She's gonna make one awesome momma to our babies one day," he purred in my ear. His words stopped me in my tracks. "Yep, you heard right. Babies, as in more than one. I'm thinking three of four." My lips quirked into an unbreakable grin. At that moment, Jax sauntered down the hospital corridor looking big and bad. Behind him Braiden and Dillon followed, dressed completely in black and looking equally as badass as Jax. Ella gave us a cheeky grin and leaped into Jax's arms, laying one damn hot kiss on his lips.

"My calendar boys, looking sharp," I murmured.

Charlie simply grunted and the men flanked us as we left the hospital.

* * *

I lay on my bed, my bed, in my room, in my house. I had been rather stiff and uncomfortable to begin with, my mind playing over the events of the last time I was in here. Charlie was beside me though, his hand following an impromptu path across the exposed skin he could reach. Not yet ready to be naked in the bed, I was in flannel pajama bottoms and a thin white tank top, so there was still a fair amount of skin accessible, and his caressing hands were soothing my fears. I spoke to Braiden only an hour ago, and he assured me that Emily was fine, she was sleeping. I relaxed a little more knowing Emily had someone watching over her. In fact, we all had someone watching over us at the moment. Between Dillon and Braiden, they had pulled together a team who were quietly keeping on our tails while Jonas Levier was AWOL. The lack of privacy and the feeling of being smothered should have angered me, but instead I felt a little more at ease. This ship was locked down tight. No Levier was getting through my laundry room window tonight, or ever. Charlie pulled me closer and nuzzled my neck.

"You smell so darn good," he murmured.

I pushed him away as he continued to tickle me, sparking to life a yearning inside me that couldn't come out to play. He was injured after all. "Stop that," I ordered weakly.

"Hell no," he growled.

I turned to look at him, suddenly feeling more than noticing the tension coiled in his strong body. I had been too embroiled in my own turmoil to notice Charlie battling his own demons. "You okay?" I asked, pushing a stray lock of dark blonde hair off his forehead.

"No," he said truthfully. "Not nearly. Two days ago I stood in a room while some asshole held a gun to you." His fingers delicately smoothed the skin under my chin where William had held his weapon. "I thought I was going to watch you die, and that has me really not okay."

I rolled my eyes. "Yet you were the one who got shot and when I got all upset over it, you told me I was being silly." It was awkward to be close to him like this. His injured shoulder was closest to me, his other arm reaching across his body to touch me. I wanted to melt into his warmth, but I didn't want to hurt him either.

"Come here." He pulled me and I moved to straddle him, only just barely avoiding his arm in his haste to have me closer. Once positioned above him he smiled, a real honest to God smile, and some of the tension left his body. "Just like this, every damn day," he murmured.

"Have your meds made you loopy?" I asked, clearly not understanding what he was talking about.

"Every day, for the rest of our lives, I want to go to sleep with you here, with me, just like this." My heart melted a little at his declaration. "Nothing between us, just you and me, skin to skin." He lifted the hem of my top and I helped him lift it off. He seemed to sigh at the sight of my breasts and immediately took his one free hand and cupped the weight gently. "You okay with this?" he asked, suddenly a little nervous that I might not yet be ready.

"Oh yeah," I moaned. "But you're hurt, so we can't do this yet." He chuckled as he teased my nipple and it felt too damn good.

"My shoulder is hurt, not my dick, Betty Boop." The aforementioned appendage was hard under my ass and I rocked a little, creating a delicious friction between our bodies. "Fuck, baby, get these off and then help me get mine off." He tugged at my pajama bottoms. I obeyed quickly, and, in too much of a hurry to remove the sling and his shirt, we left it on and I climbed back up to straddle his waist. My greedy hands roamed over Charlie's beautiful body. It was a masculine beauty, hard and unyielding, yet warm and safe. Finally I settled over his waist and dropped ever so slowly onto his hard length. We both groaned with satisfaction as he wedged deep inside me. "Ride me," he ordered and I did so gladly. Moving in a slow pace that would normally be almost torturous for us both, was now more than soothing. This was healing. Reminding us that we were alive, allowing us to feel each other both physically and emotionally.

"Just like this, every damn day," I whispered as I began to pick up our pace, our climax building steadily. Charlie's eyes latched onto mine as I gave him back the words he gave me. "Without the gunshot wound and sling though," I added. He grinned and it was wicked and sexy, and I would have come right then if he hadn't stilled me with his one free hand.

"I'm not gonna let you go, Betty Boop, you should know that right now. You're mine and I promise to give you everything, this and more, forever."

I grabbed the hand he was using to still me and brought it to my lips, kissing his palm gently. "Good, because I have no intention of letting you go. And I'd hate to go all stalker girl on your ass." I moved his hand to my breast and lifted myself slowly, slamming back down hard.

"Fuck," Charlie bit out as I rode him hard and fast until we both screamed out in ecstasy. I flopped forward, and at the last minute remembered his injured shoulder. My head nestled into the crook of his neck. As he softened inside me, I made no attempt to move, content to lay here like this for all of eternity.

"You think Dillon and Braiden would let us stay with them for a while?" I found myself asking. In a fit of worry, Charlie rolled me to the side, his eyes wide and unsure.

"Did I push you too hard? You weren't ready were you? Fuck. I don't want you to be uncomfortable in your own home, baby, this is your family's place. You need this. We can sleep in the spare room, we'll just put a mattress down on the floor or something." I put my finger over his lips to silence his rambling.

"Stop having a hissy fit, I'm fine." He arched a brow. "It's just, this place is kind of small. I thought I'd talk to the bank and see what I could do in terms of refinancing and maybe, I dunno, expand." I searched his eyes, hoping what I said next didn't freak him the fuck out. "It's not really big enough for three."

"Three?" he asked, my finger still over his lips.

"You, me and Em, if she wants to move in. I haven't talked to her about it yet, but I'm hoping she will. And I'm probably being a little ambitious assuming you would want to move in, too, but your apartment burned down, and I thought you might need somewhere to stay." Now I was rambling.

Charlie grinned. "You don't need to refinance, if I'm moving in I'll pay for the renovations. Fuck knows I can afford it and besides," he winked, "I know a guy who owns a construction company, I'm sure we can get a good deal."

My body relaxed as I took a deep breath and exhaled. It felt like all the pain and sorrow that filled my heart over the years—starting with the death of my parents—vanished. In its place, a new love existed: Charlie Freakin' Cole.

"I love you," I whispered.

Charlie's hand clutched the back of my neck, pulling me to him. "Not as much as I love you," he whispered. I would have argued, but I was too tired.

My mind drifted over my short life thus far. If it were to be penned on paper, it would be quite the tale. Born to parents who were snatched too early from the lives of two innocent little girls; two little girls who were molded under the watchful eye of an old-fashioned, yet adoring grandmother; one sister's devastation over the little sister who left her because her dreams were more important than family, only to find out that the little sister never even came close to her dreams, instead she was thrown to the wolves, her life consumed by pain and degradation. Somewhere in this story of heartache and pain, the lead heroine, I, Rebecca Donovan, found friendship with people who care for me just the way I am—there's no need for me to pretend to be someone else or to conform into someone

I'm not—I am simply accepted. I found a man who looks at me like I am the only person in the world who matters. It's fitting that he looks at me that way, because I feel exactly the same way about him. Time and time again I've been knocked on my ass, but each time I've stood back up, dusted myself off and have become a little stronger. I knew I was strong enough to stand on my own two feet, I always have been, but the crazy thing is, I no longer have to. I have people to lean on, depend on. That used to scare me, but now I feel only humble gratitude and happiness at the thought.

In the end I won. I made it out on the other side with a brand new love, loyal friends, and I have my sister back. For a short time, I feared that I was lost, that my heart had been crushed under the cruel hands of a stranger in my bedroom, violating me, invading a place I should feel nothing but safe in. But Charlie helped me find myself again and I finally feel like I can breathe once more. I know I'm not completely healed, I know there will be some lingering nightmares in my future, but in the warm embrace of Charlie's arms I feel safe.

This is where I would come home to from now on: to Charlie's embrace, to Charlie's warmth, to Charlie's heart.

EPILOGUE

Charlie

She had cried so many fucking tears, they simply didn't come anymore. She was dry, spent. I fell to my knees before her and she immediately wrapped her little arms around my neck, hanging on to me for dear life. I held her close and gathered the strength I would need to carry both of us, not physically, but emotionally.

Braiden had woken us before dawn with a loud pounding on the door, scaring the fucking shit of me, let alone Rebecca. I met him at the door, Glock in hand. She was gone, Emily had disappeared. Braiden had been watching Emily around the clock at the hospital, and finally agreed to go home to freshen up when one of Frank's boys offered to take up post at her door. He had left to take a piss, was gone not more than five minutes, and she disappeared. They had scrambled for security footage and witnessed, via CCTV, Emily wake to a phone call. She picked up the receiver, and if not for the sharp eye of Braiden and Dillon, who noticed her fist clench and shoulders tighten, we would have assumed nothing out of the ordinary. Emily hung up the phone without uttering a word, her lips sealed shut. She pulled out her IV and slid from the bed. On bare feet, in nothing but a hospital gown, she walked through the hospital, out the front doors, and straight into a waiting limousine.

Rebecca now sat on her couch, her hands hanging limply in her lap, a faraway look in her eyes. This wasn't how it was supposed to go. The bad shit was supposed to be behind us, we were moving forward, together. Braiden looked just as shell-shocked, while Dillon made phone calls from his cell in the kitchen.

"They boarded a private jet ten minutes ago," he confirmed, strolling back into the living room. Braiden's attention swung to Dillon. "My source picked out Emily easily, she's pretty banged up after-all, clearly recognizable. She was in the company of a man who could only be described as Jonas Levier. He's travelling with one other white male, unknown, but I'll find out who it is. I'm sure Jonas only has a few people that he would keep that close." Dillon turned to Braiden. "When you get to the airport, you're gonna want to find a guy who goes by the name of Marsh. I've been assured he's who you want to speak to, and he will more than likely be armed." Dillon hadn't asked Braiden to follow up on this. I guess, like me, he assumed Braiden would go looking for Emily. We had all seen the protective watchfulness in Braiden's eyes as he had watched over Emily for the last week. He even managed to get her eating and talking. Though not much, it was more than anyone else could get from her.

Braiden nodded and moved to stand before Rebecca. He sank to his knees and took her hands in his.

"Rebecca." His voice commanded attention and I found myself wondering if it was his 'master' voice. As soon as I wondered that, I wanted to kick the shit-head's ass for possibly using it on my girl. Rebecca's glassy eyes focused on him. Whatever command he had over women, in that moment, I was glad it had roused Rebecca from the catatonic state she had been sitting in for nearly forty minutes now. "I will get her back," he said with determination. "I promise you I will not come home without her, you have my word." I didn't miss the fact that he hadn't said he'd return with her alive, but I appreciated his resolve, and how much he obviously cared. Rebecca needed that, hell, Emily needed that. Rebecca nodded, her jaw set firmly. She stood with Braiden and gave him a quick hug before wrapping herself tightly around my waist. I wish I could wrap both my arms around her. Damn gunshot wound made me want to kill William Levier all over again.

"I'll let you know what I get as it comes in," said Dillon, walking Braiden to the front door.

"Appreciated," Braiden said rigidly before leaving.

"And I'll keep you both up to date," Dillon said over his shoulder to Rebecca and me.

"Thank you," Rebecca whispered.

I didn't want to think what Emily might be going through right now. I couldn't bring myself to understand why she had simply walked from the safety of the hospital and straight into his waiting limousine. The only reason I could fathom was that he threatened Rebecca's life. I knew Emily would do anything to keep her sister safe. She carried a world of guilt over the shit with William, and she would do anything to keep Jonas away from her only family. I held Rebecca a little tighter at the thought of the abuse Emily had already endured and wondered how much more she could handle before she broke beyond repair. I had no idea what kind of girl Braiden would return to Claymont with, if he returned with her at all. There was no doubt in my mind, she would carry one tortured soul.

THE END

"Strength is overcoming your worst fear."

ACKNOWLEDGMENTS

Thank you to my family who totally get my hazed out writing zone. My mum is a Photoshop genius and the legend behind my covers and merchandise, thanks Mumma. My S.I.L. and manager Kylie, you girl keep this book train perfectly oiled and moving, thank you! My W.P. Beta Team (Mum, Kylie, Trish, Kim and Nadine), thank you, thank you, thank you!

Ami Johnson! Ami, oh, Ami, what the hell did I do before you? My editing queen, THANK YOU for taking the solid, yet rough words I penned and turning them into a polished piece of perfection!

Jess and Rach at Bookslapped, thank you for EVERYTHING! Especially my last blog tour that you totally blitzed, and all future blog tours, because I will use no other, EVER!

Bloggers! Gah, you guys ROCK. I'm going to rattle off a few and miss heaps, 'cause there are just so many of you! A Love Affair with Books – Seriously, Desiree! BEST...STALKER...EVER! Bethany at The Reading Vixens, My Aussie gals: Jess at A is for Alpha B is for Books and Jodie at Fab, Fun and Tantalizing Reads. Bookslapped, TotallyBooked, Reading Renee, Can't Read Just One, A Book and a Latte, Novel Grounds, Holly's Hot Reads, Keepin' It Real Book Blog, Books Babes and Cheap Cabernet, The Book Hookers, My Fictional Boyfriend and Book Whore Page. These are just the tip of the iceberg. There are so many of you that give so much support to indie authors and it goes without saying, but I'm gonna say it anyway – Thank you, from the bottom of my heart. Without you, people wouldn't be reading my books.

Finally, my readers and devoted fans that have jumped on board the Kirsty Dallas rollercoaster and are screaming with me, right by my side! I hope I never disappoint you. I swear I'll always try and raise the bar, and take that extra step to make my reads perfectly epic adventures! I adore each and every one of you. Keep reading peeps!

Other Reads by Kirsty Dallas

Saving Ella – Mercy's Angels Book 1
Tortured Soul – Mercy's Angels Book 3
Breeze of Life

47266528R00109

Made in the USA
San Bernardino, CA
26 March 2017